# Coronado's Trail

# Coronado's Trail

## An Arizona Borderlands Mystery

# Carl and Jane Bock

ABSOLUTELY AMAZING eBOOKS

# ABSOLUTELY AMAZING eBOOKS

Published by Whiz Bang LLC, 926 Truman Avenue, Key West, Florida 33040, USA.

For information contact:
Publisher@AbsolutelyAmazingEbooks.com

ISBN-13: 978-1945772061 (Absolutely Amazing Ebooks)
ISBN-10: 1945772069

# Coronado's Trail

*Four days ago the Captain-General rode west from Tiguex, beyond the valley of the great river and out onto the high plain. Accompanying him was Don Rodrigo Maldonado. It happened that the general's saddle failed, causing him to fall under the hooves of his companion's mount. Our leader was grievously wounded about the head. Although he has survived, few doubt that this is the end of our ill-fated expedition. If the disappointments of Cibola and Quivira were not sufficient, surely now his spirit has completely broken. Perhaps, finally, we shall be permitted a return to New Spain.*

- from the diary of Pedro de Castañeda, December 17, 1541.

*Bartie Hampstead arrived today from New Haven. Picked up the metal detector in Tucson. We'll hunt artifacts. Last year's iron thing in the San Carlos Wash still intrigues me. Mysterious place: like it's haunted? Home is line shack in Lyle Canyon again. Bartie says it's a dump, and I can't say he's wrong. But still it's way better than living with Sandy and my parents at the ranch house.*

- from the diary of Jeremiah McLeod, Jr., June 3, 1995.

# Chapter 1

**I** was in my office, contemplating a week's worth of untended paperwork, when Maria Obregon called to report what looked like the remains of an old pickup, partly buried down in the San Carlos Wash. At the time I thought there were going to be more important things to worry about. Boy, was I wrong. The country is full of old abandoned vehicles, of course, but this one turned out to be a 20-year-old coffin. By the time we figured out who was buried in it, and how he got there, we'd solved an Arizona mystery that had been around a lot longer than that old truck – about four centuries longer, actually.

Stories about crime-fighting western lawmen and women seem to be everywhere these days, both fictional and otherwise, but I have yet to read one that ended up quite like this. My name is Calvin Creede, and I'm a deputy sheriff assigned to the Sonoita substation in Santa Cruz County, Arizona. Headquarters are down in Nogales, right on the Mexican border. Most residents of the county live around there or along the I-19 corridor on the way up toward Tucson. Luis Mendoza is Sheriff. He's a good guy, and he pretty much lets me handle things by myself out here in this relatively unpopulated part of his county. It is an unusual arrangement for sure, but we both like it that way. Mostly I operate outside the departmental chain of command and reported directly to him, unless things get too complicated. I didn't know it yet but some big complications were on the horizon, and my days of comparative solitude were numbered.

Maria Obregon started this whole thing off. She lives on a quarter section homestead she inherited from her late

*1*

husband. Maria works for the post office and runs a small goat dairy. She's tall and trim, dark-haired and smart, and we've known each other since grade school. I'm pretty sure we're engaged.

I answered her call in the usual way, just in case. "Sheriff's office. Deputy Creede speaking."

"Hi Cal, it's me."

"Hi. What's up?"

"I'm out here on the Rocking M Ranch, and I've found something you might want to see."

I knew Maria had a fondness for reptiles. "Is it a snake? Have you found a new kind of rattler or something? For god's sake be careful. Why don't you switch to botany or bird watching or something safe?"

"Good grief, it's not about snakes. Why would I call the sheriff's department about a snake?"

"Okay then, what?"

"The wash flooded last night, so Boomer and I decided to take a walk down here and poke around. Sometimes the water brings stuff to the surface, like arrowheads and pieces of pottery. Anyway, I've just come across a buried vehicle of some sort, sticking part way up out of the sand. I don't think it was here the last time I walked down this way."

"What kind of a vehicle?"

"I think it's a pickup, but all I can see is part of the back end. It's old and rusty. Do you know anything about somebody losing a truck on the Rocking M, maybe a while back?"

"Nope, but it could have been before my time. Ranchers used to put their old cars and trucks along stream banks to slow down erosion. I expect that's the story on this one. It got buried somehow, and then last night's flood washed it back out."

"I'll bet you're right. But here's the odd part. I was

walking away when Boomer starts to sniff and dig around in the sand. He's got a good Labrador Retriever nose, and he got real excited. I'm having to hold him back right now. So I'm wondering, you know, if there might be something down there inside it. Inside the truck, that is."

At this point just the tiniest alarm bell went off in my head. "Have you checked with the McLeods?"

"I called over there, but nobody answered. I left a message, but then I thought maybe I should talk to you."

"Can you tell what make of truck? Is there a plate?"

"I can't see a plate or any sort of a name or anything. I don't know much about this sort of thing, but it looks like it could be from the late 80's or early 90s."

"All right. I'll try to get a hold of Angel Corona, their foreman. I'll see if he knows anything, and then I'll call you back. If we decide to come out there now, do you want to stick around? We probably can find the thing ourselves."

"I'll stick around. I'm curious about this whole thing, maybe more than you, *cara*. Oh, and before I let you go, don't forget we're entertaining the parents tomorrow at my place. I'm thinking that, ah, you probably should arrive a little before six? After they're already here?"

I got the message. "Well, I suppose that's how we should handle it. But don't you think they've already figured out what's going on with us? After all we're both adults, and ..."

"Let's not do this over the phone. We'll talk about it later. Bye."

The line went dead.

I've had some experience with girlfriends, and I've walked through mine fields in Afghanistan. One thing they have in common is you never know which particular step might be the wrong one. So why was she being so touchy about going public with our relationship? I like Maria a lot, and I think she feels the same way about me. I wondered about that as I looked up the number for Angel Corona.

# Chapter 2

**N**obody answered at the Rocking M, so I left messages at the foreman's house and at the McLeods. Then I called Maria and told her to forget about it, she might as well head back home. I tried to get back to the pile of paperwork on my desk that was threatening to topple over onto the floor, but it just wouldn't happen. Instead, I stretched out a six-foot frame that isn't as nimble as it used to be, propped my cowboy boots up on the desk in front of me, and gazed past their pointy toes out the four-paneled window that is my only source of natural light. The jagged ridge top of the Mustang Mountains formed a cloudless eastern horizon, already shimmering in the early heat. A blue haze left over from last night's rain partly obscured the familiar skyline.

I thought about the boots. In most ways they're a damned silly affectation. They hurt my feet, and I rarely need to get on a horse any more. But this is cattle country, or at least it has been for most of the last 150 years. Cowboy boots are a part of the culture around here, even though it's a new century and housing developments and vineyards are gobbling up lots of what used to be ranchland. All sorts of people wear boots no matter what they do for a living, from the bartenders over at the Santa Rita Saloon to the hairdressers at Wanda's House of Beauty. For sure, nobody in the valley is going to pay much attention to a lawman wearing sneakers.

I looked again out the window. Grasslands of the Sonoita Valley had just survived nine months of drought and wind, and they had long since faded to a dry-season dusty brown. But it had rained hard the night before, the first real downpour of the summer monsoon. In a month the whole valley could be as green as a Welsh countryside. Or not. The monsoon can be notoriously fickle, especially in July. Like all us locals, I've learned the hard way not to get my hopes up this early in the season.

~ ~ ~

The telephone rang.

"Hello, this is Angel Corona over at the Rocking M? You left a message?"

"Hello Angel. Thanks for calling back. And look, this may be nothing, but Maria Obregon was out walking her dog this morning down the ravine behind her house, and she came on the remains of an old pickup sticking part way up out of the sand. Since it's on Rocking M land, I thought you might be able to tell me if anybody has ever dumped truck or car bodies along in there."

"That would be in the San Carlos Wash? No, I don't think so. But it sure could have happened, maybe back before my time. Anyway, what's so interesting about an old truck? They're all over the place in this country."

I knew that Angel Corona had worked on the Rocking M Ranch for almost forty years. It seemed unlikely that the truck pre-dated his tenure on the job, assuming Maria was right about its approximate age.

"Normally I wouldn't be interested at all. But Maria said her dog was digging around in the sand, pretty furiously I guess, as if there might be something buried down inside the cab. So I thought maybe I should take a look. Assuming you and the McLeods are okay with that."

There was no immediate response, and I thought perhaps we'd been disconnected. Sometimes a heavy rain messed with our local landline. "You still there, Angel?"

"Yep, sorry. It's just that Sandy and Janet are at their beach condo in Cabo San Lucas for the week. But sure, I suppose you and I could take a drive over there. I need to check some fence out in that direction anyway."

I wondered why the foreman seemed a bit hesitant, but decided not to pursue the matter, at least for now. "Thanks, I appreciate the offer. What if I come over right now? Maria could meet us there."

"Okay, I'll be ready. We can take a couple of the ranch ATVs, since the wash could still be pretty wet."

I got back in touch with Maria, who by this time was nearly back home. I told her Angel and I would be coming out to the truck site in an hour or so, if she wanted to walk back and meet us there. I still didn't think her discovery was going to amount to anything, but it made a good excuse to get out of the office and put off tackling the stack of paperwork languishing on my desk. Most of it had something to do with a new way of reporting overtime hours to the sheriff down in Nogales. Overtime might have been important for some of the deputies, but it had nothing to do with my job representing the county all by myself up here in Sonoita.

I ate an energy bar, locked up the office, and got into the Chevy Blazer the county has assigned to me. I drove east out of town on State Highway 82. It was mid-morning by this time, and a handful of embryonic thunderheads were building over the Whetstone and Huachuca Mountains, hopefully the portent of more rain.

On the way out of town I passed the Sonoita Shopping Plaza, still under construction. A large sign in front proclaimed that three shops were "Already Leased!" but plenty of others were still available, and interested parties were encouraged to contact "Sandy McLeod, Developer" for further information. Sandy owned and nominally ran the Rocking M Ranch, but everybody knew he had big ideas that were supposed to make him richer than he ever could hope to be in the cattle business.

When I was a boy the Sonoita Plain had been a wide

7

and treeless prairie, uncluttered by houses during the day
or by their lights at night. Now there was this ridiculous
shopping mall and, even worse, the ranchettes that were
springing up all over the place. Refugees from places like
Chicago and Dallas and Los Angeles were coming with
their pet horses and their oversized pickups belching
diesel fumes into the once-clean air. Not that I blamed
them. Who wouldn't want to live here? For a while the
stalled economy had put a stop to new developments in
the valley, but that was only a temporary delay to the
exurban juggernaut.

You might think what happened to me in Afghanistan
would have made the changes around home seem trivial.
You'd be wrong. Down deep I knew that my favorite view
was in big trouble, and sometimes it just ate my gut.

I continued driving east on route 82 until I came to the
county road that ran south along the western flank of the
Mustang Mountains. I followed it for about five miles, and
then turned left onto a well-worn gravel track winding up
across an alluvial outwash. A steady wind blew in from the
south, which was a good direction. The monsoon rains
usually came from down there.

Headquarters of the McLeod ranch were still three
miles away, nestled up against the southern base of the
mountains. Driving up into the Mustangs I had a fine view
out across the 40,000 acres of grassland that made up the
Rocking M Ranch – or had done before Sandy McLeod
started carving it up. Oak and pine-clad slopes of the
Huachuca Mountains and Santa Rita Range formed the
eastern and western horizons, respectively. To the south,
only the low Canelo Hills prevented me from having a
clear view all the way down into Mexico.

Angus McLeod had purchased the Rocking M Ranch
back in 1942. The story over in the Santa Rita Saloon was
that he had built his house so he could see the entire

8

property from his front porch. The story went on that the old patriarch would be turning in his grave if he knew what his grandson was doing to the place.

I didn't know the McLeods all that well. Janet always waved and smiled when I passed her on the road, and we exchanged pleasantries at various social functions like the county fair and rodeo. Sandy wasn't so friendly, and he always seemed disinterested in the usual things that residents of the valley talked about, like the weather and the grass. I guess he was so engrossed in his real estate developments that he didn't care how the ranch was doing as a place to grow cattle, even though he owned the biggest spread in the whole valley. Instead, he seemed almost obsessive about his new shopping mall, and about selling all those ranchettes. I'd heard rumors that the McLeod real estate empire was in trouble. Maybe that's why he seemed sort of grumpy all the time.

I continued following a two-track dirt road that curved north and up into the grass and mesquite-covered hills. Limestone cliffs of the Mustangs loomed in the background. An oversized Rocking M brand was part of a steel structure that arched over the road. Beyond it lay the sprawling ranch compound. Straight ahead of me was the original ranch house – a square two-story whitewashed adobe with wide covered porches on all four sides. A metal roof pitched down from a central peak, with dormers built into all but the northern side. Off to the left of the house were two horse barns with attached corrals, and a functioning windmill that supplied a large steel-rim stock tank. A modern one-story Santa Fe style home sat atop a low rise off to the north, surrounded by a low adobe wall.

Angus McLeod had occupied the original Rocking M ranch house until he died in 1980. His only son Jeremiah was born in that house, and Jeremiah had lived there with his wife Abigail until they had both been killed in the crash

9

of their private plane in 2001. The current owner of the Rocking M was Angus' grandson Alexander, who had been called Sandy for as long as anybody could remember. Sandy and Janet had abandoned the old house as soon as they could get the big new adobe built up on the hill. Now their foreman Angel Corona and his wife Juanita lived in the original place. That's where I pulled up and got out of the Blazer.

Angel appeared at the door. He was a head shorter than me, with chiseled features and a deep tan that testified both to his Hispanic heritage and to a life spent outdoors. He let his snow-white hair and sideburns grow a bit longer than was fashionable, but I had never seen him look anything but trim and well dressed in jeans, a long-sleeved shirt with snap buttons, and a standard wide-brimmed hat – black felt in winter, white straw in summer. Today it was straw.

We exchanged greetings and discussed the weather. It was a good neutral subject, and something everybody in the valley talked about this time of year, especially the ranchers. A strong monsoon meant it would be a good year for the grasses in the valley and for the livestock that depended upon them.

"We had a good rain here last night, Cal. How did it go out your way?"

"Likewise. That was a heavy storm. Pretty much covered the whole valley I think. And the way those clouds are building, I'll bet we're gonna get it again tonight."

The old man's eyes scanned the southern horizon. He nodded, then hesitated. "Well, maybe. But I'm a lot more comfortable talking about how it was yesterday than about what might happen tomorrow."

"What do you mean?"

"I mean the monsoon can tease a man, like somebody up there has a nasty sense of humor. Lots of days those big

*10*

wet clouds build over the valley in some places but not in others. Sometimes it seems like God is watering everybody's grass but ours. Guess I'm superstitious. Don't want to jinx it by getting all jacked up about a rain that never happens. I'll bet your Dad was the same way when he was running the Pitchfork Ranch. You still live out there?"

"Sure do. I fixed up the old stone bunkhouse for myself after I got back from the army. There's just one room besides the bath, but everything works." What I didn't tell Angel was that lately I'd begun spending some nights, most nights actually, at Maria's place.

"How's the Pitchfork doing? And your parents? They are well I hope?"

"The ranch is fine. Those folks who leased it are doing a good job. And my parents are pretty happy over in Green Valley, I think. I know Dad misses some aspects of ranch life, but they were both getting to the point where it was time to move closer to a grocery store and the doctor's office. And I know what you mean about getting teased by that monsoon."

I suggested we get on with the business at hand, and Angel agreed. "But I don't think we're going to find anything interesting."

I shared the foreman's opinion, but decided to keep things neutral for the time being. "Won't know until we get there."

# Chapter 3

ATVs are nasty noisy things, normally to be avoided. But it was the right way to head out into a wash that might have been blown out by floodwaters the night before. We drove east from the Rocking M headquarters, following Babocomari Creek downstream to its junction with the San Carlos Wash coming in from the south. A ribbon of water still flowed in the tributary, and the air was heavy with the pungent smell of head-high rabbit brush that lined the edges of the wash. Almost overnight the shrubs had turned from their dry-season gray to a brighter monsoon grayish green. A surprising amount of debris lay scattered along the cut, testimony to the power of the recent flood.

We headed upstream for about four miles, until we came to a long open stretch of bare sandy bottom. I spotted Maria and Boomer at the far end. From a distance it looked like they were standing next to a shapeless brown lump, but as we approached I could make out a wheel well and the left half of a tailgate sticking up out of the sand. The frayed remains of a tire still clung to the rim.

Maria had her glossy black hair tucked up under a wide-brimmed Resistol straw hat, and she wore a khaki sportsman's shirt with lots of pockets. She and the foreman exchanged hellos, and I asked them to stay back and hold the dog, just in case.

*13*

The old man frowned. "What's the problem? Seems like an ordinary old truck to me."

"No problem, necessarily. But if there's any evidence of a crime here, it's better that I go in before anybody else disturbs the place."

"What sort of crime?"

"No idea. Probably none at all. But Sheriff Mendoza would be plenty upset if there was something here and we messed it up."

The foreman nodded. "Okay. I've got to go upstream anyway. I want to check on a water gap fence that crosses the wash. Might have been knocked out during the flood. And by the way, say hello to Luis next time you see him. We used to be pretty tight when he lived in Patagonia. That was before he got elected sheriff. He and my youngest brother played football together at Patagonia High."

After the foreman had driven on, I approached the buried vehicle while Maria held Boomer. I started by walking around its perimeter. There were no signs of recent disturbances in the sand except two sets of fresh footprints, one human and the other canine.

I called back to Maria. "Did you see any footprints when you first got here?"

"Nope. I hope it was all right for us to walk right in like that. Perhaps curiosity got the better of me."

"That's all right, I understand."

I pulled a camera out of my daypack and photographed the truck from all sides. Then I untied the spade Angel had attached to my ATV and began to dig, carefully at first and just along the place where the back bumper was sticking up. The sand was loose and easy to move. About two feet down the center part of the tailgate appeared. It bore the symbol of the Ford Motor Company. I dug further, exposing the rest of the bumper, and below that an old rusted license plate. I brushed sand and dirt away until I was able to make out numbers and letters. It was an Arizona plate, but any stick-on tags showing the registration years were long gone. I took a small spiral-bound notebook out of my shirt pocket, and wrote down the plate number.

I went around to where the front half of the pickup presumably lay buried under the sand. Some very large boulders lay just below the surface. It was obvious that any further excavation would require a backhoe or some similar piece of heavy equipment. I needed to get permission from the McLeods to do any more digging. They probably wouldn't object, but it would have to wait.

Just then Angel Corona came around the bend, moving fast, so I decided to hold off calling Nogales for information about the license plate. The foreman pulled to a stop, but left the ATV running. I walked over in his direction. No point in encouraging the man to come any closer. "That didn't take long. Were there any problems upstream?"

"Nope. Looks like that fence held in the flood. I'm surprised, given the amount of water and debris that must have moved through here last night." Angel gestured toward the buried pickup. "Did you find anything down there?"

"Yeah, I was able to dig out the tailgate and a license plate. It's a Ford, with an Arizona plate." I consulted my notebook. "The number is TRJ 897. Does any of this sound

*15*

familiar?"

"No, not really. Like I told you, there's lots of old abandoned vehicles in this country." Angel stared at the truck, and I thought maybe he was about to say something more. Instead he just looked down at his feet, and kicked at a piece of driftwood sticking up out of the sand.

"So you have no idea how this old truck might have gotten here?"

"Nope."

"All right. I'm going to run a trace on the plate. I'll let you and the McLeods know what I find out."

I turned to Maria. "Do you want a ride back home? The only problem is going to be Boomer. I guess he'd have to run along beside us."

"No, that's fine. We'll walk back. It isn't far. Will I see you tonight?" She hesitated. "I mean, you are coming over for dinner, right?"

"Sure, see you then. And thanks."

Angel Corona shot me a look, but kept quiet. We got on our ATVs and drove back downstream toward the Rocking M headquarters, while Maria and Boomer headed off on foot in the opposite direction. By now thunderheads were building over the Huachuca Mountains in earnest, and I heard one low rumble as we pulled into the Rocking M yard.

# Chapter 4

**D**ark clouds continued spreading across the southern horizon as I drove off McLeod land and back down to the county blacktop. The air smelled moist, as if it might have been raining already in the San Raphael Valley, down on the Mexican border.

"Get on up here," I said aloud to the rain gods. Then I had another thought. "But as long as I am asking favors, please stay out of the San Carlos Wash for the next couple of days."

I was getting an odd feeling about that old truck. Maria said Boomer had wanted to dig down around it. Now that I had the make and the plate, I would learn something about its history. Yet the foreman of the Rocking M had seemed almost deliberately uninterested.

~ ~ ~

Margaret Brumbaugh had served as Santa Cruz County Clerk and Recorder for thirty years. She was a treasure. All her files were in order and up to date, all the time. She had quickly and adroitly adapted to the computer age, but she insisted on keeping paper copies of everything anyway. And she was a local, having been born and raised on a small ranch in the valley.

Anybody at departmental headquarters with access to a computer could have run a trace on the license plate I had unearthed in the San Carlos Wash. But it was Margaret I called, just as soon as I got off the Rocking M. There were two reasons. First, she probably would be able to get me more information on the history of the truck, and more quickly. Second, I wanted to avoid getting staff in the sheriff's office stirred up about something that might not be important after all.

"Clerk's office. This is Margaret."

"Good afternoon, Mrs. Brumbaugh, this is Calvin Creede calling from up in Sonoita?"

"Good afternoon, Cal. How can I help you? And please call me Margaret."

"Yes ma'am. Well, I've come up with a license plate on an old Ford pickup, and I was wondering if you could tell me something about its history - who bought it, who registered it last, that sort of thing."

"Do you have the VIN number? That would be a big help. Is there a stick-on tag showing the year?"

I explained the circumstances as to why I had neither the VIN nor a tag. "But I do have the plate number, so I'm hoping you can run that. I'd be interested in who purchased the vehicle and when, and whether there were any subsequent owners."

I read her the letters and numbers.

"Okay. This may take a while. Let me call you back. Shall I reach you on your cell or at the office?"

"Either one. I'm on the way back to town. Should be there in about twenty minutes. I'll wait for your call. And thanks."

~ ~ ~

More than an hour passed before Margaret Brumbaugh called back.

"I was able to get some information on that truck you found. If I may ask, what sort of case are you working on?"

"I'd rather not say right now, Mrs. Brum – ah, Margaret. I know you wouldn't break a confidence, but most likely this will turn out to be nothing important."

"I wouldn't count on that, in light of what I found out."

That sounded interesting. "Go on, please."

"Well, in the first place, that plate belonged on a 1990 Ford 150 pickup, and there's no record that anybody ever moved it to another vehicle. Second, it first was registered to Jeremiah McLeod, who evidently bought the truck new in that year."

"Were you able to find out the last time the truck was registered?"

"I'm getting to that. So anyway, I checked all the records for that vehicle. Took some doing I don't mind telling you, and I had to call in a favor from a friend who works in the state office up in Phoenix. But here's the deal, at least as far as the official records are concerned. Title to that truck was switched from Jeremiah McLeod to Jeremiah McLeod, Jr., in 1993. It was registered for the last time, in his name, in 1995. There are no records after that. No indication of a sale or trade. Just nothing."

"I didn't know Sandy McLeod was Jeremiah. I thought his real name was Alexander."

"I assume you're talking about the McLeod who owns and runs the Rocking M Ranch? The guy building all those houses in the valley? That's not who owned the truck. It was his older brother. They always called him Scooter, but his real name was Jeremiah McLeod, Jr. Don't you know the story about him?"

"I didn't even know Sandy had a brother."

There was a slight pause. "Well that's right, of course you wouldn't. You were only a kid in 1995, when Scooter, uh ... went away."

"What do you mean 'went away'?" Angel Corona's peculiar reaction down in the San Carlos Wash was taking on greater significance.

"He just disappeared that summer. Nobody knew where he went, or at least nobody talked about it. As I recall there'd been some trouble before he went off to college. We heard some stories about drugs, maybe a DUI. That was a long time ago, and I can't remember the details. Not sure I ever really knew them, probably because the McLeods tried to cover it all up. Sorry I can't be of any more help."

"You've been a big help. And thanks for getting me this information so quickly. Whoever was running the Sonoita office in 1995 likely handled the case, since it involved a missing person. I expect the sheriff can fill me in on the details, although I think he was just a deputy back then."

"I expect he can, Cal. Luis has always had good political instincts, and this case involved one of the most prominent families in the valley. If it helps any, I think the deputy assigned to Sonoita back then was Barney Stroud. Last I heard he was living in a retirement home over in Sierra Vista. Might be dead though, by now. My contacts aren't what they used to be since Fred and I moved down here to Nogales."

# Chapter 5

**B**ecause I was the only lawman stationed in the valley except for the Border Patrol, I was on duty essentially 24-7. That meant staying in uniform just about all the time, and sometimes driving a county vehicle on personal business. The uniform was a pretty simple deal really, just the badge, a sidearm, and a regulation shirt, in addition to my customary boots and blue jeans. Luis Mendoza wanted each of his deputies to look like one most of the time, but he also expected us to be discreet. Although we had not discussed it specifically, I had decided that such discretion would apply when I stayed over at Maria's place. This was going to be one of those times, so I headed home to swap out the Blazer for a 2004 Jeep Cherokee I'd had since college. It now spent most of its down time in a shed next to my little stone bunkhouse on the Pitchfork Ranch, except when it was parked at Maria's.

I changed out of my uniform and put my sidearm and badge in the jeep. I drove back to Sonoita, and then headed east to the village of Elgin. At one time Elgin had been a center of regional activity in the valley, with a school and a railroad hotel. But the railroad was long gone and Elgin's only gas and grocery place closed in the 1970s. A few years later they even shut the post office, and now the town was little more than a rural crossroads with a few private residences and a small winery.

I took the right fork just past the winery, and turned south. The Mustang Mountains were at my back, under a partly cloudy sky. I drove until I came to a small hand-lettered sign on the side of the road:

*21*

**Nanny Boss's Dairy**
**Milk, Cheese, and Soap.**
**Registered LaMancha Goats.**
**M. Obregon, Prop.**

I turned east down the two-rut track leading back to Maria's house and outbuildings. Nanny Boss was the name of her first goat, and the ruling matriarch of her little herd. Dust billowed out behind the Cherokee and then blew forward ahead of me, driven by a strong wind that had shifted to the west. The remnants of last summer's grass lay along the sides of the road, beaten and bleached by the sun and the wind. I tried to imagine some new green shoots, but it was way too soon for that. The jeep's windows were rolled up tight against the dust, but to little avail. By the time I reached the clearing in front of Maria's house I could feel the grit on my teeth. It was amazing how the Arizona wind and sun sucked moisture out of the soil, even in one day.

Maria lived in a modest adobe that she and her late husband Tony renovated the first summer they were married. Tony's great-grandfather had built the original structure as a simple three-room square that included a living area along the east side, with a kitchen and single bedroom at the west end. The house had grown into its present rectangle with the addition of a bathroom and two more bedrooms, signaling the arrival of both indoor plumbing and various offspring.

I parked my jeep under the canopy of a huge mesquite that grew next to the west wall of the house, then stepped out into the buzz of a thousand bees dutifully collecting nectar from the flowers over my head. At least some of them were provisioning hives that Maria kept in a field at the south end of the property. Her mesquite honey was among the best in the county.

North and east of the house were corrals, two sheds,

and a small barn that comprised Maria's goat dairy. Two hundred yards beyond them I could see the tops of desert willows lining the San Carlos Wash, over on Rocking M land. A handful of goats were milling around in one of the corrals, and Maria's big brown and white billy goat was among them. I was barely out of the jeep, but already he had given me the evil eye. We didn't get along, and I had a sore backside to prove it.

I walked around to the front door and knocked. Nobody answered, so I knocked louder and looked in the window. The response came from behind me. "I'm out in the barn milking the last couple of goats. Go on in and help yourself to a beer. And take a look at something I put on the table."

When Maria and Tony first moved into the house they had torn out the inside walls of the original structure, creating a larger living space that afforded a fine view of the Mustang Mountains off to the north. The two remaining bedrooms were at the east end, one of which Maria had turned into an office where she kept records for her dairy.

I walked inside and across to the kitchen area that now took up the southwest corner of the main room. I pulled a bottle of *Bohemia* out of the refrigerator, and then turned my attention to a green piece of paper lying on the table. It had the following words printed on one side:

*KELP*

*[Kin for the Ecological Liberation of Plants]*

*Whereas grasslands of the Southwest are precious and fragile.*

*Whereas horses, cattle, sheep, and goats are destroying these grasslands and all the living things that need them.*

*Therefore, we must take action to rid the valley of these vermin.*

23

*Take heed.*

What the hell? I turned the paper over, but the other side was blank: no name and no address. How had Maria come by this and what did it mean?

Just then she walked in through the front door. Boomer came charging up, tail wagging, and licked my hand. I lifted my beer up out of range of the dog's eager pink tongue, and held up the green sheet of paper with my other hand. "Where'd you get this?"

"It came in the mail, post-marked Tucson. Sent first-class."

"Was there a name or return address on the envelope?"

"Nope. But a whole lot of them turned up in the post office three days ago, addressed mostly to different ranchers in the valley. I delivered them all over the place. Has anybody complained to you about it?"

"Not yet, but I expect they will. What about the postmaster? Did she get any feedback? This note seems pretty threatening."

"I haven't heard anything yet, but I didn't go in to work today so maybe she did."

"Let me know if you learn anything more. And I'd like the envelope if you still have it. We need to find out who's behind this. I don't think there's a legal issue here, but there could be if the threats get more specific, or if something happens."

"Like what?"

"Who knows? Maybe harming or rustling somebody's cattle? This '*KELP*' bunch, if there is one, could be some kind of eco-terrorist group. Livestock grazing is a hot-button issue for some of those types."

"Well, nobody'd better mess with my goats. If I catch anybody out there ..."

"If you catch anybody out there, you call the sheriff, that's what you do, okay?"

"Sure. Right after I grab the shotgun that's up there over my door, and back 'em into a corner with it. *Then* I call you."

I decided it was time to change the subject, but I also made a mental note to see what I could find out about an organization called *KELP*.

"You want a beer? Shall we go out on the patio?"

"Thanks, but let's drink it in here. It's still too hot outside, and I've got to attend to those *chimichangas* we're having for dinner."

I went to the refrigerator again, and got Maria a bottle of *Pacifico*. It was her favorite. She kept the *Bohemia* around just for me. We agreed that any Mexican beer was better than the horse piss in a bottle that passed for most of the big-name U.S. brews.

"So when you were walking down the San Carlos Wash today, what were you after?"

"Pretty much anything. You know, artifacts and stuff. Oh, and snakes I suppose."

Snakes again. "Did you find anything? Besides that old pickup, that is?"

"I found an arrowhead and two pieces of broken pottery. But I didn't keep them."

"Why not?"

"When I studied anthropology at the university, the professors explained all the reasons it was a bad idea to collect things made by Native Americans. So I just took pictures and wrote down the locations in a little notebook I carry."

"So you don't have any sort of a collection?"

"Not Indian stuff. But once in a while treasures come to the surface that could date from when the Spanish or the first *gringos* lived on the land, and sometimes with

*25*

them I just can't help myself."

"What have you got? Can I see?"

Maria went to the closet in her office, rummaged around for a bit, and came back with a cardboard box that she laid on the kitchen table. Inside were some purple glass bottles, a rusted hunting knife with a bone handle, and what apparently was her most treasured item - a hollow sphere that looked like it was made of copper or brass. It was about an inch in diameter, with a hole in the bottom and a loop at the top.

She handed me the little ball. "I have no idea what this might be, but it looks old doesn't it?"

I turned the object over in my hands. "Sure does."

Normally I would not have shared information about an open case with a private citizen. But I was certain that Maria could keep a confidence. Besides, she was the one who had found the truck in the first place, so I decided to bring her up to speed. "Speaking of things in the San Carlos Wash, aren't you interested in what I found out about that buried pickup?"

"You know I am, *amigo*. I thought you'd never get around to telling me."

I filled her in on what I'd learned about the truck's history from Margaret Brumbaugh. She was as surprised I had been about the existence and mysterious disappearance of Sandy McLeod's older brother.

"I guess we were both too young at the time to remember it. But it must have been a hot topic of gossip in the valley. And nobody ever heard from the brother again, after the summer of 1995?"

"Apparently not, from what Margaret said. But I haven't checked the case files yet. I hope they still exist. And I need to have a conversation with Sandy McLeod. That will be task number one on Monday. Sandy and Janet are down at their Mexican beach house through the weekend."

"Aren't you going to check inside the front end of that old truck? I told you about how Boomer was acting."

"You bet I am. I expect Sandy will be anxious to help, but one way or another it's going to happen. Didn't you think it was odd, though, how Angel Corona reacted when I told him the make of the pickup? I can't say for sure, but it's almost as if he was sorry you'd found the thing in the first place."

"Yeah, I noticed that. You know it really would be helpful if you knew a bit more about this mysterious older McLeod boy before talking to Sandy. They called him Scooter? I'll bet our parents will remember the case. Why don't we ask them about it when they're here tomorrow for dinner?"

"That's a good idea. But don't tell them about the pickup yet. I'd like to keep that quiet for a while. We'll just need to come up with some other way to start a conversation about the McLeods."

I decided this was the right time to change the subject. "There's something else I'd like to talk about now, for just a bit, if that's okay."

"About what?"

I paused and took a sip of beer. "About us. I want to talk about us. You know I ... just think we ... I mean ... oh Hell, Maria, you know what I mean."

Maria rolled her eyes. "How can I know what you mean, Deputy Creede, when you haven't said anything yet? You were like this even in grade school. I liked you a lot back then, mostly I suppose because of your curly black hair and your blue eyes. But you never could get to the point. Now stop mumbling and tell me what's on your mind."

I sipped again, and fiddled with the wet ring the bottle had left on the table. "That's not fair. You don't seem any more willing than I am to talk about us. About our relationship. But I think it's time, don't you?"

Maria shifted her gaze to somewhere over my right shoulder. Her standard bemused look had gone away. Eventually she spoke, quietly at first and then with more force.

"You're right. But this is hard for me." She paused. "So here is what I think." Another pause. "I think you and I have something special. I think we could make a good life together, and most days that's just what I think we should do. Most days, really, I wish we'd gotten together before Tony and I were married. And before you married Martha. It might have been easier then. Now, it's not so easy."

"Why not? We're more grown up now than we were back then, when maybe we both made some mistakes. I sure did with Martha."

Her dark eyes flashed. "I'll never think of Tony as a mistake, Cal."

"Sorry. I didn't mean it like that. All I am saying is, Tony and Martha are out of our lives now. Now, it's just us. Can't we just take it from there?"

"Of course we can. But you have to be patient. You have to understand how hard it was for me after Tony died."

"I'm sure you still grieve his loss, Maria. It was a terrible blow. Nobody, including me, would expect otherwise."

"Yes, but there's more to it than that. It has taken some years, but now I feel pretty good. Good about this place and about my dairy business, which is finally starting to get somewhere. And of course I'm happy about you."

Maria paused long enough to take a drink from her *Pacifico* and wipe a beer bubble off her chin. "But here's the hard part. I also feel good about my independence. It's like I'm proving something to myself, about what I can do.

And it's a good feeling."

An awkward silence followed, and then I guess we both realized it was time to lighten things up.

"So anyway, Deputy Creede, it seems you've got a handful, huh? I mean, being in love with an uppity broad who wants it all?"

I followed her lead. "Some of my best friends are uppity broads, especially if they know how to make good *chimichangas*. And it's starting to smell really good in here. When are we gonna eat?"

Later that night, in the midst of our lovemaking, the second storm of the summer rolled down off the Huachucas and swept across the old Obregon homestead. "That was thunderous," Maria said afterwards.

I laughed, and hoped the rain had stayed out of the San Carlos Wash.

# Chapter 6

The next evening Maria and I and both sets of parents were seated around her table in the little adobe house at Nanny Boss's Dairy. Mom and Dad (that's Doris and Harold Creede) had arrived about five-thirty, with Maria's folks, Cecilia and Ernesto Contreras, as passengers. I showed up fifteen minutes later.

The Contreras family lived in the small town of Patagonia, about 12 miles down the road from Sonoita. For years they had run Ernie's Auto Service, where she kept the books and he was the head mechanic. Up until his retirement Ernie had kept the vehicles at the Pitchfork Ranch in good running order, and so my parents had known the Contreras' for better than forty years. That afternoon Mom and Dad had taken the southern route on their drive over from Green Valley, down to Nogales on Interstate 19, and then up through Patagonia on highway 82, picking up Maria's parents on the way.

Conversation around the Obregon table was having trouble getting started.

Mom spoke first. "Well, here we all are."

Mrs. Contreras was next. "Yes, here we are."

Another awkward silence followed, eventually broken by my father.

"Please pass the enchiladas. Those are just too good not to have seconds. Don't you agree Ernie?"

"I sure do Harold. I think I'll have another one myself."

Mom nodded approvingly at Maria. "I don't know how you do it, my dear. I mean what with doing your job for the post office, and then keeping up this dairy. When did you find time to put together such a delicious meal?"

"Well, I had yesterday off from work, and then Cal helped out. He, uh, came by here for a while yesterday afternoon on some business. And so I put him to work chopping things."

Ernie Contreras perked up. "What sort of business?"

I recognized this as an opportunity to change the subject in a favorable direction. It required just one small fib. "Nothing much, really. There was a call about some cattle loose on the county road, and I thought maybe a water gap fence had broken on the Rocking M Ranch."

I pointed out the window in the direction of the San Carlos Wash. "You know, because of the rain we had Thursday night. It's not my job to round up cattle, of course. But it is my job to keep the roads safe, and there's always a lot of traffic through here on Friday night. Mostly it's folks from Tucson driving too fast, trying to get a camping spot down at Parker Canyon Lake before they're all taken for the weekend."

Maria took her cue. "It seems like Angel Corona has his hands full these days. Sandy McLeod spends so much time with his development projects that he doesn't help out much at the ranch. Was his father a good rancher?"

Ernie Contreras did not hesitate. "You bet. Jeremiah McLeod was a fine cattleman, just like his father. One of the best. But his boys, well, that's another story."

Now we were getting somewhere. "Maria and I were talking about that the other day. We heard somewhere that Sandy had a brother, but neither of us remembers him."

Mom swallowed a last bite of enchilada and put down her fork. "Jeremiah Jr. was two years older than Sandy. Everybody called him 'Scooter.' I was teaching at the Elgin grade school back when the McLeod boys were growing up. I remember them well. They were bright, good students, but very different."

"Different how?" asked Maria.

"Scooter was quiet, artistic, and always sort of moody, even as a boy. Sandy, on the other hand, never met a stranger. He was very popular among his classmates. But there was something about him that always put me off. I enjoyed teaching Scooter more than Sandy, in spite of his quirks. Scooter went to Yale, you know, just like his father."

"So what happened to Scooter?"

Cecilia Contreras spoke up. "It was very strange, and tragic too. He was home from college for the summer. What year was it, Ernie? Some time in the mid 1990s, I think. Anyway, one day he just disappeared. Nobody could figure it out. The sheriff's office investigated of course, but nothing ever turned up. His parents were frantic, as any of us would be. But then the weeks turned into months, and the months into years, and they never found him or heard from him again.

"It haunted them up until the day they died – not knowing what had happened, whether he might be alive out there someplace. You could see it in their eyes whenever they came into the shop or we met them around town. I can't imagine what it must be like to live with something like that."

"Me, I think the McLeods always had their suspicions about what happened to Scooter," said Ernie Contreras. "He'd been in some trouble, you know."

I definitely wanted to hear more about this. "What kind of trouble?"

"Trouble with the law. He had a DUI during high school. Then a couple of years later the Patagonia town marshal caught him selling drugs. That was in the summer too, but earlier than the summer he disappeared. Maybe two years before, I can't remember for sure."

33

I wanted more details. "Was he arrested? How did the case turn out?"

"Oh, he was arrested all right. But I don't think he ever did any jail time, because of his father's influence in the community. Also, I think he testified against a drug dealer as part of a, ... what do you call that when somebody gets out of legal trouble by helping on another case?"

"A plea bargain?"

"Yeah, that was it. A plea bargain. He testified against one of the Trujillo boys in return for probation. It was either Paco or Pedro, I can't remember which."

Cecilia Contreras interrupted at this point. "It was Paco, dear, don't you remember? They put him in jail, and then he died. But I think Pedro's still around."

I knew something about the Trujillo family. They had homes in Patagonia and in Nogales, Sonora. Various family members had been prosecuted over the years for smuggling both drugs and people into the U.S. There also were rumors about worse crimes, about rivals who died or disappeared, but nothing ever was proven.

Maria steered the conversation back to the McLeods. "What happened to the boys' parents?"

Dad apparently knew a lot about this. "Jeremiah liked to fly. He had his own plane that he kept at the ranch. He and Abby died together when he crashed trying to land during a thunderstorm. I think it was in 2001. That was when Sandy took over the ranch."

Ernie Contreras rolled his eyes. "Sure, if you could call it that. From the very beginning he was more interested in real estate than in cattle. He'd gone to the University of Arizona and majored in business. That kid always has had dollar signs in his eyes. And there's one other thing about Sandy. He and Scooter pretty much hated each other's guts."

Cecilia interrupted. "Oh I don't know about that,

34

Ernie. They were just different, that's all. I don't think you know very much about sibling rivalry." She paused and looked around the table. "I don't suppose any of us does, since Cal and Maria are both only children."

Nobody knew what to say in response to that. My mother apparently decided it was a signal to draw the evening to a close, because she pushed back her chair and stood up. "Anyway, it's getting late, and I know you kids have to work tomorrow. Maria, let me help you with these dishes."

"That won't be necessary, Doris. Cal and I will clean up. And thanks for coming, everybody."

On the way out to the car, my mother drew Maria aside. I watched the two of them with their heads together, and wished I could hear what they were talking about.

# Chapter 7

**S**andy McLeod was waiting outside my office when I showed up for work on Monday morning. He was slouched against the hood of a late-model Mercedes sedan, smoking a cigarette. As I pulled into my usual parking space, the rancher/developer stood up, dropped the cigarette onto the gravel and stubbed it out with the toe of his lizard-skin boot. Sandy was of medium height, slim, with curly red hair that was fading to gray around the temples.

"Morning Deputy."

"Good morning, Mr. McLeod. I was about to call you."

"I expected that might be the case. Angel filled me in on what you two found on the ranch last week. He came over as soon as Janet and I got back from Cabo. I had to be in town early this morning, so I thought I'd just come on over. Did you find out anything more about that pickup?"

"Yes I did. Why don't we go inside? Would you like some coffee?"

"No, thanks, I can't stay that long. Got to get over to my shopping mall. There's a crew coming to put up drywall in one of the new suites. Speaking of which, I was talking to your boss at Rotary breakfast the other day, and I asked him if maybe the department might want to lease you a new office in my development." Sandy paused to wave his arms around. "This place you're in now looks kind of run-down."

"Oh? The sheriff hasn't mentioned that to me. But anyway, come on in and let me tell you what I found out."

We settled in the office, me in a brown leather swivel chair behind the desk, my guest in an old wooden straight-backed number I'd liberated from the Pitchfork when my parents moved out. I'd been hoping to discuss things with the sheriff before talking to Sandy McLeod, but now there wasn't going to be time for that.

"After I left your place on Friday, I did a successful trace on the license plate attached to that old truck. It was first registered to Jeremiah McLeod in 1990. It was new that year, a Ford F-150. Then, in 1993, the registration showed a new owner, or what I assume was a new owner – Jeremiah McLeod, Jr."

A look flashed across Sandy's face. What was it? Fear? Anger? Hope? I couldn't be sure, so I played ignorant. "Are you Jeremiah McLeod, Jr.? And do you remember that pickup?"

"I remember the truck, but it never belonged to me. I wasn't named after my father. That was my older brother. We called him Scooter."

I noticed Sandy McLeod used the past tense. "I don't believe I ever met him. Does he still live around here?"

"No, he ... uh, he's gone. We ... uh, we don't know where he is. But he was declared legally dead several years ago."

"When did you last see him?"

"In the summer, when he was home from college."

"Do you recall what year that was?"

"I think it was 1995."

"That's interesting."

"Why?"

"Because 1995 was the last year that anybody renewed the registration on that pickup."

I expected a response, but didn't get one. Sandy McLeod just sat there staring out the window, his pale blue eyes squinting against the morning sun. There may have been a pained look, but I couldn't be sure. Finally, he turned back in my direction, unsnapped his shirt pocket, and fumbled inside for a pack of cigarettes. "Do you mind if I smoke?"

"Sure, go ahead." I watched the other man light up, as I dug a heavy old glass ashtray out of the top center drawer in my desk. "With your permission, I'd like to make arrangements to excavate the area where we found that truck."

"Why? When?"

"Well, right away I suppose. There could be another flood. As to why, that's pretty obvious, isn't it? I mean, with your brother's disappearance, we might find something – some evidence – about what happened to him. You said he just disappeared that summer. Nobody had any idea where he might have gone? Has anybody ever heard from him since 1995?"

"No. We never heard anything. He was just gone." Sandy took one nervous puff on his cigarette, then stubbed it out in my ashtray. He exhaled, enveloping both of us in a pale blue cloud. "Your department searched for him, of course, eventually contacting other law enforcement agencies. Even the FBI, I think. And after everybody else gave up, my parents continued looking on their own. But they - that is *we* - never had any luck."

I decided not to mention how Maria's dog had reacted around the place where they had found the truck. No point in upsetting the man any further at this point. "So, would it be okay for us to do that, Mr. McLeod? To dig it out of the sand?"

"Sure, go ahead. Just let me know when it's going to happen, so I can tell Angel."

"I think the easiest way to get in there is through Maria Obregon's place, since the San Carlos Wash is right out behind her house. But we'll need to cut your fence. We'll repair it afterwards of course, and we'll make sure no livestock get out. So is that okay?"

Sandy McLeod waved a hand in dismissal. "Sure, that's fine. Like I said, just let Angel know." The rancher/developer turned away and resumed his stare out the window. He coughed once, then stood up. "Well, I've got to go now. They're expecting me over at the mall. Oh, and you might want to give Luis a call, about getting a new office suite."

There had been something decidedly odd about the man's reaction to the discovery of his brother's old truck. Neither he nor Angel Corona seemed to care all that much. What was going on here? If I had a family member that disappeared, and if something turned up that might lead to new information, any sort of information, I'd be pretty excited. I'd jump at the chance. I'd dig up that truck myself, even if the law didn't want to do it.

It was time to get going on the cold case of Jeremiah 'Scooter' McLeod. And it was past time to have a talk about it with my boss down in Nogales.

~ ~ ~

When I first accepted the job as deputy assigned to the Sonoita Valley, Sheriff Mendoza had set up a protocol he wanted followed whenever something important came up in the northeastern part of the county. I'd been an officer in the Military Police during the second half of my hitch in Afghanistan, which had included training and some experience in crime scene investigations. So I had latitude to act on my own, at least in the early stages of an investigation, as long as I kept the sheriff in the loop. Luis Mendoza trusted me to do the right thing. He just didn't want any surprises.

I dialed the number that got me straight through to his personal cell phone.

"Mendoza."

"Morning Luis, this is Cal Creede. There's a little thing going on up here that we need to discuss, if this is a good time."

"Sure. What's the problem?"

I proceeded to describe what I knew about the case of Scooter McLeod and his pickup truck, including Sandy McLeod's peculiar reaction to the news.

"And so there are several things I need. First, I want to dig up the vehicle. Second, I need to get a look at all the files from the McLeod missing persons case, assuming we still have them. And I would like to have a talk with whoever conducted the original investigation. Margaret Brumbaugh thought it might have been somebody called Barney Stroud, and that maybe he was living at a retirement place over in Sierra Vista."

There was no response, so I went on. "Oh, and finally, can you think of any reason why Sandy McLeod might not want me involved in this?"

It was like he hadn't heard the last part. "You've been talking to Margaret?"

"Uh huh, to run a trace on the buried truck."

"I'm not sure you needed to get the County Clerk involved in this. My office staff could have done that for you." The sheriff did not sound happy.

"Sorry. I thought Margaret could get me the full story quicker, and that she might remember some things about the case since she grew up around here. Anyway, is it okay if I proceed? Can you have somebody get the files organized? I could come down later this week to pick 'em up."

It was dead quiet on the other end of the line. Over the years Luis Mendoza and I had developed a solid, almost familiar, working relationship. But now something wasn't right.

Eventually he responded. "Sure, go ahead with your investigation. But I have one condition. If there's nothing interesting in that truck, just let it go, okay? I'm guessing there are more pressing matters that need your attention besides a twenty year old missing persons case. If you do find anything, then we'll probably need to get my people in crime scenes involved.

"And I'll get somebody to dig up those old files, assuming they still exist. Last I heard Barney Stroud was living over in Sierra Vista, but the same thing goes there. Don't bother him until you've finished with the truck and we've talked about it."

I rang off with a promise to get back in touch if anything turned up. Afterwards, I remembered that the sheriff had avoided answering my most important question. Why might Sandy McLeod be stonewalling the investigation?

# Chapter
# 8

**R**amirez Backhoe Service did a brisk business in the valley, mostly digging holes for septic tanks and ditches for water and sewer lines. It was going to take some finesse excavating around the McLeod pickup without damaging any possible evidence. I was pretty sure Manny Ramirez was up to the task, so I looked him up in the office copy of the local phone book, and punched in the number.

"Ramirez Backhoe, this is Ruby."

"Good morning, Mrs. Ramirez, this is Calvin Creede calling from the Sheriff's Department. May I speak to Manny please?"

"He's out on a job right now. Can I take a message?"

"I have need of his services, to help me unearth a truck that's stuck out in the San Carlos Wash. I think it should take two or three hours at most. Do you think he might be able to do that?"

"I keep his schedule and make the appointments. The job he's on now will probably take until tomorrow morning to finish up. But he's free tomorrow afternoon. What happened? I'll bet somebody got stuck in that flash flood, right? Some people just never learn."

"It's something like that. Tomorrow afternoon will work fine. Do you know Maria Obregon's place? Tell him to meet me there right after lunch. Oh, and we'll be doing a bit of cross-country driving, so he'll want to hook his trailer to a four-wheel drive vehicle if he has one."

"Sure, we know where Maria lives. We bought some of her goat cheese last week. It was pretty good, too. I'll tell Manny to bring the big truck. You say the vehicle is stuck in the San Carlos Wash? I suppose things have dried out by now from the storms we had last week. But we'll need to be careful. It'd be a real mess if Manny buried his rig in the sand out there, you know, because then we'd have to charge you whatever it cost to get him out."

"It should be okay, unless we get another rain tonight. If that's the case, I'll get back to you. Otherwise, tell Manny I'll see him tomorrow."

Next I called Angel Corona to tell him we would be out to dig out the pickup truck the following afternoon. The Rocking M foreman said that he'd scheduled a doctor's appointment in Sierra Vista, so he wouldn't be around. I was just as glad.

~ ~ ~

The sheriff liked his deputy in the Sonoita Valley to go out on a general patrol at least four days a week, just to check on things and to assure residents that the department was on the job. Since there was nothing else pressing, I decided to do my rounds.

Sonoita lies at the crossroads of two state highways. Route 82 runs northeast from Nogales toward Tombstone over in Cochise County, while route 83 begins at the Interstate east of Tucson and terminates down near the Mexican border. The only place they meet is in Sonoita.

I got in the Blazer and headed south on 83, across the grasslands and up into the oak covered slopes of the Canelo Hills. Then I turned back north on a county road that led into Elgin. This took me past Maria's place, but she would be out on her mail route so I didn't stop. From Elgin I drove north to the junction with highway 82, and then east between the Mustang and Whetstone Mountains as far as the county line.

Grasses on the slopes of the Mustang Mountains were showing the first hint of green. There were some puffy white clouds building over the Whetstones, but it wasn't serious, at least not yet. Good thing, since another flood could jeopardize tomorrow's planned excavation.

On the way back to Sonoita, I passed a big semi that was moving way too fast on a curvy section of the highway. I turned around, put on my lights but not the siren, and followed the big rig until the driver found a place to pull over. He was a produce hauler from Nogales, bound for Dallas with a load of Mexican corn and tomatoes. This sort of traffic was heavy on route 82 because it was the shortest distance from the border for truckers heading east on Interstate 10. I wrote the man a $300 ticket for excessive speed, and advised him that a better way was to go straight north out of Nogales toward Tucson. It was Interstate the whole way, straighter and safer, and the speed limit was higher. The driver nodded, but he didn't say anything. He knew about that route of course, including the fact that it was farther and took longer. He wasn't about to change despite the risk of hefty speeding tickets, because his bottom line was the difference between fuel costs and what he got paid on delivery.

It was a never-ending contest between produce truckers and the law along the whole length of highway 82 in Santa Cruz County. I had made more than my share of the traffic stops, particularly in Sonoita itself. The speed limit dropped to 35 just outside town, but veteran truckers usually slowed down well ahead of that point without resorting to their engine brakes. They had learned the hard way about a local deputy sheriff who seemed to have a thing about those brakes. What they didn't know was the reason. It wasn't just that the citizens of Sonoita deserved a quiet community, although that was part of it. The full truth lay elsewhere. Something in the sound of engine brakes took me back to a dark night with the infantry along a dirt road just outside Kabul. I hated that feeling, and did everything I could to keep it buried.

45

# Chapter 9

The sun had just dipped below the skyline of the Santa Rita Range as I drove into Sonoita from my little house on the Pitchfork Ranch. It was Monday, and time for my only regularly scheduled nighttime appearance in town. The heat of the day had faded, and there was no wind. A ribbon of dust hung motionless in the air behind my jeep as I drove down the familiar road heading west off the ranch where I'd grown up. I pulled onto the pavement and turned south on route 83 toward the Sonoita crossroads.

A band of peach-colored sky heightened to orange at the terminus of a cloudless western horizon. It would not rain on this night, but when the monsoon returned there would be thunderheads adding texture and even more spectacular colors to the evening sky.

I walked into the Santa Rita Saloon about seven-thirty, out of uniform and technically off-duty. It was Sonoita's oldest watering hole and eatery, and my personal favorite. The place had a loyal clientele, especially a group of locals who referred to themselves as The Regulars. They came to eat or at least to drink there several nights each week.

I hesitated just inside the door, waiting for my eyes to adjust to the interior darkness, and then to take a preliminary survey of this night's customers. A long high bar ran most of the length of one wall, with a mesquite-fired grill at one end. There were six booths opposite, to my right. Two battered pool tables filled the back of the room, and behind them were restrooms with signs indicating which one was for Cowboys versus Cowgirls. Four booths and about half the bar stools were occupied. I recognized a handful of The Regulars, mostly at the bar. There were other customers as well, some familiar and some not.

Monday used to be dead for business in the Santa Rita Saloon, because The Regulars needed at least one night off to recover from the weekend. Then three years ago Frenchy Vullmers, who owned the place, decided to make it two-fers from five to nine. The idea was to attract new customers. It hadn't worked, but it had caused The Regulars to postpone their recoveries until Tuesday. And it ended up costing Frenchy, because everybody drank twice as much for the same price. Also, fights among the doubly inebriated crowd sometimes added expenses in broken glass, barstools, and mirrors. Frenchy deeply regretted having ever conceived of two-fers night, but The Regulars threatened to take their business to a bar across the highway if he quit having it.

The first big fight had broken out on the third two-fers Monday, two years ago. Nobody could remember exactly what started it, but in the end I'd had to call in help from Nogales to break it up. Six cowboys, four motorcycle types from Tucson (two of them female), and worst of all two soldiers from Fort Huachuca, ended up spending the night in Luis Mendoza's Nogales jail. The sheriff had been annoyed, first because he hated driving the forty-five miles to this end of the county, and second because of complications involved in dealing with the military. He suggested strongly and unambiguously that henceforth I was to spend the last couple of two-fers hours at the saloon to head off trouble. Luis told me I could buy dinner out of petty cash, but I always paid out of my own pocket. I figured I had to eat anyway, and so it wasn't right to stick the county with the bill.

I slid into a booth opposite my old friend Al Truetline, a charter member and one of the most regular of The

Regulars. Al, a native and local entrepreneur, had hired me to pump gas at his Quick Stop filling station back when I was in high school. Inside the station, Al's wife had operated the Good Eats Cafe that served the locals chili and pie for lunch.

Frenchy came over to take my order.

"You got any prime rib tonight?"

"Cal, you know we hardly ever have prime rib on Monday. Usually it is *finis* by Sunday."

"Well, how about a steak sandwich then? And a bowl of your cowboy beans. And a bottle of *Bohemia*."

"Right. I'll have your sandwich up in a minute. So tell me, what's the action around our beloved Sonoita?"

"Not much, I hope."

By anybody's definition, Frenchy Vullmers was a local character. He was tall and heavy, with close-cropped gray hair. The haircut was left over from a twenty-year career in the Army. His massive gut had grown to its present proportions only since he'd retired and bought the Santa Rita. Al Treutline had once suggested that Frenchy must be "drinking up the profits." Everybody loved that one so much that Al had to buy the house a round. In fact, Frenchy had ballooned to his present 270 pounds not from drinking but from inactivity. Tending bar and supervising the kitchen and grill just didn't compare with life in the Army.

Frenchy's real name was Patrice Vieumilliers, and he had been born some 60 or 70 years ago in the southwest of France. His life's journey from the vineyards of Bordeaux to the ranchlands and vineyards of the Sonoita Valley had been complex, to say the least. None of the Regulars knew all the details, and neither did I. What we did know was that Frenchy had been in the Foreign Legion, and then he had volunteered for service in Viet Nam. His final hitch had been a special assignment at nearby Fort Huachuca.

*49*

The Regulars liked Patrice Vieumilliers. He served a good drink at a fair price, he kept the pretzel baskets full, and he cleaned the restrooms at least every other day. But they couldn't handle his name. To The Regulars, Patrice sounded like a girl's name, so they changed it to Frenchy. Nobody objected to Vieumilliers, but neither could they pronounce it. After circling around a variety of approximations, they had finally settled on Vullmers. Frenchy didn't care as long as The Regulars stayed that way.

Most of the Monday night fights started out and ended up strictly verbal. The likelihood of escalation to actual physical violence depended a great deal on the conversational themes that happened to arise. Some of The Regulars liked to bait outsiders by commenting on such things as the length of their hair (too long on bikers, too short on soldiers), and by being overly familiar with their women. But mostly The Regulars were a friendly bunch and the conversations were simply a selection from topics of local interest. Various themes-du-jour would come and go, usually increasing in intensity while declining in cogency as the levels of intoxication rose, until the combatants finally exhausted themselves or actually forgot what they were talking about. Relative silence might then fall over the saloon, except for the clink of ice, the snap of billiard balls, and the sounds of Johnny Cash or Willie Nelson coming from an ancient Wurlitzer beside the bar - still three plays for a quarter.

~ ~ ~

This particular Monday began quietly. Regulars kept drifting in, along with three bikers from Tucson I didn't recognize and some cowboy types that I did. By eight o'clock Frenchy was doing a good business, albeit at half price. There was some talk about the weather. The startup of the monsoon was always a good topic for conversation and wager. Was it going to be a wet summer or a dry one? Then somebody from Tucson claimed that monsoons in the old days were lots wetter than today, and that it had something to do with global warming. The locals greeted this with an ominous and stony silence.

I held my breath. Weather used to be such a nice neutral topic. That was before the energy companies started buying just enough pseudo-scientific cover for politicians willing to pander to folks who found the reality of a changing climate just too inconvenient. Al Gore had it right, but at some level he was like Cassandra, doomed to crying hopelessly in the wilderness.

I never got a chance that night to find out where The Regulars fell out on the climate-change denier scale, because another topic broke the silence, and that was rattlesnakes. Al Treutline started off by stating that rattlesnakes could climb, he'd seen it himself. He'd heard about an old cowboy who'd been killed when a rattler dropped out of a tree onto his horse. The horse had spooked and went over a cliff. Al Treutline winked at me, took a long pull on his fourth Bud Light, and waited for a challenge.

"That's a load of cow crap," said Sally Benton. "Everybody knows rattlers can't climb. They can't even get over the three-foot wall around my verandah, let alone up a tree. But they sure as hell can swim. I've had to pull more than one out of my swimming pool when somebody left the gate open."

Most of The Regulars agreed loudly with Sally Benton. She was right on both counts, of course, but that wasn't the real agenda. Sally Benton owned the V-9 Ranch over near the Huachucas. Her late husband, Arthur T. Benton III, had been an investment banker who bought the Vee in the early 1970's in order to lose money in the cattle business. The first year that Sally ran the ranch by herself she'd accidentally made a profit. It had taken her accountant six months to cover it up, and she had not made the same mistake again. For one thing, she sank a major amount of capital into a herd of very fancy Herefords, including a bull valued at something just shy of half a million dollars. In the dry Arizona grasslands it would take years just to break even on that sort of an investment.

At first The Regulars had been wary of Sally Benton. Her frosted hair, carefully applied makeup, and abundant turquoise jewelry were as alien to most of them as her green Jaguar sedan. But Sally had proven herself otherwise unpretentious, and she was a knowledgeable and steady tequila drinker. Most important of all, she was always good for at least one round for the house.

None of The Regulars chose to disagree with Sally about anything, and there was no more talk about rattlesnakes. Even Al Treutline dropped the subject. I eased back into my booth, relieved that the argument had subsided. Rattlesnakes were just the sort of topic that could erupt into real trouble.

It was quiet for a while, until a biker drifted up to the bar for a refill. He wore jeans and a white T-shirt with a pack of Camel's rolled into one sleeve. How retro was that? His complete outfit also included a black leather vest with a faded logo on the back, and some sort of engineer's boots with too many buckles. His hair was long and slippery, and there was a stainless steel chain looping from his belt to something hidden in a back pocket.

"Piece 'a cake shootin' a rattler," said the biker to nobody in particular. "Ya just pull one off in their general direction, the snake whips out and strikes at the slug, zaps hisself right in the head!"

The biker cackled and looked up and down the bar, pleased with himself. What he probably didn't know was that The Regulars had all heard that apocryphal story about bullet-eating snakes before. It was standard Western lore, along with the myth about rattlesnakes chasing people.

A quiet voice came from somewhere down the bar. "Bull."

The biker turned toward the voice, swaying slightly. Three cowboys sat motionless, all wearing this year's style of droopy felt hat, each staring down into his own beer. The other bikers had stopped their pool game and were watching the bar intently. The original storyteller glanced over to his companions, then focused back on the three guys in the hats.

"Which one 'a you expert cowpunchers got a problem?"

Nobody moved.

"What I'm sayin' is, I'll bet you guys ain't real cowboys at all. Prob'ly never even *seen* a rattlesnake outside a zoo. Probably just a bunch a' *computer* programmers or something."

The largest of the hats put down his beer and turned toward the biker, who had finally managed to say something at least half true. The trio included no cowboys, and none had ever seen a rattlesnake except squashed on the highway. But they were produce haulers from Nogales, not computer programmers.

The trucker rose and moved up the bar. "At least I'm not some pea-brained welfare rat specializes in puttin' his baseball cap on backwards and ridin' a wore-out Harley."

Frenchy Vullmers looked nervous. "Now boys."

Sally Benton tried to intervene. "How about drinks all around, on me?"

Al Treutline quickly got on board. "Sounds great. And you know, speakin' of snakes, I saw this big diamondback once ..."

53

But the biker would was not to be put off. "Stuff it old man. Me an' Hopalong Cassidy here are havin' a conversation."

Unfortunately, the time had come for the sheriff's department to get involved. The biker felt somebody grip his arm tightly, from behind. It was me. I spun him around and gave him a close-up view of my Santa Cruz County Deputy Sheriff's badge. "I would like you and your friends to move on out of here."

"But they ..."

"Please?"

After the bikers had left, I turned my attention to the trio of truckers. They were semi-regulars, usually peaceful enough, and I didn't want to provoke any more hostility. The one who had spoken was named Dave.

"Now look, Dave, that almost got really bad there. Why'd you have to provoke that kid?"

He looked rueful. "I dunno, Cal, it's just that sometimes those punks really get to me. I mean, coming in here and makin' up a bunch of bull. Who was he trying to impress?"

"You know that was just drunk talk. And you darn near got Frenchy's place busted up again, basically over nothing. I'd appreciate it if you'd watch yourself in the future. There's nothing to prove by riling up a biker."

"Yeah, okay. Sorry."

"Oh, and Dave? Next time you and your friends want to masquerade as cowboys in here? Well, try to remember that it's July, and everybody has switched to straw hats by now. Those felt numbers you guys are wearing tonight are a dead giveaway."

There was no trouble the rest of the evening. But just before closing time something happened that eventually proved highly significant. There was an older man at the bar, bald and thin except for an exceptionally prominent beer gut. I didn't recognize him, but he seemed well known to some of The Regulars. At one point the man turned to Al Treutline and spoke in an unnecessarily loud voice.

"Hey, Al, you really go for those light beers, right? So, do you know why a light beer is like making love in the bottom of a canoe?"

Frenchy Vullmers quickly interrupted.

"Now Barney, let's watch it there. We've got ladies present, and we don't like no bad jokes being said!"

The Regulars started to drift home about nine, and by nine-thirty only Frenchy Vullmers and I remained. As usual, I volunteered to help him clean up. As usual, Frenchy said thanks but it wouldn't be necessary.

"Well, then I guess I'll head on home. Here's fifteen bucks for the meal and the beer. Oh, but before I leave, you gotta tell me. Why *is* light beer like making love in the bottom of a canoe?"

"That's a very old and a very poor joke. And you're not going to get the punch line from me. I guess you'll have to ask Barney Stroud if you really want to know."

"Did you say Stroud? Was that Barney Stroud?"

"Sure, that was Barney. Don't you know him? It was before my time, but I think he used to have your job."

"I learned that just recently. Does he live around here?"

"Over in Sierra Vista someplace, in one of those retirement communities I think. You know, where you have your own place but there's meals and medical help right there? He's too old to drive anymore, but Al Treutline goes and gets him once in a while. I think they go way back."

"When did Barney retire from the sheriff's department?"

"I do not know for sure. But I heard Al say once that he retired sort of early, and then he got a job working as a rent-a-cop at the bank over in Huachuca City."

"Any idea why he left the department?"

"Not really. Like I said, it was before my time. But Al once told me he thought it had something to do with those people that own the Rocking M Ranch. The McLeods aren't they? I don't know them. They hardly ever come in here. I guess this isn't their kind of place. Al says they're stuck-up, and maybe he's right."

# Chapter 10

I was anxious to have a talk with Barney Stroud, now that I knew the former deputy was alive and in reasonably good shape, and that he'd been involved with the case of Scooter McLeod. But I'd given my word to Sheriff Mendoza that I would wait until we had learned more about the buried pickup. So on Tuesday morning I was just sitting in my office thinking it was going to be a dull day, when the telephone rang. You'd think I'd have learned by now.

"Santa Cruz County Sheriff's Department."

"Hello, Cal, is that you? Listen, this is Ollie Swade, and I got a big problem. You need to get out here right away!"

Ollie Swade had become one of the loudest complainers in my end of the county, and given to strange notions that sinister and elusive forces were threatening him and his little run-down ranch. He ran too many cattle on too few acres, and his place looked like it. It was a joke over in the Santa Rita Saloon that Ollie's cows must have learned how to eat rocks. Only a pension from the railroad kept Ollie Swade off the county welfare roles.

I sighed inwardly. "What's up, Ollie?"

"Well, this morning I seen these buzzards circling around over my windmill? So I go out, and there's one of my cows lyin' there dead and all bloated-up. And there's a knife stuck in her belly, which is bad enough, but that's not the weird part. There's some kind of note pinned on it, you know between the knife handle and the hide? It's printed on green paper."

"Did you touch the knife or read the note?"

"Nope. I just beat it back to the house and called you.

57

Didn't want to get close enough to read what was on the paper. I been watchin' those crime programs on the TV, and I know about - what do they call it – containing the crime scene? No, *contaminating*. That's it. Contaminating the crime scene. And I didn't want to do that, because we sure as hell got a crime here. That cow didn't stab herself."

"OK, Ollie. I'm on my way out."

I loaded a small backpack with my camera, a roll of yellow tape, some evidence bags, and plaster for casting tire or footprints, just in case. I was now ready to drive the short distance east across the valley to Ollie Swade's little ranch. If in fact the cow had been killed, this was serious business. Besides crimes against persons, there were few things more serious in ranching country than killing or stealing livestock.

~ ~ ~

Ollie lived on a treeless twenty acres out in the middle of the valley. I turned off the county road and drove down a dirt track leading to a small wooden house with a tin roof. There were deep ruts in the road, suggesting that somebody had driven down the track multiple times shortly after the rain. By now it had all turned back into dust.

Beyond the house were a 500-gallon propane tank, a small metal barn, a cattle trough, and an empty corral. An ancient battered Ford Econoline van was parked in the barn. A dozen calves and mother cows were attempting to graze on the barren land off beyond the corral. Most of the animals were clustered around a stock tank being filled by an ancient windmill. The windmill groaned and squeaked under a steady breeze, but only the smallest flow of water trickled into the tank. Turkey vultures rocked and circled overhead. There was no sign of any green grass, in spite of the recent rains.

The old man was on his front porch, sitting in one of

two decrepit wicker rocking chairs. I pulled the Blazer to a stop, and got out. I shaded my eyes from the sun's glare reflecting off the tin roof, in an attempt to get a better look at the man seated in the comparative gloom of his covered porch. He wore faded bib overalls on top of a ragged t-shirt that probably had been white in its original condition. His boots were the lace-up type, but I noticed they were untied. A sparse head of snow-white hair topped a long face with pale watery eyes. He looked surprisingly pallid for somebody who presumably spent a lot of his time outdoors.

"Well howdy Creede. I'm surprised you got here so soon, seein' as how all that's happened is somebody's killed one of my cows. I figured you probably had more important things to do, like bust some trucker out on the highway or get a cat down out of a tree for some rich lady over in Bobcat Creek Estates."

"Now come on, Ollie. I'm here, and you knew I'd take this seriously. After all, I grew up on a ranch."

The old man hesitated, stared off toward the Canelo Hills for a while, and then went on. "Yeah, sure. Sorry. It's just that sometimes I get the feeling people don't care about us old timers any more. Come on up and cool off a bit, why don't you? Then you can go out and see my cow. She ain't goin' nowhere. Want something to drink? All I got is water. Oh, and some bourbon, but maybe it's too early for that."

The outside walls of Ollie Swade's house consisted of vertical wooden planks, long since bleached gray by the sun and wind. Bits of white paint clung to the rafters under the overhanging roof. There was no way to see inside, because the door was closed and an ancient swamp cooler was built into the only window on the front of the house. It hummed and gurgled as I sat down in the other chair. The old man kept rocking, and he eyed me expectantly.

Nothing seemed to be happening, so I nodded and made ready to stand up. "Let's go out and look at your cow first, then we can come back here and talk and maybe have something to drink."

"Sure. I guess so. Damn, here it is only nine o'clock or so, and already hotter than a pistol. Looks like we ain't gonna get any rain today, neither."

I noticed that Ollie's hands trembled as he rose unsteadily from his rocker, and that his forehead was beaded with sweat. The old man pulled a dirty red bandana from the hip pocket of his bib overalls, and mopped his brow. As we stepped of the porch together, I picked up a strong body odor that reminded me of my old high school gymnasium. There were rumors about the man's health, and I wondered how long he could go on living out here all by himself.

Three vultures flapped noisily up off ground as we walked past the windmill. The scene was pretty much as Swade had described it. A full-grown black and white cow was lying on her side, belly swollen to the bursting point, legs pointing stiffly away from the body. The eyes already were gone, probably the quick and early work of insects and birds. There was a large hole in the lower abdomen, from which something had been pulling the intestines. It could have been vultures or coyotes, or maybe even a stray dog. Up higher on the exposed side a small knife held in place a green piece of paper. It was identical to the *KELP* note I'd seen at Maria's.

"See, what did I tell you? Some sonofabitch has gone and killed one of my animals! And left some kind of a note besides!"

"Okay, Ollie. You stay back here while I walk in for a closer look."

"I'm goin' back to the house right now. It's too hot out

here." The old man shuffled off, still mopping his head with the bandana.

I walked slowly around the dead animal from a distance of about ten feet. There was one clear set of human footprints. Somebody had approached the cow from the direction of the county road, apparently milled around a while, and then turned and headed back in the same direction. The prints were deeply embedded in the dried mud. Assuming the footprints belonged to whoever had stuck the knife in the cow, they indicated three important things. First, the person had come in from the road, not from the direction of the house. Second, he or she had come since the rain, most probably some time in the last two days. Finally, the prints were short and relatively narrow, as if a woman or a small man had left them.

There were three other aspects to the scene that puzzled me, and they raised serious doubts about Swade's version of what had actually happened. First, based on my experience with such things, the state of decomposition indicated that the cow probably had been dead for five days or more. Second, the KELP note was smooth and clean, not at all the way a sheet of ordinary paper would look after being subjected to a heavy rain. Finally, the knife was way too small to have inflicted a fatal wound to such a large animal, at least not right away. The cow would have wandered or staggered around for hours, if not days, before bleeding out. How could the *KELP* note have survived intact?

I walked in for a closer inspection, photographing the carcass and the footprints from various angles. Then I put on my gloves, extracted the knife, and placed it and the note in separate plastic bags. I found an old bucket next to the stock tank, added plaster and water, and poured the mixture into three of the best-preserved footprints. There was no sign of Ollie, but I noticed his front door was ajar, and I felt sure he had been watching me.

All the evidence suggested that somebody had pinned the knife and note on Ollie Swade's cow after she already was dead. Nevertheless, something akin to vandalism had occurred here, and of a very peculiar sort. If this was the work of *KELP*, it was one more reason to find out just who the hell they were.

I spread some yellow tape on the ground around the cow, secured it with rocks, and walked back toward the house to rejoin Swade on his porch. A trace of a sneer crossed his flushed face. "So, who do you suppose killed my cow, mister Hot-Shot Deputy?" The guy just wouldn't back off with his attitude.

"It's too soon for that, Ollie. Let me start by asking you some questions. I know you're worried and I don't blame you, but this thing is complicated. I don't think the knife actually killed your cow."

"Yeah, well, it sure looks that way to me."

I told him my reasons for suspecting otherwise. "When did you last see her?"

"It was just this morning, right before I called you. You think I'd wait around on something like this?"

"No, I mean when did you last see her alive?"

The old man paused before answering.

"Well, I guess I'm not really sure. Why?"

"Because it looks to me like she's been dead for several days. I'm surprised you didn't see her when you were out tending to your stock."

"Yeah, well I didn't, okay? I've been having trouble."

"What kind of trouble?"

"Oh, its just that I'm not doing real good anymore. Most days I just stay inside, next to my swamp cooler. The well's working fine. The cows have access to water and some grass, so don't you start in on me. I've got enough trouble with those ecology fruitcakes around here."

"Who's that?"

"You know, them people with the bird club. There's others too. And now this deal with the note. Look, I know what kind of reputation I've got. Seems like half the county has it in for me. Those twenty-five years on the railroad was hard work. All along I was dreaming about getting a little place like this. And now I just want to run a few head of cattle, live out my life, and be left god-dam alone. Is that too much to ask?"

"Who won't leave you alone, Ollie?"

The old man didn't seem to hear the question.

"You know when I first come out here Sonoita was just a place where two highways met up. You could get some gas and a cup of coffee and some ranch supplies at Al Treutline's place. Except for Al most everybody was in the cattle business. Now some of those big ranchers, like the McLeods, well they've decided to become developers. That Sandy McLeod, he's a piece of work. Greedy bastard. You know he's tried to buy my place? Well, I told him to go to hell."

I wondered why Sandy McLeod would be interested in Ollie Swade's little ranch. Didn't he have enough land already? I also wondered why Ollie hadn't sold out.

"You know we all did okay too, back then, just being ranchers. You could sell some steers and maybe have a couple bucks left over at the end of the year. We had dry summers and wet ones, but mostly it rained and the grass was good, and nobody hassled you about grazing it either."

Ollie Swade's grass sure as hell didn't look good now. Over time the mind could play tricks. Many ranchers talked about how hard it rained and how thick the grass grew in the good old days, but the weather records showed that things really hadn't changed. Still, I sympathized. Ollie and I were worried about some of the same things.

63

We'd both known Sonoita when it was free of housing tracts and vineyards, when stars of the wide night sky had shown uninterrupted by the lights of Tucson and Fort Huachuca. And we both knew it would never be the same.

"So you don't have any idea who these *KELP* people might be?"

Ollie shook his head. "Never heard of 'em."

"I've put some yellow tape around your cow. I'll try to get out here later today to make pick up the casts I made of the footprints out there, once they've dried. Don't disturb anything in the mean time. After I'm done with that you can get her hauled away. And don't worry, we're going to figure this thing out."

"I don't think I'm gonna haul her away. I'll just let the buzzards and the coyotes have her. Who the hell cares?"

It wasn't until I'd left Ollie Swade's place, on the short drive over to Maria's, that it struck me. I'd grown up surrounded by ranchers in the Sonoita Valley, and they came in the full range of styles and political persuasions. But I'd never met a single one that didn't care passionately about his cattle, except maybe Sandy McLeod and now, apparently, Ollie Swade. Why else would he be willing to let that dead cow just rot away to nothing right outside his own front door?

# Chapter 11

**M**aria and I were having left over burritos at her place while I waited for Manny Ramirez and his backhoe. She was pressing me about this KELP business, so I decided to catch her up on the doings out at Ollie Swade's ranch.

"There were footprints at the scene and I collected the knife. We may have a better idea who was out there after the lab techs down in Nogales examine the forensic evidence. Which reminds me, I've got to call the sheriff and ask him for some help."

"What sort of help?"

"We need to find out just who's behind this *KELP* business before it escalates into something more serious." I swallowed one last bite of burrito and pushed back from the table. "Have you seen any more of those *KELP* flyers around? Or envelopes that looked like the one you got?"

"You mean like tacked up somewhere? No, I haven't seen any of the flyers besides mine. As to the envelopes, you know I can't talk about what I see in the mail without a court order."

"Not even to me?"

"Not even to you, mister. And by the way, did you know that Luis Mendoza is my godfather?"

"Yeah, I think I heard that. Maybe it explains why he keeps telling me what a great person you are. I think he's dying to find out what our, uh, relationship is about. I'm not quite sure what to tell him. What *is* our relationship about, Maria?"

"Let's work on that tonight, okay?"

I hoped she meant it.

Maria went back to work at a quarter after one, and Manny Ramirez showed up five minutes later, towing his backhoe behind an enormous Dodge 4X4. I got in the Blazer and led Manny and his rig back to the Rocking M boundary fence. We chose a section where the barbed wire already was pretty saggy. I stepped out with my wire cutters, opened a section of the fence, and motioned Manny on through. I'd brought along some extra wire, which I used to patch the fence back together, but just loosely for the time being. A full repair would come later, once we finished dealing with whatever turned up in the buried pickup – if anything.

I pulled around Manny and headed downstream. We startled a big-eared antelope jackrabbit that ran straight down the wash ahead of us for better than two hundred yards before it finally decided to peel off into the brush lining the creek bed. The sand in the wash was mostly dry by now, and we had no trouble getting where we needed to go. The afternoon sun was heating things up, absent even a hint of cloud cover, and there was almost no breeze. It was dead quiet except for the faraway rasp of a lone cicada, probably coming from a stand of cottonwoods down in the Babocomari wetlands.

Manny hopped down from the high cab of his big black Dodge and walked over in the direction of the old pickup. He wore a faded John Deere ball cap, an Arizona Diamondbacks t-shirt, blue jeans, and black cowboy boots. He pushed the cap back farther on his head and contemplated the half-buried vehicle. "Boy, she's really stuck down in there. Just what would you like me to do?"

"I don't want the truck moved or disturbed, if at all possible. But I need to be able to get down to where I can look at the whole chassis."

"Why? From what I can see that old wreck isn't worth salvaging. Why not just leave it there?"

"I can't really talk about it. Let's just say we, the Sheriff's Department and the McLeods, are anxious to find out more about that truck than we can see from what's already sticking up out of the send."

"Well, sure then. But this could take a while, and it's gonna cost somebody."

"Don't worry. The department will pick up the tab, and you know we're good for it."

Manny Ramirez proved to be a true artisan with his backhoe. First he dug a wide trench all the way around the truck, down to the level of the front wheels. Then he began shaving the sand, rocks, and rubble away from the cab, the hood, and the buried part of the bed. It took about two hours before the job was done, and by then the full outline of the old truck was exposed.

Manny cut the engine, and hopped down off his rig. "Do you want me to dig the sand out of the bed and from inside the cab? I can't do that with the backhoe, but I've got a pick and shovel in the back of my truck. Maybe we could work on it together."

"No, this is fine. I'll take it from here. Be sure to re-attach the fence on your way out. And thanks. Please tell Ruby to send me the bill."

After Manny had loaded his backhoe back on the trailer and driven off up the wash, I set to work, first with a shovel and then with a trowel and a whiskbroom. I started with the bed, because it was the easiest to get at. I carefully dug out all the sand and rocks, examining each shovel-full for anything interesting. Nothing turned up. Then I brushed away what little debris remained over the hood, and attempted to check things out inside the engine compartment. But the hood wouldn't budge. This was frustrating, because I had hoped to find the VIN number that would have been stamped somewhere inside. That would have to wait.

Finally, I turned my attention to the cab. The windows were gone, and all that was visible inside was sand and rocks. This presented a dilemma. It would be easier to see what was inside if I could pry open one or both doors, but that would significantly disturb the scene. Should I back off now and get a full investigative crew up from Nogales? I decided instead to take photographs and then to proceed on my own. After all, it might rain tonight.

I photographed the truck from every angle and then got a pry bar and a heavy-duty hammer from my vehicle. I started with the driver's side door. It proved to be a bigger job than I'd anticipated because the hinges and the latch were rusted shut. Leveraging the pry bar into the gap that separated the door from the frame accomplished nothing except to break off old bits of rusted metal. After several fruitless attempts at this, I went after the latch and hinges themselves, using the pry bar and hammer to break them apart. Once freed from these attachments, the rest of the door eventually gave way, albeit in multiple pieces. Some sand and gravel spilled out, but most of the contents of the cab remained firmly in place.

There was nothing obvious inside, but I took more photos anyway. Then I got the trowel and whisk broom and began to scrape and brush away at the debris. It was slow going, but after digging for about fifteen minutes the trowel hit something different. It wasn't necessarily harder or softer than the sand, but it definitely was different. I dropped the trowel and began to brush the sand away by hand. What gradually emerged was a rounded object, more yellow than gray. It didn't look like one of the smooth river boulders that characterized the San Carlos Wash. It looked like the top of a human skull.

I'd seen enough. It was time to call in some high-powered help.

# Chapter 12

On the way back to Sonoita, I stopped off at Ollie Swade's place to pick up the casts I'd made of the footprints next to his dead cow. There was no sign of the old man, and I noticed that his van was gone.

I drove back to the office, made myself a late cup of coffee, and called the sheriff. He didn't let me get past the hello part. "I just got off the phone with Sandy McLeod."

"Oh?"

"Yeah, he's after me about moving you into a new space in his mall. He said he'd already talked to you about it. What do you think?"

"I suppose it would be okay, but that's not what I'm calling about."

"Then what?"

There were two things, of course. I decided first to catch him up on the deal with Ollie Swade's cow. "So I was wondering if you've heard anything about this KELP organization down your way."

"Nope, not a thing. Do you want me to check with my other deputies?

"Yeah, that would be great. I'll ask around up here, but maybe you could find out if they have any sort of statewide or national profile, or maybe a criminal record. We need to find out who these people are. And I should get the knife and footprint evidence down to your lab as soon as possible. Any chance you could send somebody up here for it?"

The sheriff hesitated. "Sure, I suppose so. Is there some reason you can't bring the stuff down here yourself?"

"Yeah, actually, there is. We just finished digging out the rest of that pickup on the McLeod place, and I think there's a skeleton inside."

"Jesus. Are you sure?

"All I saw was the top of a skull. But it looks human, so I'm thinking we probably have a crime scene here. The front of that truck is packed with sand and rubble."

It stayed quiet on the line, so I went on. "Obviously I'm gonna need some help out here. There could be all sorts of evidence in the vehicle besides the body, and it will be all mixed up with the debris. And we need to get moving on this. Another rain could really mess things up."

On previous occasions I had found the sheriff to be decisive and clear-headed when it came time for action. This time, I got only silence.

"You still there, Luis?"

"Yeah, I'm here."

I could almost hear the man sigh over the phone, but then I guess he made up his mind. "Okay, then. Nobody – I mean *nobody* – goes near that truck until we get a forensics crew on the site. And obviously that includes the McLeods. There's a new guy just joined the department, Larry Hernandez. I'm going to send him up your way to help secure the truck site. Do you know Larry?"

"We've met. Seems like a good guy, and he's from the valley if I remember right. Have him give me a call, so I can tell him how to get out there from Maria's place."

"Good. You and he are going to take turns camping by the truck tonight, and I'll try to get a crew out there in the morning. As you know, the county commissioners are too damned cheap to hire their own medical examiner, so we use the one from Pima County. But I like her. Name's Gail Tanner. You should give her a call, since you can tell her where to meet. Hang on, I've got the number here someplace."

There was a pause while he looked up the contact for Dr. Tanner. I wrote down the number, then the sheriff continued. "Oh, and one more thing. Somebody needs to call the McLeods and let them know what's going on. Do you want me to do that?"

"No, I'll do it. But, if it's all right with you I'll wait until Larry gets here. Then I'm going to drive over to the Rocking M headquarters and deliver the news in person."

"Any particular reason?"

"Sure. I'm interested to watch Sandy McLeod's face. There was something odd about his reaction when I told him about the truck the other day."

"Odd how?"

"I can't say for sure. But he seemed sort of distant, not like I'd be if somebody just told me something about my long-lost brother."

"You know people have different ways of dealing with grief and bad things in their lives. Be respectful. The McLeods are an old and important family in this county."

"Sure, I understand. Oh, and while I have you, I want to go see Barney Stroud, and I'd like to read those old files on Scooter McLeod."

"Yeah, I guess it's time for that. Go ahead and see Barney. And I'll get those files copied. Maybe I'll bring them up to you myself. I'd like to take a look at that truck scene. We'll meet up at Maria's place, right?"

"Yep."

"Okay. I'll see you first thing tomorrow."

So now we had a plan, which was good. If it eventually resolved questions about the disappearance of Scooter McLeod twenty years ago, that was good too. With all this good stuff at hand, then why didn't Sheriff Mendoza share my enthusiasm? Was he holding something back, or was it just in my head?

# Chapter 13

I called the office of the Pima County Medical Examiner, identified myself, and asked to speak to Dr. Tanner. A secretary explained that she was out, teaching a class at the University of Arizona in forensic anthropology. "She spends Tuesdays over there, lecturing, supervising the lab exercises, holding office hours, that sort of thing. I can have her call you tomorrow if you'd like."

"Well, this is pretty urgent. I wonder if there's a way to reach her on campus."

"Of course. Let me give you her cell. She always has it on, except during lectures."

I thanked the secretary, rang off, and punched in the number she had given me.

"Tanner speaking." The voice was strong yet distinctly feminine.

"Dr. Tanner? This is Calvin Creede. I'm a deputy sheriff down in Santa Cruz County, and I understand from our sheriff that you help out with crime scene work when there's a need."

"I do when it is appropriate, yes. What's the problem?"

"We may have found a corpse in an abandoned vehicle."

"I see. And the condition of the body?"

"Pretty much a skeleton I expect, but maybe with clothes. Most of it's still buried, so it's anybody's guess what might turn up when you start digging."

"Digging?"

I explained a bit more about the circumstances.

"Just how much of the skeleton have you seen?"

"I dug into the cab far enough to reveal the top of the skull. Then I quit."

"That's a good thing. Do you know about how long the body's been buried?"

"If we've got this figured out right, it's been in there almost exactly twenty years. If we're wrong, well, that's why I called you. We need an expert. I gather you teach a class in forensics at U of A, in addition to your work as a medical examiner. So I'm guessing you've had experience excavating bodies, identifying skeletons, preserving evidence, that sort of thing?"

"Of course. That's one of the things we do here. I can have a crew there first thing tomorrow morning, two former students actually, if you think that's soon enough. Oh, and how do I get there?"

I gave her directions to Maria's place, along with my cell number. "Tomorrow will be great. But I was hoping you could make it down here yourself, rather than just sending your crew. My boss is kind of nervous about this whole thing."

"Oh, I'll be there. This sounds like an interesting case. And besides, getting out in the field is just about my favorite thing. Plus maybe, after this case is settled, I might be able to use it as an example of how we apply forensic archaeology in a real world case."

"If we ever get this thing figured out, I don't suppose that would be a problem. It would be up to the sheriff, of course. See you tomorrow."

I called Maria, who had just come home to feed her goats, and explained what was happening.

"I told you Boomer had found something in that old truck."

"So Nanny Boss' Dairy is going to become something of a staging area over the next twenty-four hours, at least. And is it okay if Larry Hernandez crashes in your living room tonight? He's a new deputy Luis has assigned to help me on this case. We're gonna take turns standing guard over that truck and its contents. The medical examiner will be coming in the morning, with her crew, but I don't think they'll be needing anything from your place."

"No problem, I guess. Just try to keep everybody away from the barn and corral. Sometimes my animals get reluctant to let down their milk when strangers are around. And did you say 'her'?"

"The medical examiner? Yeah, her name is Gail Tanner from Pima County. She's on call for Santa Cruz when we need help."

"That's interesting. I took an anthropology class from a Dr. Tanner at the U of A. It was about forensics."

"Yep, that's her. Listen, I gotta go. I'll see you later tonight. I'm gonna call Larry Hernandez now. He should be coming through your place as soon as I tell him how to get out there."

"Just one more thing, then, in case I miss you tonight. If I'm gone in the morning before Dr. Tanner gets here, say hello for me. Tell her I'll swing by at lunchtime. There's something I'd like to talk to her about."

"What's that?"

"Oh, nothing related to the pickup. I just want to show her that little metal sphere I showed you the other night. The one I found down in the wash? Maybe she knows what it is."

Everything seemed to be falling into place.

I should have known better.

# Chapter 14

**I** called Larry Hernandez, who turned out to be on patrol somewhere near Lake Patagonia, so he didn't have all that far to go to reach the Obregon homestead. I gave him directions, and told him to meet me at the crime scene. "You shouldn't have any trouble finding me. Once you're in the creek bed, just keep driving downstream. It's about two miles."

I got in the Blazer and headed back to the San Carlos Wash, which was when the whole day fell to pieces. I was reattaching the Rocking M boundary fence when an engine noise came from somewhere off to the north. It was loud and high-pitched, as if somebody was in a hurry.

I jumped back inside and drove downstream as fast as I dared. I rounded the last bend upstream from the crime scene just in time to spot old green and white Chevrolet pickup heading north. The bed of the truck was filled with cut mesquite, as if somebody had been collecting firewood. Sand sprayed out from behind the rear wheels as the driver attempted to negotiate the wash at a high speed. The person driving looked like a man. The truck had an Arizona plate, but it was too far away to get any letters or numbers.

I gunned the Blazer, confident that my four-wheel drive SUV could catch up. It would have worked too, except for a patch of wet sand that the other driver had successfully avoided but I did not. Instead, I drove straight into a quagmire. I shifted into reverse, but it was too late. The front wheels spun in place, and sank slowly into the sand. I was hopelessly stuck.

I got out of the Blazer, slamming the door in

frustration, and walked around to the front end for a closer inspection. It was buried clear up to the bumper. I listened in vain to the sounds of the other vehicle fading off into the distance, then pulled out my cell and dialed Larry Hernandez. Fortunately, there was a good signal. Unfortunately, he was too far away for us to have any chance of catching the green and white Chevy.

Larry arrived about twenty minutes later driving a new four-door Jeep Rubicon, courtesy of the county. He got out carrying a shovel and walked over to where I was standing next to the Blazer.

"That doesn't look too good."

"No kidding."

Larry was in his early twenties, with high cheekbones and straight black hair reflecting the Indian portion of his Mexican heritage. He stood about two inches shorter than me, but looked more powerfully built, especially in the arms and chest. He insisted on doing most of the digging, despite my protests.

"I'm the one that got it stuck in there, Larry. It was my screw-up."

"Yeah but I'm younger than you, and I have bigger shoulders. And besides, it's my shovel."

The sun was dipping toward the Santa Rita Range by the time we got my vehicle fully back on dry sand. There still was no wind, nor any sign of thunderheads. I was thinking about that green and white pickup. It must have been my day for old trucks.

"You stand the first watch, Larry, while I drive over to Rocking M headquarters. I've got to talk to the McLeods before they hear from somebody else about what might be going on out here. I'll be back to relieve you in a couple of hours. Or maybe three hours, tops. Maria said there's some *refritos* in the fridge we can warm up, and I'll put on a pot of coffee. It's going to be a long night. She said it was okay if we take turns crashing on her couch."

"That's mighty nice of her."

Innocent enough reply, but was there a look? I wondered how much the folks down in Nogales knew about me and the goat lady.

~ ~ ~

Iced tea on the McLeods' veranda was pleasant in the cool evening air. A half dozen hawk moths were busy extracting nectar from the *Agastache* flowers planted inside their adobe wall, and an occasional bat swooped in from somewhere out on the grasslands. I told the couple what we had found and what we planned to do.

Janet seemed particularly distressed. "Oh my. Do you think it might be Scooter? When will we know? Can we come over in the morning and watch?"

"I would prefer that you not come just now. I promise I'll let you know as soon as we find out anything. Of course that could take a couple of days or more, depending on how easy it is to make the identification. Actually, you may be able to help with that. Sandy, do you remember whether your brother regularly wore any distinctive items like jewelry at the time of his disappearance? And - sorry, I know this may be difficult - but do you remember who his dentist might have been?"

Sandy McLeod did not immediately respond. When he did speak, it was in the same flat tone he'd used the day before.

"It was a long time ago. Scooter wore just ordinary stuff. So, I guess I can't help you on that."

"And what about the dentist?"

"My brother and I started going to Dr. Rojas down in Nogales when we were kids. Janet and I still go there; his daughter now runs the place."

"Thanks, that may help. Oh, and before I go, do either of you know anybody around here who drives an old green and white pickup? Maybe somebody in the firewood business?"

"Why? Do you think it might have something to do with Scooter?"

I'm not inclined to be secretive or deceptive, but my instincts told me not to reveal the circumstances under which I had encountered the vehicle. "Probably not. But I saw a truck like that earlier today, with an odd-shaped load of mesquite, and I just wondered."

Janet McLeod glanced over at Sandy. "Doesn't one of Angel Corona's grandsons drive a green and white pickup? I think I saw it down by the house when they had their family reunion last spring."

Sandy shrugged his shoulders. "I can't really remember. And besides, there's got to be more than one truck like that in this country."

"Would this grandson be in the firewood business?"

"I have no idea. Why don't you ask Angel?"

I stopped by the Corona house on my way out. Both Angel and his wife were on their porch enjoying the evening light.

Angel spoke first, in response to my query. "Doesn't sound familiar. I have two grandsons, you know, Ramon and Oscar. They live down in Patagonia. But I don't think either of them cuts firewood, and I don't recall a green and white pickup."

Mrs. Corona sighed. "We don't see them very often."

I thought she looked sad.

# Chapter 15

It was ghostly quiet in the San Carlos wash until just after midnight. By then the light cast by a half moon was just bright enough to illuminate a cottontail rabbit that made the fatal mistake of crossing the open sand. She had been easy prey for a Great-horned Owl perched in a tall desert willow, and her scream broke the silence when the owl's powerful talons pierced her brain.

I read somewhere that the Navajos think an owl is bad luck. If there was anybody buried in that old truck, he or she was way past luck of any kind. Other than the rabbit and the owl, the only moving things that Larry Hernandez and I experienced through all that long night were mosquitoes.

Larry had taken the watch at sunrise. I was back at the house, just starting my second cup of coffee, when Gail Tanner drove up on a late model Chevy Suburban, accompanied by two young male assistants. Maria was out in the barn feeding the goats. The doctor was younger than I had expected, maybe late 40s, and she had the appearance of someone who spent a lot of time outdoors. She got out of the truck, brushed a loose strand of straight brown hair away from her deeply tanned face, and introduced herself.

"Good morning. Mr. Creede? I'm Gail Tanner, and I'd like you to meet Bob Wilkins and Jeff Garcia. They'll be helping me with the examination today."

We shook hands all around, as Maria joined the group. She nodded to the two assistants, and then spoke directly to Dr. Tanner. "You may not remember me, but I attended your forensic anthropology class a while back."

Gail Tanner smiled in recognition. "Of course I remember you. You always sat in the front row, and you asked really good questions." Then she turned back to me. "Well, Mr. Creede, shall we get started?"

Maria interrupted. "I was wondering, Cal, could I borrow Dr. Tanner for just a minute or two before you all drive down the wash? There's that thing I wanted to show her, and this way I won't have to find you later on."

"Sure I suppose so, as long as it doesn't take too long. The sheriff and somebody from crime scenes should be here any minute. As soon as they get here, we're heading out. I'm anxious to get this job done before there's any chance of a storm coming up. And I expect Larry needs a break."

Maria went inside and retrieved the cardboard box from her house. She pulled out the little metal sphere she had found the previous summer in the San Carlos Wash, and handed it to Gail Tanner. "I know some people think it's not right to collect things like this. I mean, not just to keep it for yourself. And I never take anything that looks like it might have had something to do with Indians. But with this ..."

Gail Tanner shook her head. "No, that's all right. Let's see what you've got here." She held the object up in the morning light, turning it in her hand as she examined it from all angles. Then she handed it back to Maria.

"Well, my field is forensics and not archaeology, so I'm no expert. I've never seen anything quite like that, but if I had to guess I would say it's Spanish or Mexican, and possibly quite old. It could be valuable. I mean to science, not necessarily in terms of dollars."

Maria nodded. "What should I do? Do you want to take it?"

"No, I don't think that would be appropriate. I have a better idea. Why don't you take it yourself to the Arizona

State Museum on campus and show it to the Head Curator, Dr. Rincon. I'll call him when I get back to Tucson today, and tell him to expect you. Okay?"

"Sure, that would be great. You don't think he'll be ... mad, or anything?"

"No, I'll take care of that. But be sure to bring all the information along with you, about where you found it and when. Just where *did* you find this?"

"Last year, over in the San Carlos Wash. But it wasn't by the pickup, where Cal is about to take you. It was upstream from there, in the opposite direction from my house, so it couldn't have had anything to do with that buried truck."

I wasn't so sure.

~ ~ ~

It was a little past 8:30 and the sheriff still hadn't showed up, which wasn't like him. I decided we shouldn't wait. Gail Tanner rode with me to the pickup site, with her assistants following in their van. Larry was glad to see us, and happily went back to Maria's for a quick cup of coffee.

I was impressed with the care, competence and efficiency with which Dr. Tanner and her assistants tackled the job of finding out what was inside Scooter McLeod's old pickup. They started in from the passenger side, because the bit of skull I had unearthed the day before suggested that the body was behind the steering wheel, and apparently they wanted to uncover it last. Each scoop of gravel was sorted through a sieve, and any object of interest was bagged and labeled along with a note describing its approximate location. The crew made sketches and took photographs as they worked.

About 9:30 I heard a vehicle approaching from upstream, and shortly after that a county Explorer pulled to a stop next to my Blazer. Luis Mendoza was driving and he had a passenger. They both exited the vehicle and walked over in my direction. The sheriff was a big man, in his middle fifties, with a tanned craggy face and a full head of dark curly hair. An expanding waistline was the only outward sign that many years in a tough job might be taking a toll. He was in full uniform, including a regulation shirt and tie, and a dark brown dress jacket with a star on the breast pocket and four gold bands around each sleeve.

The sheriff introduced me to Sergeant Joseph Ortega, head of crime scenes. Actually, I had met Ortega before, but I didn't know him on a personal level. He looked to be in his late forties, medium height, with close-cropped reddish hair and one of those scraggly beards that made it look like he'd forgotten to shave for a couple of days.

A few minutes later Larry Hernandez showed up, and the sheriff called the whole group together. He handled the introductions, thanked Gail Tanner for coming on such short notice, and then made it clear that everybody was free to get back to work.

Luis motioned Joe and me aside. "I stopped by your office on the way out here. As long as I was there, I picked up the knife and footprint casts you said came from that rancher's place with the dead cow. I'll take them back to Nogales today. We should have something for you in a couple of days. Oh, and the reason we're late is my SUV crapped out in Patagonia. Broken fan belt."

I asked him about the McLeod case.

He nodded. "Copies of the department files on the McLeod disappearance are on your desk. I didn't take time to read all of it. You probably should do that before you go over to see Barney Stroud. They're mostly his notes, I think."

"I heard Scooter McLeod might have had a record. Is that in the file as well?"

"Yep, that's one thing I did notice, and actually I remember the case. He was busted right after he graduated from high school on a DUI, and then a couple of years later on a drug charge. Oh, and one more thing. Sandy McLeod had his brother declared legally dead in 2003, two years after his parents were lost in that plane crash."

"Tell me about the drug arrest."

"He got caught selling marijuana in Patagonia. A small amount, so it wasn't a big deal. Just kid stuff, really."

Up to this point Sergeant Ortega had not said anything, probably because he hadn't been around at the time of Scooter McLeod's earlier troubles. However, he clearly was anxious to get in on things. He pointed in the direction of Gail Tanner and her crew. "Are things under control here? Do they have any idea yet about who might be in that truck?"

"Nothing so far. Oh, and would you check on a dentist in Nogales named Rojas? Apparently the McLeod kids were his patients. There might be some dental records we could use. I understand his daughter now runs the office."

Ortega took a small spiral notebook out of his shirt pocket, and made some notes. "We'll get on it."

All the forensics team found in the first hour were a few coins, an ordinary kitchen spoon, and the remains of an old ballpoint pen. They didn't make their first major hit until late morning. It was a medium-sized rock hammer, old and rusted, lying on the passenger side floorboard. Gail Tanner placed it carefully in a plastic bag, walked over to where we were standing, and held it out for me to see. "This is interesting, because it's not something the average cowboy would be carrying around. More likely a geologist."

I thought of one other possibility. "Or perhaps an archaeologist?"

"Maybe. Depends on what they were doing out here."

At that point Bob Wilkins called out. "Dr. Tanner? I

think we're pretty much done here, except for the body. We've brushed away as much of the debris around it as we can. How do you want to proceed?"

"Very carefully, as usual. Mr. Creede, Mr. Ortega, Mr. Hernandez, would you give us a hand? We want to get this skeleton on the ground intact if possible."

Actually, it was more than just a skeleton. There were pieces of skin and hair on one side of the skull, some dried flesh on what was left of the face, and a lot of skin and sinew on the ribs and leg bones. Most of the clothing had rotted away, but we couldn't see the feet or lower legs because they were still wearing the crusty remains of a pair of leather cowboy boots.

Dr. Tanner bent over the body. "We shouldn't have any trouble getting DNA off this corpse, if it comes to that. What's the matter, Mr. Hernandez, you look a little pale. Surely you fellows have seen a dead body before."

"Yes, ma'am, but not like that." Larry excused himself and walked upstream into the shade of a tall rabbit brush. It didn't bother me nearly as much. I'd seen worse things in Afghanistan. Much worse, actually.

Gail Tanner got down to business once we had laid the corpse out on the ground. She used a probe, a toothbrush, and a hand magnifying lens to explore all parts of the body. After about ten minutes she asked to see the rock hammer.

"Well I'll be damned."

"What?"

"Looks like you may have a murder on your hands. Not only that, I think we've got the weapon. Look here, on the right side of the skull. This hole isn't the result of decay or from some animal chewing off pieces to get the calcium."

Joe Ortega bent over the body for a closer look. "How can you tell?"

"Well, first of all the hole is too regular and too round. And if you look inside you can see pieces of bone that were broken off and pushed in."

Apparently the sergeant wasn't sure what he was seeing, and told her so.

"That's a puncture wound. No doubt about it. And the rock hammer we found? It fits in that hole perfectly." Then she did a demonstration. "See?"

"So whoever did this left the murder weapon in the truck? What else can you tell me?"

"I'll need to look at this skeleton in more detail once we get the body up to the morgue in Tucson. But from what I can see the victim was a young male, maybe in his early to mid-twenties, without any obvious signs of bodily trauma except that wound to the skull. And we found something around his neck, on a chain. It might be a small coin of some sort, with a hole punched into it. Probably gold, given the lack of oxidation."

She handed Ortega the evidence bag, along with a small magnifying lens. He held the bag and its contents up to the light, and peered at one side and then the other with the lens. Then he asked if I would like to have a look.

Duh.

There was a figure on one side that could have been the Virgin Mary, and on the back were some initials. As best I could see, there were three letters in a row, an "A", followed by another "A", and then an "S."

Jeff Garcia walked over from the truck. He was carrying something. "It was down in the seat, beneath where the body was. I think it's a belt buckle."

We all gathered round as the young assistant put the buckle in a plastic bag, and handed it to Gail Tanner. It may have been silver, with an engraved design, but I couldn't tell because it was pretty tarnished.

The medical examiner held the buckle up for a closer

inspection. "Looks like there are two letters, again probably initials. The first one looks like an 'A' and the second one could be an 'M.' Gentlemen, I'd guess we're standing over the remains of 'A. M.' here, or maybe of 'A. A. S.' Any idea who he, or they, might be?"

The sheriff and Joe Ortega looked at Larry and me. Larry shrugged. I couldn't be sure, but I knew who to ask. I told the sheriff what I planned to do.

He agreed. "You go ahead with that, Cal. Joe and I will help Dr. Tanner finish up here, then we'll make arrangements to get the body up to the morgue in Tucson. Keep us posted on what you find out."

"Will do. Oh, and I have a request about what we found here today. For the time being I'd like to keep that medal and belt buckle, to see if anybody around here recognizes either of them. I'll make sure they're locked in my office safe."

The sheriff frowned, but then nodded his agreement. "Yeah, I can see why you might want to do that."

From his expression, I wasn't sure Ortega was all that happy with the plan, but apparently he had sense enough not to get in the sheriff's face about it.

# Chapter 16

For the second time in twenty-four hours, I drove to the Rocking M Ranch. Angel Corona was on his porch, but I didn't stop. It was the McLeods I had come to see. There was a decision to make, and it was a tough one. Should I show them any of the items we had found in the buried pickup? I decided that was not a good idea, at least for the time being.

Janet was home, but apparently alone. She answered the door so promptly I suspected she'd been watching from the window.

"Hello, Cal. Have you found something? Is that why you're here? Was it - I mean is it - Scooter in that old truck?"

"Well, there was a body, but whose body is anybody's guess at this point. Is Sandy here?"

"No, he's up in Tucson on business. Is there something I can help you with?"

"We found some things with the body, and I need to ask you a couple of questions. First, do the initials 'A. M. ' mean anything to you? Or 'A. A. S.'?"

"What sort of things?"

"I'd prefer not to say at this point, Janet. But can you help me with those initials?"

She thought about it for a while. "Well, obviously the 'M' could stand for McLeod. As to the 'A,' it could be Alexander. That is my husband's real name. Oh, and there's one other possibility I suppose. The boys' grandfather, the man who bought this place, his name was Angus. What were those other initials?"

"A. A. S."

"Off the top of my head, I can't think who that might be. Scooter's real name was Jeremiah, so I can't see how ..."

I thought about the other thing we found in the buried pickup, besides a corpse and two pieces of jewelry. "One last question and I'll let you go. Was your brother-in-law interested in geology, or maybe archaeology?"

"I didn't know Scooter all that well. He went to Yale, though, and I think he studied anthropology and forestry, or something like that."

"Okay, thanks. And would you ask Sandy to come by my office as soon as possible."

Janet McLeod's shoulders had sagged. Her gaze held steady, but I could see the pain in her eyes. "It must be him. Scooter died in that old truck didn't he?"

"It's beginning to look that way, but we won't know for sure until we've finished the autopsy."

*And they don't need to know it was murder*, I thought to myself. *At least not yet.*

~ ~ ~

Back in the office I read Barney Stroud's notes on the McLeod case while eating a sandwich. The file was brief, and not all that helpful. Jeremiah McLeod had reported his son Jeremiah Jr. ('Scooter') missing on July 20, 1995. They had last seen him two days earlier when he and a college roommate from Yale, who was visiting at the time, had come for dinner. The parents had written down a list of Scooter's friends and acquaintances, and Deputy Stroud had interviewed the ones he could find. But it was all to no avail. He had contacted other law enforcement agencies, from local to national and including the FBI, but no leads ever turned up. The young man and his truck had simply vanished.

There were two other pieces of paper in the McLeod file, in addition to copies of the town marshal's reports on

Scooter's legal troubles in Patagonia. One was a newspaper account describing the deaths of Scooter's parents in a crash of their private plane in 2001. The other was a copy of the certificate declaring Jeremiah McLeod, Jr., legally dead. It had been filed in response to a request made by Alexander McLeod in 2003. Barney Stroud couldn't have placed either of these documents in the file because he'd retired from the department in 1996.

# Chapter 17

The town of Sierra Vista is about an hour's drive east of the Sonoita Valley. It had grown up adjacent to Fort Huachuca, dating clear back to the time when the Buffalo Soldiers were trying to catch Geronimo. Sierra Vista has remained a military town, but it has been diluted in recent decades by a substantial influx of Sun Belt retirees.

I pulled my Blazer into the parking lot of the Coronado Vista Manor, an assisted living facility on a quiet side street in the southeast part of town. I had come for my interview with Barney Stroud, armed with a list of names and events I had extracted from the McLeod case files. It seemed the logical place to start on what almost certainly was going to be a cold case murder investigation.

Stroud was expecting me, and he turned out to be much more helpful than his old notes. The old man rose unsteadily from a chair in the small reception room next to the main entrance. We shook hands. He was wearing a loud Hawaiian shirt with parrots and palm trees on it. I guessed he'd put it on just for the occasion. He was tall and gaunt, and almost completely bald, with a potbelly that stuck out well beyond his shrunken chest.

The former sheriff's deputy pointed toward an interior courtyard. "Let's go through here. I spend too much time in that damned room of mine as it is, so I'd rather talk somewhere's else. There's lots of snoopy old geezers in this place with nothing better to do than listen in on other people's conversations, but most of 'em are too deaf to hear anything over the noise of that fountain."

We settled in cheap white plastic yard chairs beside a

splashy water works. The place was protected from the wind, but not from the sun. The air smelled like chlorine. I brought out a list of questions I'd jotted down back in the office, got the man's permission to turn on a small tape recorder I'd brought along, and began my interview.

"First, please call me Cal. And I want to thank you for talking time to talk to me about this case."

"Forget it. Truth is I'm bored out of my skull most of the time. There's only just so much television and bingo and sing-alongs I can tolerate. I can't drive any more, you know, since I had my stroke. And I don't like most of the organized outings they put on here. Can't stand shopping malls, for one thing."

"Do you get out of here very often? I think I saw you at the Santa Rita Saloon the other night."

"Oh yeah? I don't remember seeing you. But that Al Treutline, he's an old friend of mine. He comes and gets me maybe once a month and we have a couple of Frenchy Vullmers' steaks and some beers. It's a nice break from here, and I usually see an old acquaintance or two from back in my Sonoita days, though lots of them's dead now."

"Anyway, like I told you over the phone, we think we may have found Scooter McLeod's body inside his pickup in the San Carlos Wash on the Rocking M Ranch."

"And the pickup just showed up there?"

"No, we think it was there all along, but somehow it got buried in the sand. We had a big storm the other night, and the wash ran. When the water receded, part of the truck was sticking up out of the sand. We dug the rest up and found his body – or at least somebody's body – inside."

"So you're guessing it's been there all along? I mean since he disappeared? That's really spooky, thinking about Scooter's parents spending their last years wondering what had happened to their son, and he was just a little ways out there all that time. Hell, you can probably see that place from their front porch."

"At least now Sandy won't have to wonder what happened to his brother anymore. Assuming that it's Scooter we found, which seems likely."

The old man shifted uncomfortably in his chair and scratched the top of his head. "I don't expect Sandy's spent all that much time worrying about it anyway." Then he chuckled and farted, more or less at the same time.

It was all I could do not to wave a hand in front of my nose. "Why not?"

"Not sure. But from the very beginning he just didn't seem all that worked up. And some of the other folks I talked to said those two brothers never really did get on."

"Speaking of the other folks, I brought a list of names of people you talked to back then, and I'd like to ask you more about some of them, if that's okay."

"Shoot."

I consulted my notes. "Well first, tell me about the roommate from Yale that was visiting the ranch that summer. Somebody named Barton Hampstead?"

"Yeah, he was the first person the McLeods got hold of when Scooter went missing. He was already back at Yale, in summer school I think. He told the McLeods that Scooter had seemed fine when he left, but they hadn't talked since."

"Did you speak to Hampstead?"

"Yeah, but he didn't really say anything more than what the McLeods had already learned. I asked him how long he'd been at the ranch, and why he was there. He said he'd been there most of the summer, up until that point. As I recall, he told me he'd been there for a while the summer before too."

"Doing what?"

"Digging for stuff, apparently."

95

"Digging for what?"

"He didn't say exactly. He said both he and Scooter were interested in archaeology."

"Do you know if they ever found anything?"

"Like what?"

"I don't know, maybe some Indian artifacts?"

"I never asked, and he never said."

That topic seemed like a dead end, so I moved on to the next person on my list. "One of the other people in your notes was a girlfriend of Scooter's. Somebody named Angela Salerno?"

"Yeah, I never actually got to talk to her that summer. But I did speak to her parents, Ray and Vicki. You've probably heard of them."

"Maybe. I'm not sure. Are they the ones who developed Bobcat Creek Estates?"

"That's them. They owned the original ranch that was the land for the development. It was their partner, Jay Hancock, who did the construction and marketing. But everybody got rich on the deal, that's for sure. And it was a high class operation, not like some of that cheap stuff Sandy McLeod keeps putting up."

"So you talked to the Salernos? Did they know anything about Scooter?"

"Nope. They said their daughter was traveling in Europe that summer, and so they hadn't seen him around at all. But I guess the summer before, and then over Christmas break, Scooter had been at their house almost every day, moping around Angela like a lovesick dog. Ray didn't seem all that thrilled about it, either, which surprised me since the McLeods were one of the most prominent families in the valley. And they're Catholics too, like the Salernos."

I was surprised that Barney Stroud remembered so many details about a case that was two decades old. "Did you ever track down Angela?"

"Nope. Never did. Couldn't see the point, really."

Apparently Barney Stroud had trouble seeing the points of things, his good memory notwithstanding. "Did you ever confirm that she actually was in Europe that summer?"

"Didn't do that either. Maybe I should have, now that you mention it. But you gotta remember, this was just a missing persons case back then. And Scooter, well he was different from his father and brother. Sort of a free spirit as far as I could figure out, and not all that close to his family. So we decided he'd probably just gone off on his own somewhere, which of course he had a legal right to do. Nobody was thinking about murder."

"Okay. There's one other thing I wanted to ask you about, and then I think we can wrap this up. What can you tell me about Scooter McLeod's drug arrest in Patagonia?"

For the first time that afternoon, Barney Stroud seemed reluctant to talk. When he did, it was to offer only a short comment.

"The Patagonia marshal's office handled that one. I wasn't involved."

"But Scooter's file has a copy of the arrest record and the disposition of the case. And it occurred before Scooter disappeared. Didn't you see any possible connection?"

"No, not really. Why would there be?"

Up until this point, Barney Stroud had been more than forthcoming, almost too anxious to talk. Now I had the feeling I was being stonewalled.

"We both know what's in that file, Barney. When Scooter McLeod got caught selling marijuana, he ratted out his supplier in exchange for no jail time. That supplier was a guy named Paco Trujillo. Paco got killed in a knife fight in the county jail while he was awaiting trial."

"Your point being?"

"I'd think that's obvious. The Trujillos are a big family down in Nogales, rumored to be involved in some pretty shady business. The oldest son gets killed in jail, and he's there because of Scooter. Seems like an obvious motive for murder to me."

"Well, like I said, nobody was thinking about murder back then."

That was all Barney Stroud could be persuaded to say about Scooter McLeod's drug arrest. I stood up to leave, and the old man followed me out into the lobby of the Coronado Vista Manor assisted living facility.

"Before I go, Barney, there is one more question I wanted to ask. It's personal, if you don't mind."

"What's that?"

"Why did you retire in 1996?"

Stroud hesitated. "It was time, I guess. I'd done my twenty years. Maybe I just got fed up with the rat race."

Rat race? Even now, twenty years later, I'd scarcely describe my job as a rat race. "Then you went to work as a security guard at a bank in Huachuca City?"

"Yep. It didn't pay all that much, but I had my pension from the county. Boring as hell, though, just standing around in that bank lobby all day. Kinda' like this place."

I didn't think my predecessor looked bored. I thought Barney Stroud looked afraid.

# Chapter 18

**M**y talk with the Barney Stroud had been surprisingly helpful. That was good, because as things turned out it was the only conversation I would ever have with the man.

There was time for a quick meal before heading home. The main road leading from Sierra Vista onto Fort Huachuca included at least one of every fast-food franchise I'd ever heard of, along with some truly unique cultural crosscuts. I decided to skip the Chinese hofbrau and the all-you-can-eat Korean taco bar. A billboard next to the taco place extolled the virtues of the El Cortez Condominiums, one of which was that they were right across the street from something called the Sushi Ke-bob. That one sounded mildly interesting, but there was no clue about its location. In the end I opted for safe if predictable, and did the drive-through at one of those standard chain burger places.

I've got to admit that fast food is a secret indulgence, and one I don't get to satisfy all that often. In most other ways, including the late-day traffic, Sierra Vista is a crowded and noisy mess that I was glad to escape for the relative peace and quiet of the Sonoita Valley.

Still, the trip had been useful, and I contemplated what lay ahead as I drove. The sky was nearly dark now, but there were flashes of lightening far off to the south, somewhere down in Mexico, too far away to even hear the thunder. The monsoon might be coming back, but it wouldn't be tonight.

The case of Scooter McLeod was about to get very busy, with all the possible leads I had gotten from the case file and from Barney Stroud. There was the old girlfriend, Angela Salerno, and the old roommate (or whatever he was) called Barton Hampstead. I would need to track them down if that was still possible. I wondered if the Trujillo family remained active in the business of smuggling drugs and people across the border between Arizona and Mexico. I hadn't heard their name mentioned lately, but I wasn't all that involved in things down in Nogales. There were two other items that might or might not have anything to do with the case, but that required my attention anyway. One was the green and white pickup that possibly belonged to Angel Corona's grandson. Whoever was driving, what had they been doing that evening in the San Carlos Wash? And then there was the puzzle of Ollie Swade's cow and the flyers from *KELP*. I'd almost forgotten about that.

It was time to make another call to Luis. I debated bothering the sheriff after hours, but I decided it couldn't wait. After all, Luis said to always keep him in the loop. I punched in his private number (yeah, I know, driving and dialing and all that). He answered on the second ring, and I brought him up to speed.

Luis Mendoza did not hesitate. "Obviously it's getting too busy up your way for just one person. You need help. I'm going to assign Larry Hernandez permanently to your office until things calm down. His parents live in the valley, so he can stay with them. I assume you two have been getting along. You let him handle the daily routine. I'll make sure he knows that he's working for you. Okay?"

"Thanks, that's a big help. He was real helpful today out at the crime scene." I left out the part about where he dug me out of the sand. "And while I've got you, there's a couple more things. First, can you nudge Gail Tanner on the autopsy? I'd like to know for sure if we've got the remains of Scooter McLeod before I get too much farther into this."

"Will do. What else?"

"Three things. First, I need your advice about whether I ought to show Sandy McLeod the stuff we found in the buried pickup, or maybe just tell him about it. I didn't show any of it to Janet this morning, but I'm tempted to with Sandy in order to get his reaction."

"Well, normally we wouldn't share that sort of thing, especially this early in an investigation. But I take your point, so go ahead. Just be sure he doesn't mess with the evidence bags. What else?"

"Have you had anybody check on this *KELP* organization I was telling you about? I'd almost forgotten about it because of everything else that's going on. But Ollie Swade's gonna be all over me if we don't look into it, even though I'm sure his cow was dead before the knife went in."

"Yeah, I was going to call you about that. We did find something, although I'm not sure it's the same deal. Out in northern California they had a situation with some people who were trying to sabotage oil tankers and refineries in the Bay Area. I think they were protesting harm to the sea life. They called themselves KELP."

That sounded interesting. "Was there much damage? Was anybody hurt? Did you get a name?"

"A whole bunch of their flyers started showing up and there was a little vandalism, but nobody got hurt. Apparently the thing blew over pretty quickly. This was a couple of years ago, and nothing has happened since. But all the vandalism was directed against facilities owned by one corporation, Davenport Petroleum. And according to the report we got from the Richmond police department, a person of interest in the case was a woman named Eloise Davenport, aka Muffy."

"Sounds like more than a coincidence."

*101*

"It was. Turns out this woman is the daughter of the head guy and majority stockholder in the company. And she has a record of environmental activism. Pretty weird, huh? But they never could connect her or anybody else to the case, and so it just got put on the back burner."

"Interesting. I think I'll try to find out if anybody named Davenport has been around Sonoita lately."

"Good idea. So, you said there was something else? I gotta' get going. The wife and I were about to head out to the movies when you called."

"One more thing. According to the case file, when Scooter McLeod got busted by the Patagonia marshal he turned on his supplier, Paco Trujillo. And then Paco got killed in jail. I was wondering what has become of the rest of the family. I remember when I was going to Patagonia High the Trujillos were rumored to be a big deal in town, but I haven't heard anything lately. Is there anybody still around I could talk to that might know something about all that?"

"I'm ... not sure. You're thinking one of them might have had something to do with Scooter McLeod ending up dead?"

"Well sure, doesn't that make sense? If the family was at all tight then there's a pretty good motive." There was silence on the other end of the phone. "Luis, are you still there?"

"Yeah, but I've gotta' go. Let me check into this. And do me a favor? Please stay away from the Trujillos for the time being. There's lots of other leads to pursue. I'll get back to you."

"Yeah, sure, but what's the deal?"

The line had gone dead.

# Chapter 19

**M**aria and I were finishing an early breakfast of *chorizo* and *huevos*. It was early and still cool, but the sun already had backlit the eastern horizon, throwing a pale light across the barn and corrals visible through her front window. In another hour it would be too bright to sit here comfortably, but we would both be at work by then. Maria's day always started with milking the goats, and they got really crabby about it if she wasn't out there just after dawn.

She took a bite of chorizo and washed it down with the last of her coffee. "So, I've got an appointment with Dr. Rincon Friday up in Tucson. Want to go along?"

I couldn't remember who Dr. Rincon was, and I had a momentary panic that it might be Maria's physician. Why might I need to go along?

She must have noticed the puzzled look on my face. "You know, the man at the State Museum. Dr. Tanner said he might look at that little sphere thing I collected down in the wash."

That was a relief. "Oh sure. But I probably can't make it, with everything that's going on around here. Speaking of which, I've got a favor to ask. Remember that *KELP* note you got in the mail?"

"Of course I do. What's the favor?"

"Well, we've traced an organization like that to California and come up with a name. Have you been delivering mail around here to anybody named Davenport?"

"You know I can't talk about things like that. It's a violation of a federal statute."

"I can find out from the county clerk if the name is on the county tax rolls. I just thought you might be able to save her and me the trouble. Couldn't you maybe just give me a hint?"

"So you're asking me to break the law? Really?" Maria's dark eyes flashed, but she started up again before I could attempt an explanation. "A hint? All right then, here's a hint. You might take a drive up Lyle Canyon and look for a car with California plates."

"Thanks, I'll do that."

"And here's another hint. I know you take your job very seriously, and I respect that. So you might just afford me the same courtesy, okay?"

"Don't you think that's being a bit asymmetrical?"

"What?"

"Well, it's not like I don't share things about my job that are pretty confidential."

"That's different."

I didn't see how it was so different, and almost said so. She stopped me by putting a hand up right into my face, palm out. I got the message, and turned my full attention back to finishing breakfast.

We both ate in silence for a while, and then it was Maria who broke the ice. "Sorry. I think you owe me one, that's all."

"One what?"

"My choice."

I guess that meant I was off the hook.

~ ~ ~

The drive back into the Canelo Hills and up Lyle Canyon took me into a world very unlike the Sonoita Valley. First, oaks came to dominate the landscape. Farther on juniper and pine mixed with the oak, and soon the sweet smell of pine resin filled the air. Lyle Creek flowed much of the year, watering a ribbon of stately sycamores. I drove in their shade whenever the winding county road dipped near the canyon floor.

I kept my eye out for any sort of vehicle with a California license plate. I could radio the number down to Nogales and get a pretty quick trace. But if it did belong to somebody named Davenport, what was I going to say? I thought about that for a bit, and came up with a plan.

About ten miles into the canyon I spotted a late model Volvo with the right kind of plates parked next to a big stone house set down along the creek. The name 'Wahlberg' was carved into the flat side of a split oak log at the side of a drive leading down to the house. I'd heard of the Wahlberg Ranch, but I didn't think the family was from California.

I couldn't get a signal on my cell phone, so I punched the talk button on the radio.

"HQ, this is Sonoita Station. Come in. Over."

Nothing.

"Come in Nogales, this is Calvin Creede. Is anybody there? Over."

Still nothing. What was wrong with the county communications system now? I took a chance and drove on down the gravel lane.

A woman came out the front door as I pulled up. She was young, short, and shapeless as far as I could tell. Her straight brown hair framed a round face and blue eyes rendered owl-like by thick plastic-rimmed glasses. A cherubic smile seemed frozen in place. She was wearing some sort of mud-green dress that looked as if it had been made from a burlap bag.

I stepped out of the Blazer. "Good morning, ma'am. I'm Deputy Creede from the Santa Cruz County Sheriff's Department. Are you a member of the Wahlberg family?"

"No, actually I'm not. I bought this place from the Wahlbergs last spring."

"As it happens, I'm actually looking for a Ms. Davenport. Would that be you by any chance?"

"Yes, I'm Muffy Davenport. Why are you here?"

The woman kept smiling, but for some reason I was not feeling all that welcome. "Is there some place we could talk, ma'am?"

Muffy chose not to invite me into the old stone ranch house. Instead we sat in two plastic yard chairs under the canopy of a huge sycamore. I admired the tree. She followed my eyes.

"Yes, it is one of our most cherished gifts, isn't it? You know that sycamores once thrived along all the creeks in these mountains, but they usually can't reproduce by seed now that cattle have destroyed the watershed."

"You mean cattle eat the seedlings?"

"Maybe, but the main thing is the cows eat the grass that once held the rain in the soil, so now all the water runs off instantly in flash floods, scraping all the baby trees out of the canyon." Muffy blinked and smiled.

I wondered if that were true, and worried about how I was going to get around to the subject that brought me to this place. She solved the problem for me. "It's just another example of how the ranchers are ruining the land. We've *got* to get this information out. Out to the people, so they will rise up and put a stop to this ... this ecological immorality!"

The young woman's face had flushed, and red blotches mottled her throat. "I suppose you're here about the letter?"

"Well, yes. Now you have every right to your opinions, and in fact I think I share some of them. But if your goal is to reduce grazing, I'm not sure your flyer is the best way to go about it. You know ranchers are a pretty passionate group themselves. It's hard to say how they're gonna take this, especially after word gets out about the cow you killed at Ollie Swade's place."

The young woman stirred in her plastic chair and blurted out in a voice pitched distinctly higher than before.

"Don't you accuse me of something you can't prove, Mr. Creede! You can't tell me what to do! I'm not the one destroying this land. It's *them*! *They* don't care how many plants die! Why can't they see what they're doing? Well, I just don't know. All I know is they've got to be stopped before it's too late!"

Muffy Davenport was still smiling, but now a fire burned in her owl eyes.

"We KELPers got our start in California. Out there, it was the oil tankers discharging waste, killing the marine vegetation, our wonderful kelp beds. And we showed *them* something! Oil companies are big and powerful, so I'm not afraid of a handful of redneck cowboys. And I don't know anything about a dead cow. Who is, uh, what was that name you said?"

"Ollie Swade. Your flyer ended up pinned with a knife to one of his cows, Ms. Davenport. I think you know that. Killing or even harassing livestock is a serious crime in this country. If I can prove you had anything to do with this, I intend to enforce the law. And I certainly can't guarantee your protection from some of the locals if you keep pushing this thing. For your own safety I strongly recommend you stop distributing those flyers. Sooner or later, somebody is going to figure out where they're coming from."

Muffy seemed to have herself under control again. "I'm not frightened by your threats, and I certainly don't need your protection."

As I was leaving the old Wahlberg Ranch, now apparently the southwestern headquarters of KELP, I noticed a stack of mesquite firewood piled up against the side of the garage. I couldn't put my finger on why, but somehow it looked familiar.

# Chapter 20

**L**arry Hernandez was putting some of his things in the office when I came in after lunch. He grinned up at me. "Hi boss."

"Glad to see you know your place. Getting settled okay?"

"Sure. Guess I'll head out on patrol. You can get me on the radio or my cell if you need help with anything."

"Will do. I noticed Sandy McLeod's car over at the shopping mall. I'm gonna go over and see him. I want to talk to him about the stuff we discovered in the pickup yesterday, and ask him about some of the people Barney Stroud mentioned."

"Is Barney the old guy that used to have your job?"

"That's him. He lives over in Sierra Vista now, but he was in this very office back when Scooter McLeod went missing."

"He give you any good leads?"

"He did lots of talking. I think he's bored to death over there. Funny though, there was one topic that seemed to shut him up."

"What was that?"

"When I asked him about Scooter McLeod's drug arrest in Patagonia. As soon as I pushed him for details on that, he pretty much stopped talking."

Larry stopped shuffling his papers. "What details are those?"

I filled my new assistant in on the particulars, about how Scooter had turned on his supplier, Paco Trujillo, who subsequently died in prison.

Larry's face darkened and his eyes briefly flicked away.

"Does he have a brother named Pedro?"

"Yep, that's the one. Why?"

"It's just that I've heard Pedro is some bad *hombre*, Cal. You be careful."

"I gotta go where the evidence leads me."

"Still, you watch your *espalda* on this one, my friend. I wouldn't want to end up running this office alone."

~ ~ ~

I walked the short distance down the road to where the partially occupied Sonoita Shopping Mall was under construction. It was hard for me to be objective about Sandy McLeod, because I resented what he was doing to the valley. No doubt I was being cynical and selfish. After all, the cattle business was pretty bad these days, and housing developments brought jobs for local people who needed them. Like Al Treutline said, "You can't stop progress." Al, for one, was anxious to ride progress for all it was worth. He wasn't in Sandy McLeod's financial league, with his little Quick Stop gas and grocery. But he seemed content with his current enterprises, and he was certain things soon would get better. I liked Al Treutline, but I could not share the man's boomtown philosophy.

The Sonoita Shopping Plaza consisted of an L-shaped array of one-story business suites, opening to the south and east. The structure was faux adobe crowned by a terra-cotta tile roofline, like so many of the low-end tract houses springing up all around the outskirts of Tucson. Sandy McLeod's real estate office occupied one of the larger spaces, tucked into the northwest corner. Adjacent to it, along the west side, were a small yarn shop and a hair and nail place called Wanda's House of Beauty. Other suites were in various stages of completion, but none appeared close to being ready for occupancy. I wondered which one Sandy had in mind for the Sheriff's Department. There were no cars around except the developer's Mercedes. For a business center supposedly under active construction, the place looked pretty damned dead.

The parking area wasn't paved yet, and my boots crunched on newly spread gravel as I walked toward the back corner of the complex. The front of the real estate office was all glass. A spacious front room was sparsely but well-furnished, with a couple of desks, some file cabinets, and a seating area in one corner with two low leather couches and a round black coffee table. There were some oak bookshelves, mostly empty. One wall was adorned with various maps and an artist's rendering of how the mall would look when it was finished. Another section was hung with sketches of various Santa Fe style homes that I assumed were those available in one of the realtor's housing developments.

I was on the verge of tapping on the door, which was ajar, when I heard a voice coming from a back room. Nobody else was talking, and I realized I was listening to half a telephone conversation. It seemed like a good time to do a little snooping.

"... and the escrow on that loan is way too high anyway. We don't need to hold anything like that much insurance until more construction starts. And I'm not really sure when that will be, given the slow-down."

There was a pause.

"I know that. You think I haven't tried? I got all I can handle up here as it is. I need to get my hands on some more water, and I'm still tryin' to move those east side lots."

Another pause.

"Well, why don't *you* talk to the county planners? Seems to me you don't have anything to do anyway, except baby-sit your money."

A much longer pause.

"Aw jeeze, where did you hear that? News sure does

travel fast around here. But believe me, it's not going to be a problem. Those titles are clear as crystal."

A shorter pause.

"Yeah, it probably is him. And even if it isn't, you know we had him declared dead years ago. We're golden on this, if we can just keep the rest of the money boys calmed down. Believe me, your investment is solid."

At this point Sandy McLeod emerged from his back room, and spotted me waiting outside the front door. He was still holding a phone. "Uh, I gotta go. Somebody's at the door."

I knocked, hoping he would think I'd just come on the scene. He waved, and I walked inside.

If Sandy suspected anything, he didn't let on. "Afternoon, Cal! Hope I didn't keep you waiting. That phone's *always* ringing."

"No problem. But if this isn't a good time ..."

"No, no, it's fine, Cal, fine. Come on in. What can I do for you? Is it about that new office we were talking about the other day? Because you couldn't have come at a better time. Let me show you around the mall, and we'll see if there's a spot that suits you."

"Maybe another time. I'll have to clear it with the sheriff first, 'cause the department's budget is pretty tight these days. No, I wanted to talk to you about a couple things we found in the buried pickup if that's all right. See if you recognize them. And I want to run some names by you. Okay?"

"Sure, I guess so. Janet said you came by yesterday." The rancher turned developer pointed to the corner seating area. "Let's sit over here. Like some coffee?"

I declined the offer of refreshments as I handed him two plastic bags, which he seemed reluctant to take. He gave the medal only a cursory glance, and then set it back on the table. The bag with the belt buckle was different. He held it up to the light, and examined both the front and backsides.

"I recognize this for sure. It was my grandfather's. I remember Dad gave it to my brother on his 16th birthday."

We had arrived at a critical moment. "So, then it looks like it was Scooter we found in that truck. I'm sorry, Sandy. I know this must be a shock."

Sandy fidgeted with the belt buckle. "Yeah, it sure is."

"I'm curious about one thing, though, if you're up to talking some more about this."

"What's that?"

"Your name is Alexander, right? So the first initial on that buckle, the 'A,' would fit you, not Scooter. Why didn't your Dad give you the buckle?"

"I can't remember. I think maybe Scooter asked for it. Or maybe it was just that he was the first grandson of Angus McLeod."

It didn't seem like a satisfactory answer, but I decided to change the subject. I pointed to the other bag lying on the table between us.

"What about that little medal? Do you recognize it? And the letters on the back, do you have any idea who that might be?"

Sandy put down the bag with the buckle and picked up the other one. "No, I don't think I've ever seen this before. It looks like a holy medal, but the initials 'A. A. S.' don't mean anything to me."

"Barney Stroud – he was the deputy that had my job back when your brother went missing – he said Scooter had a girlfriend named Angela Salerno. I wondered if those were her initials."

"I suppose that's possible."

"Did you know Angela? Is she still in the area?"

"I remember she and Scooter were a big item their senior year at Patagonia High. Then Scooter went away to

Yale, but I think maybe they kept seeing each other when he was home on vacation. I'm not sure about that, because it was a long time ago."

"What happened to Angela?"

"I have no idea. You might ask her parents, Ray and Vicki. They live over in Green Valley."

"Thanks. There's one more person Barney mentioned that I wanted to ask you about. Somebody named Barton Hampstead. I think he was your brother's roommate at college. Apparently he was visiting out here the summer Scooter went missing."

"Bartie? Sure, I know Bartie. Actually, he lives in Tucson. He has a big fancy house up in Sabino Canyon. But he comes down to the ranch sometimes."

"Why? Is he a family friend?"

"No, not really. Bartie's a pretty weird guy. Rich as lords from inheriting a family fortune, I've been told. I even tried getting him to invest in one of my projects, but it didn't work out. He just likes to come down here and poke around, looking for stuff."

"What kind of stuff?"

"Artifacts, I think. He's interested in archaeology. I hear his house is crammed with things he's dug up from various places in the Southwest."

I was reminded of the rock hammer we'd found in Scooter McLeod's pickup. I decided a trip to Sabino Canyon was in my future, along with a visit to the Salernos in Green Valley. Maybe Maria would like to go along.

~ ~ ~

*The army was marching south up the Nexpa River when we came upon an area recently burned, as a result of which the grass was fresh and very fine. Our horses were much weakened for lack of green forage, and so Captain-General Coronado ordered a halt in order for our stock to replenish themselves before resuming the journey back to New Spain. He himself also was in much distress with headaches and abdominal discomfort, both likely a residual from his fall at Tiguex. An Indian in our party mentioned to our ensign-general, Don Pedro Tovar, that there was a curative spring at the headwaters of a stream called the Babocomari that happened to enter the Nexpa from the West near the point where we were camped. Don Pedro inquired as to the distance to this spring, to which the Indian responded that it would be a two-day ride. Upon hearing this news, Don Pedro reported to our commander that he might wish to visit this spring in hopes of curing his various ailments. The Captain-General agreed, and I am among those twenty-five soldiers to have the honor of accompanying him on the ride, while Don Pedro and the other captains remain with the main camp on the Nexpa.*

- from the diary of Pedro de Castañeda, May 10, 1542.

~ ~ ~

*Big hit with the metal detector today in San Carlos Wash. Copper for sure. Maybe the bolt from a crossbow arrow? We celebrated with steaks and beer at the Santa Rita Saloon. A local guy, Ollie Swade, came to our table. Said he'd heard we were treasure hunters. Said he had some things he'd like to sell. Showed us a small potsherd and some purple glass. Said he had more at home. I accused him of looting public land. Swade stomped off mad. Bartie said it was a bad move, because now we weren't going to get a look at the rest of the old man's stuff. We had a fight, and it ruined our night out.*

- from the diary of Jeremiah McLeod, Jr., June 28,199

# Chapter 21

It was Friday morning, and Maria and I were on our way up to Tucson with a stop planned for Green Valley later in the day. We drove north out of Sonoita on highway 83. The hills were showing their first hint of green, a result of the recent rains. The sky was a brilliant uninterrupted azure, the air clean and crisp. I rolled down my window and let in the sweet smell of new desert grass. After about 10 miles the road crested a low rise that marked the northern boundary of the Sonoita Valley. From there we followed the winding highway down into a landscape of creosote bush, palo verde, and barrel cactus. This was a different place, the Sonoran Desert. It was the image most people associated with southern Arizona, especially those folks driving along Interstate 10, usually hell bent on getting to southern California from Texas, or the reverse. It was fine with me if the magical oaks and grasslands just over that rise to south remained unknown to most of them.

Understandably, Maria wanted to know more about the mystery of the buried pickup. "So, were those the remains of Scooter McLeod you found in there?"

"Looks like it. We'll have to wait for the coroner's report, but Angus McLeod's belt buckle was there with the body, so I'm going on the assumption it was Scooter until we hear otherwise."

It was going to be a busy day. I would drop Maria off at the University of Arizona campus for her meeting with Dr. Julio Rincon at the State Museum. Then I planned to head up into Sabino Canyon to meet with Barton Hampstead, in hopes of learning more about the last days

*117*

of Scooter McLeod. Afterwards we'd drive down to Green Valley, where Maria could visit with my parents while I went to see Ray and Vicki Salerno, the parents of Scooter's girlfriend, Angela. Maria had with her the metal sphere she wanted to show Dr. Rincon. I had my briefcase. Inside it were the same evidence bags I'd taken to Sandy McLeod's office the afternoon before.

As we drove into the brown cloud that hung over downtown Tucson, I took the opportunity to ask Maria what she knew about the Trujillo family.

"Not much. Why do you ask?"

"You remember at dinner the other night your parents mentioned that Scooter had been mixed up in a drug deal with Paco Trujillo? I obviously need to pursue this angle on his possible murder, but everybody's been warning me off, especially Luis. "

Maria frowned. "Any idea why?"

"Besides the obvious one that the family has a bad reputation? No. But Luis said he would talk to them, and I should pursue other aspects of the case. Which is what I'm doing today."

"I think my parents told me something a couple of years back about the old *patron* of the family - Herman Trujillo is it? I think he might have had a stroke or something and died. So maybe they aren't what they once were."

"I don't know about that. But if Luis doesn't do it pretty soon, I'm going to have to talk to Pedro Trujillo myself. If the old man is dead, the son should be running things."

I delivered Maria to the south edge of campus and drove east on Speedway Boulevard toward the base of the Santa Catalina Mountains. From there I followed a winding road up into Sabino Canyon, to the home of one Barton Hampstead. I was driving the jeep and out of uniform, but I carried a badge in my wallet and a sidearm concealed under my light sport coat.

A massive double door carved out of mesquite marked the entrance to Barton Hampstead's old adobe home. The landscaping was natural desert, including a scattering of tall saguaro cacti. Hampstead answered the door himself and invited me to follow him into a single large room that apparently served as a combination kitchen, dining, and living room. The ceiling was a least fifteen feet high, and supported by beams made out of the trunks of pine trees. The furniture was heavy and dark, and the walls were lined with glass-front cabinets filled with artifacts that looked to me like a combination of Native American and early Spanish or Mexican.

Barton Hampstead himself was a real vision, tall and heavy-set with a completely bald head and a full Santa Claus beard. He was barefoot, and he wore a bright green robe that looked like it might have been Asian or middle-eastern. He pointed to a matched set of leather armchairs, but offered no refreshments. Nobody else was around, as far as I could tell.

We got settled and I thanked the man for agreeing to see me.

"What can I do for you, Mr. Creede?"

"I was hoping you could tell me something about the disappearance of Scooter McLeod. I understand you spent some time on the Rocking M Ranch the summer it happened. Maybe you and he did some archaeological exploring together?"

Hampstead nodded. "I was there for a while, yes. But that was years ago. Why do you ask?"

"We may have found his body. In fact, I'm pretty sure we did. From the original reports of the missing persons case, it appears that you were one of the last people to see him alive. Naturally, we are anxious to trace his

*119*

movements just before he disappeared."

"Do you suspect foul play?"

"We do." I chose not to elaborate, but waited for a response.

Barton Hampstead was not immediately forthcoming, but eventually he must have realized it was his turn. "Well, I'm not sure I can be all that helpful, but I'll tell you what I remember of that summer. Scooter and I were roommates at Yale. We shared an interest in southwestern history and archaeology, and we hatched this idea that we might be able to dig up some interesting things on his dad's ranch."

"Did you ever find anything?"

"Nothing worth mentioning. A few potsherds, some purple glass bottles, nothing of value."

"This was in the summer of 1995?"

"If that was the summer he disappeared, yes. But I was out there for about a month the previous year as well."

"Where were you when Scooter disappeared?"

"I was back at Yale, just starting a summer school class, when I got a call from his parents. They wanted to know if I'd seen him, if maybe he'd gone back to Connecticut with me. He hadn't, of course."

"When, exactly, was this?"

Barton Hampstead yawned and scratched his head. "I can't tell you the exact date, but I was there for the second session, the one that began in late July. I guess he must have gone missing just a little while after I left on my drive back to New Haven. But you must know all this. Somebody from your department got hold of me back at Yale right after Scooter vanished, and I gave him all this information then."

"Yes, but it's good to have personal confirmation. And just for the record, you never saw or heard from Scooter McLeod again?"

"That's correct. Now if that's all, Mr. Creede, I have an

appointment downtown in about an hour. So, if you could excuse me?"

Hampstead rose from his chair, but I didn't follow his lead. "Actually, there are a couple more things I need to ask you about. It shouldn't take long."

The man sighed conspicuously, but eventually sat back down. "What things? You know I really haven't got much time."

"First, how well do you know Scooter McLeod's brother Sandy? Did you see a lot of him during those summers?"

"I don't remember much about Sandy. Scooter and I didn't live at the main ranch house. We had our own place over at the mouth of Lyle Canyon. Some sort of old line shack, as you say in cowboy land. It had power and water back then, but that was about it. Anyway, that's where we kept all of our stuff, and where we slept and ate most days."

"So you never saw Scooter and Sandy together?"

"Oh, I wouldn't say never. But the brothers didn't seem at all close. I think there was some kind of a problem there."

"What sort of a problem?"

"I don't know for sure. But Scooter complained sometimes that his brother, and his father for that matter, didn't respect his interests. I wouldn't have minded staying at the headquarters ranch house, really, because that old shack was a dump. But Scooter just didn't want to do it."

"Sandy tells me you still come down to the Rocking M sometimes. Why is that? Are you interested in his real estate developments?"

Hampstead actually rolled his eyes. "Not in the least. The man has no class. And besides, I don't need any more investments."

"Then why do you go down there?"

"Because they let me poke around the place. My hobby is exploring for artifacts, as you can see from what's here in this room. My collection is all perfectly legal, of course. I never hunt anywhere except on private land. And the Rocking M is nearly all private, except for a couple of small leases from the Bureau of Land Management and from the State of Arizona. That makes it unlike many ranches around Sonoita, where much of the land is public. But you probably know that."

"I do. But tell me, is there something about the Sonoita area that could be particularly important to southwestern history?"

I thought Hampstead hesitated about two seconds too long before he answered.

"No, not really. It's just a place I happen to know well. Now, you really must excuse me before I miss my appointment."

Once again, the man started to rise from his chair. That's when I unsnapped my briefcase, pulled out the evidence bag containing the little holy medal and chain, and held it up. "Have you ever seen this before?"

For the first time that morning, Barton Hampstead showed what appeared to be genuine interest. "Where did you get that?"

I handed him the bag. "We found it around Scooter McLeod's neck. Do you know its history? If you turn it over you will see the initials 'A A S' on the back. Do you have any idea who that might be?"

Hampstead examined the medal. "Well, I remember that Scooter had a girlfriend. I think her name was Angela. It could be hers, I suppose."

"Was Scooter wearing that medal when you last saw him?"

"I really can't remember."

"Did you know Angela?"

"Yes, I met her a couple of times. She was from the area, I think. But that was in the first summer, in 1994. I don't think she was around that second summer."

Next I took the belt buckle out of my briefcase, and showed it to him. "Do you know if this was Scooter's?"

"May I see that?"

"Sure, just be sure to keep it in the bag." I noticed that Hamstead's hand was shaking as he took the buckle from me.

"Yes ... yes, this was his. He never wore it at Yale, but he always had it on in Arizona."

Up until this point, Barton Hampstead had impressed me as someone who was arrogant and bored, as if conversation with a rural deputy sheriff was somehow beneath his dignity. Now a completely different expression came over his face. I thought he looked wistful.

~ ~ ~

On the way back downtown I got Maria on her cell and asked if it was too late for me to meet with her and Dr. Rincon at the museum. Maria set it up, and forty-five minutes later all three of us were seated around an oak table in the curator's office. I would have gotten there a lot sooner, but finding a place to park anywhere near the University of Arizona campus turned out to be a nightmare.

The Santa Catalinas, partially obscured by smog, were visible out a large window that made up most of the west wall of the curator's office. The other walls were built-in bookshelves, crammed to overfilling from floor to ceiling. The place smelled faintly of pipe tobacco.

Julio Rincon was in his mid-forties, be-spectacled, with a high forehead and a deep tan. He wore an immaculate tan linen suit and a pale yellow dress shirt accented with a burgundy tie. On the table between us was the little sphere that Maria had brought, along with her notes and photographs showing its location.

"Your friend Maria has brought us something most interesting, Mr. Creede. We believe it is a type of brass bell, sometimes called a Clarksdale bell. They were carried by the early Spanish explorers, perhaps to decorate their horses' bridles but also as gifts for the Indians. They are quite rare, and virtually unknown in this part of Arizona. We are most grateful to Maria for bringing this one to us. However, as I have just finished explaining to her, we would prefer in the future that she leave any such objects *in-situ* and let us come down to examine the sites ourselves."

Maria blushed. I thought she looked especially beautiful. I wanted to give her a hug, but clearly it wasn't the right time or place. Instead I turned my attention to the curator. "I have a question."

"Is it related to the bell?"

"Perhaps, but probably not. I was wondering what you could tell me about a man named Barton Hampstead."

Julio Rincon's face immediately lost its academic composure. He removed his glasses and stared hard right at me.

"Are you asking this in an official capacity, Mr. Creede?"

"Well yes, I suppose I am."

"Then I guess I'd better watch myself. Let me put it this way. That man is not friend to this museum, nor to archaeology in general."

"Why not?"

"This is difficult. Do I have your assurance that what I say will remain confidential?"

"You do, unless what you tell me has a direct bearing on a criminal case."

"I understand, of course. But then all I am prepared to

say is that we do not look with favor upon individuals who collect and hoard artifacts for themselves."

"Even if they do their hunting on private property?"

"That can make it legal, technically, but it still doesn't make it right. Also, and please understand that nothing has ever been proven, there are questions about just where and how Mr. Hampstead obtained some of the things known to be in his possession."

# Chapter 22

We were on Interstate 19, making the short drive from Tucson south to the retirement community of Green Valley. The San Xavier Mission was off to our right, shining in brilliant white contrast to its drab desert surroundings. I was reminded of how much the Santa Cruz River Valley must have changed since the Spanish friars chose this spot for a major frontier outpost. Today the once-verdant river channel was scarcely more than a barren sandy wash, and there was no sign of any new green growth in the mesquite and desert scrub on either side of the highway. But there were some thunderheads building over the Santa Rita Range off to the east. Sometimes after a heavy downpour the Santa Cruz could still run full to its banks.

Maria asked me about Barton Hampstead. I described his physical appearance. "A pretty strange guy. I need to find out more about the man, that's for sure."

"Like what?"

"Well for one thing, where he got his money. That estate of his up in Sabino Canyon couldn't have come cheap. And Barney Stroud over in Sierra Vista suggested that his relationship with Scooter may have been more than just that of a college roommate. Hampstead hinted as much to me today."

"You mean the two of them might have been involved in this business of collecting prehistoric artifacts?"

"That could be part of it."

"There you go, sounding all mysterious again."

I changed the subject. "That sure is interesting about the bell you found. I wouldn't worry too much about Dr.

Rincon chastising you for taking it. After all, if you hadn't found it the museum would never have come into its possession."

"I suppose so. But I'm not taking anything home from my little walks, ever again. He's right, you know. From now on I'll just notify the professionals when I find something interesting, and let them decide whether or not to dig."

"When we get to Green Valley, I'll drop you at my folks' place and head on over to the Salernos. You might as well tell Mom and Dad what I'm up to, since afterwards I may want to ask them about Angela. But just give them the general outline, not all the details."

Maria seemed puzzled. "What do you mean, exactly?"

"I mean you should tell them that we found Scooter McLeod in the truck. But they don't need to know how he probably died."

~ ~ ~

The town of Green Valley included a wide range of accommodations. My parents lived in a modest southwestern style patio home, built carefully and tastefully into native desert landscaping. The house belonging to Ray and Vicki Salerno was something else entirely. It was a two-story plantation-looking sort of thing, adjacent to a golf course, all white except for a green roof. A wide staircase led up to an oversized entranceway framed by twin columns. A late model Cadillac sedan was parked in front of the detached three-car garage. I followed a circular drive to the front of the house, got out of the jeep, and surveyed the property. The whole thing was wrong. Its opulence spoke to the success of the Salernos' real estate ventures, but it seemed like the couple must have had no sense of place. Where had these people come from before they bought Bobcat Creek Ranch? It was before my time.

I climbed the front stairs and rang the bell. A distinguished elderly Hispanic gentleman came to the door and invited me to join the Salernos on the patio beside their pool. Ray Salerno rose as I approached. He was dressed in golf attire, including tan slacks and a striped polo shirt. He was a short man with wide hips and an oversized head with black hair (dyed?) combed straight back. Vicki Salerno was a full six inches taller than her husband, but similarly dressed. She was thin but not scrawny, with short frosted blond hair that almost certainly would have been gray if it weren't for constant attention. The couple appeared to be in their mid to late 70s, but very well-preserved. I introduced myself.

Ray Salerno pointed to an unoccupied wicker chair. "Please sit down, Cal. May I call you Cal? Would you like some iced tea?"

"Yes, thanks. And Cal is fine."

"I'm guessing you might be Harold and Doris Creede's boy?"

I nodded.

"We knew them when we were all in the ranching business over in Sonoita. How are your parents? What are they doing these days?"

"They're fine. In fact, they've retired and they live right here in Green Valley."

"Is that right? Well, well, we must all get together some time, don't you think Vicki?"

Ray Salerno went right on without waiting for his wife to reply.

"But tell me, Cal. What is it that we can do for you? Frankly, we were a little puzzled when you called the other day. It's been so many years since we lived in Sonoita that I'm not sure how we might be of help. You said this involves a missing person?"

"That's right. It's about Jeremiah McLeod, Jr. You

probably knew him as Scooter. He disappeared in 1995, and I believe we just found his body. We have some evidence suggesting that he was murdered, which is why Sheriff Mendoza has decided to reopen the case."

I had expected a big reaction, but none was forthcoming. The Salernos said nothing. They just sat there. It did seem as if Vicki Salerno's iced tea glass rattled just a bit as she set it down on the marble-topped patio table.

I decided to drop my second piece of news. "We have examined the case file put together at the time Scooter McLeod disappeared. It indicates your daughter Angela might have been acquainted with him around that time. Is that correct?"

Ray Salerno glanced quickly at his wife, then looked back at me. "She may have been. But surely you're not suggesting she had anything to do with this?"

"I'm not suggesting anything at this point. But I would like to speak with Angela, if that's possible." I extracted the holy medal from my coat pocket. "And I wonder if you recognize this medal. It may have Angela's initials on the back. We found it on the body."

Ray Salerno shifted in his chair and stared out toward the golf course. He barely glanced at the holy medal, and he did not respond. It was Vicki Salerno who spoke: "May I see that, Mr. Creede? Angela isn't here. In fact, we ..."

Ray immediately interrupted. "We don't see her anymore."

"Can you tell me how to reach her? And do you happen to know if she is married?"

This time Vicki spoke up before Ray even had a chance. "The last we knew she was teaching school some place in Colorado. But that was two years ago. We got a Christmas card. There was no return address, but it was postmarked Fort Collins. I don't know if she's married. I tried information, but the phone company didn't have a listing. I wanted to go back there to see my only child, but ..."

Ray Salerno interrupted again. I was getting the feeling he did a lot of that. "She knows where we live, Vicki. If she wants to come and see us, she knows how. I'm not going to chase after her like we did the last time back in Chicago. Now if that is all, Mr. Creede, we're due to meet some friends on the golf course."

Vicki Salerno had begun crying quietly. She turned the holy medal over in her hands, and then looked up at me with tears streaming down her face. "May I keep this?"

"I'm sorry, but for now it's evidence. And I do have one more question before I leave. Do either of you know a man named Barton Hampstead?"

The couple glanced at one another, look puzzled, and shrugged. Both shook their heads. I excused myself and rose to leave. They made no effort to follow. Just before I reached the door I heard Vicki start to cry again, much louder than before.

I stepped out into the sunlight, and thought about what had just happened. Tension in the Salerno household had been palpable. Obviously I had reopened an old wound. It was time to dig further into the history of Angela Salerno's relationship with her parents, as well as with Scooter McLeod.

# Chapter 23

I drove back to my parents' house and walked in through the kitchen door without knocking. My mother was cleaning up some dirty dishes. Dad and Maria must have been somewhere else.

"Hi Mom, I'm starved."

She smiled. "Boy does that take me back. Sit down and let me fix you something. We just had egg-salad sandwiches. Is that okay? And Maria told us about Scooter McLeod. Now I understand why you were pumping us for information about him over dinner the other night."

"A sandwich would be great, thanks. And for the record, we had no idea when you were there last Saturday what was going to turn up in that old truck."

My mother frowned and muttered something I couldn't hear.

"Anyway, I wonder what you can tell me about Angela Salerno. Her parents couldn't or wouldn't help much. They admitted that she and Scooter knew each other, but that was about it. They don't seem to have much of a relationship with their daughter, but Mrs. Salerno was really broken up when I showed her a little holy medal we found on Scooter's body. I think it must have been Angela's."

My mother nodded. "I remember Angela, but it was a long time ago. She went to Elgin School with Scooter, and I think they continued together at Patagonia High. As I recall, the Salernos moved over to Green Valley about the time that Scooter McLeod disappeared, but I don't think Angela was around then. She must have gone off to college or something."

133

"How well did you know the Salernos, Mom? It was news to them that you even lived here in Green Valley. Where did they come from originally?"

"They bought the Bobcat Creek Ranch back in the 60s some time, I think. We didn't know them all that well, really."

"Didn't know who all that well?" My Dad had just walked into the kitchen.

"Ray and Vicki Salerno, dear. Cal is trying to learn something about their daughter Angela, because she may have been a friend of Scooter McLeod's."

"That Ray Salerno, he wasn't a real rancher, and he never had much to do with those of us who were. They moved out here from some place in New Jersey. It was only a couple of years afterwards that they started that big housing development on their place. And boy, did they make a bundle. Got real snooty about it, too. Nobody missed 'em when they moved over here to Green Valley, I'll tell you that much."

I filed this away and took a bite out of my sandwich. "And what about Angela, Dad? Do you know what became of her? And by the way, where's Maria?"

"Angela's their daughter? I've got no idea. I left Maria in the living room. I just showed her a coffee table book about early southwestern Spanish exploration. She can't seem to put it down."

At this point Maria called out from the other room. "Cal, we'd better get on the road. It's getting late and I need to feed and milk the goats."

~ ~ ~

Maria made a fateful suggestion as we were preparing to leave Green Valley. "Let's take the shortcut home, through Box Canyon. It's quicker, and I really do need to get back to the dairy."

I had my doubts, and pointed to the eastern horizon.

"Boy I don't know. Look at those clouds. That road is bad enough in good weather. You know what it can be like when the washes run up there. It may be the shortest route from here to Sonoita, but it sure won't be the quickest if we get stuck. Why don't we play it safe and go home by way of Nogales?"

But she was not to be deterred. "Sometimes I wonder why you ever got this jeep. It was made for roads like the one in Box Canyon, and it must get bored running on pavement all the time. And besides, it's not raining yet." Then she made a noise like a chicken, which explains why forty-five minutes later the left front wheel of my Cherokee was buried up to the axle in mud.

The road into Box Canyon started out easily enough, heading straight across a broad mesquite savannah that covered the western alluvium of the Santa Rita Range. Then we crossed a series of normally dry washes and began a steep climb up the south-facing side of a deep canyon. I negotiated the washes with little difficulty. It was along the canyon wall that we ran into trouble. The gravel road was narrow in spots, and I instinctively avoided its outside edge for fear of driving off into space. It was a prudent strategy, of course, except that I was so busy avoiding the precipice on my right that I failed to notice the ditch on my left that was running full of water.

So there I was, on my back in the rain and the mud, trying to secure a jack under the front bumper of my jeep. Lightning flashed against a black sky above the crest of the mountains, suggesting even worse weather ahead.

Maria leaned out the passenger-side window and called out to me. "Why don't you call Larry? I'm sure he'd be glad to come and help."

I twisted my body out from under the jeep and looked up at her. "Not gonna do it. He had to rescue me once already this week."

135

"Oh please, Cal. Don't tell me this is going to be one of those moments."

"What moments?"

"Oh you know, one of those times 'when a man's gotta do what a man's gotta do'? Sometimes I wonder what's the matter with you men when it comes to asking for help."

That's when I lost it. "Oh damn it to hell, Maria, why can't you just be quiet for once and let me do my job!"

A deservedly ominous silence followed, broken only by the rumble of approaching thunder. I scooted back under the jeep and continued to wrestle with the jack. Twice it slipped off the bumper, causing me to bark my knuckles against the frame as the front end of the jeep swung sideways even farther over into the ditch. Now there was blood mixed with the rain and the mud, and still I was no closer to getting us out of there.

Maria could not have failed to hear my cursing reference to the jeep's mother. Her voice was muffled from up inside the jeep. "Sorry. It's just that I'm really worried about my goats."

"Yeah? You know if it weren't for those precious goats of yours, we wouldn't even be in this mess. Can't you call somebody to go over and feed them, or whatever it is that needs doing?"

Maria tried that, but she couldn't get a signal.

It took thirty more minutes, but I finally managed to raise my vehicle up high enough to slip some rocks under its left front tire. I released the jack and stowed it behind the back seat, then got in front next to Maria. We did not make eye contact. But the makeshift rock platform held, and I had no difficulty getting the jeep back onto solid ground.

We continued our journey up the mountain amidst thunder, lightening and very heavy rain. There were no more incidents, but neither was there any conversation.

136

The whole ugly episode had brought me to a place I didn't want to go. Memories of an awful night in the Afghan desert came flooding back. I'd been trying for seven years to forget that night, but the nightmares just wouldn't go away.

The storm had subsided by the time we reached Elgin, but I could hear the roar of the Santa Carlos Wash in the distance. At least the rain had covered the whole valley, and it would help the grass. It was a good thing we had gotten the remains of Scooter McLeod out of there before they washed off downstream someplace.

I pulled up beside Maria's house, but I did not cut the engine. She started to get out of the jeep, but then stopped when she realized I was making no effort to follow. Of course she was puzzled. "Aren't you coming in?"

"No, I don't think so. I've got some things to do at the Pitchfork."

I'll give her this much credit: she had the good sense not to ask what those things might be.

# Chapter 24

### Sheriff Luis Mendoza

**T**he Sheriff of Santa Cruz County realized he had been stalling. He dreaded having to deal with Pedro Trujillo, his one-time friend and longer-time adversary. But the autopsy results had come in on the body that had turned up on the Rocking M Ranch. Dental records proved it was indeed Scooter McLeod, and the forensic evidence pointed inescapably to murder. The man had been killed, probably with his own rock hammer. So now it was time. He could find no more excuses.

It wasn't that he was afraid of Pedro Trujillo. He was long past such personal concerns. He just couldn't see any clear path to resolution of the case, and any dealings with Trujillo on the McLeod matter could easily compromise other ongoing investigations. The Sheriff already had decided not to tell the feds about his plans, and he hoped they didn't get word.

Pedro Trujillo and his father Herman certainly could have taken their revenge on Scooter all those years ago. God knows they had a motive. It was Scooter's testimony that had sent Pedro's brother Paco to jail, and to his subsequent death at the hands of another inmate. But there wasn't the least bit of forensic evidence tying any of the Trujillos to the McLeod murder, and tracing their whereabouts in July of 1995 was as good as impossible. Luis Mendoza had only one hope – that Pedro himself might let something slip. That was unlikely. Both the old man and Paco had done time for drug smuggling, but never Pedro. There were two possible reasons for this fact, the least likely of which was that he wasn't really involved in the family business. Pedro had always been smart and careful, clear back to when they had been classmates at Patagonia High.

It had taken most of a day, but a meeting had been arranged. It would not be in any of the homes owned by the family. Rather, they would meet in Pedro's restaurant in Nogales, Sonora. It was not the sheriff's choice, but he decided not to push the issue.

He dressed in civilian clothes and walked across into Mexico without a weapon. He had his Sheriff's Badge, but he knew better than to show it at the border or anywhere beyond. *El Restaurante Camarón* was on a dingy back street in Nogales, away from the main tourist district. But the food was exceptional, especially the fresh seafood brought in daily from Guaymas. Pedro's place was well known to many *gringos*, and there was a good lunch crowd when Luis arrived. He identified himself to the headwaiter, a distinguished man in a dark suit who escorted him to an office at the rear of the main dining area. At least they could meet in private.

Pedro Trujillo rose from his chair as the Sheriff entered the room. "Luis, my old friend, it is good to see you. It has been how many years now since we've actually had a chance to talk? Please sit down. Let's have some of my shrimp for lunch, and maybe a bottle of *Pacifico*?"

"Sure, that would be fine."

Pedro made the briefest of nods to the waiter, and turned his attention back to Luis. "You are looking well, though I must say your belly is not so flat as it was when we played football together for the Patagonia *Lobos*, eh? I myself have tried to stay in shape, but the years take their toll on us in different ways I suppose."

The man did cut a fine figure in a white *guayabera* trimmed in blue. But his black hair looked dyed, and Luis

Mendoza noticed tobacco stains on the thin fingers of his right hand. Also, wasn't there just the slightest tremor?

"But you probably did not come here to talk about the old days," Pedro continued. "Our paths have diverged since then. You are now the Sheriff, while I am a mere businessman."

The Sheriff decided it was time to get to the point. "I am sure you know that I know what sort of business has occupied you all these years. You and your father and your late brother, that is."

Trujillo fixed the Sheriff with a level stare. "And what sort of business would that be?"

"Your family is in the drug business. And maybe in the people importing business, too."

"As you well-know my friend, I have never been convicted of any crime. Never once. My father and brother, yes, they have made those mistakes. But I run a restaurant, and it is a good one as you can see. It is true that the profits from this place have permitted me to expand into other ventures involving import and export, but of goods not people. All legitimate. I know about the activities of your department, that your men are following mine. As for your *Federales*, hell, everybody but the Coast Guard is after me. Don't you think they would have found something by now?"

Luis felt his temper rise. "We'll see about that. Things will play out, and someday you'll get caught."

The other man only shrugged. "But why have you come here today to tell me all this – to insult me in my own place? The only reason I agreed to see you is I held out the hope you might want to make amends."

"Amends? No way. But you are right about one thing. I did not come here to ask about your business ventures."

"What then?"

"I came to ask you about Scooter McLeod."

*141*

"I am not sure I know who that is."

"Yes, you do. He's the guy who ratted out your brother in a drug bust back in the 1990s."

The other man shifted in his chair. "Perhaps I do remember him. But that was years ago. Why ask about him now?"

"We found his body last week, up near Sonoita. The evidence indicates he was murdered."

"What does that have to do with me?"

"Don't patronize me, Pedro. Scooter McLeod disappeared in 1995. Can you account for your whereabouts in July of that year? And for your father?"

Pedro Trujillo thought for a minute, or at least pretended to do so.

"Let's see, then. I was a student up at ASU in Tempe that year, so that is where I must have been."

"But this was in the summer, Pedro."

"Ah, of course it was. But you see I worked for my uncle in Phoenix during summer vacations, so that is where I must have been."

"And what about your father?"

Pedro Trujillo's face darkened.

"Five years ago my father had a stroke that left him a mere vegetable. It took him all this time to die, but he finally did, just last month. But why are you patronizing me, my friend? You must know all such things. It is your county, after all."

"Do I have permission to visit your mother?"

Pedro Trujillo did not hesitate. "No, you do not. She is old and frail, and besides she has no knowledge of anything that could be of interest to you. I insist that you leave her in peace."

They were interrupted by a knock on the door. A young man in a short white coat entered carrying a large tray covered by a linen cloth.

"Ah, here is our food, Luis. Please, let us stop all of this unpleasant talk and enjoy our meal. I have a feeling it may be the last time."

The Sheriff indulged in a short laugh. "Perhaps you have that feeling. I, on the other hand, am quite certain we have not seen the last of each other."

~ ~ ~

On his walk back across the border, Luis Mendoza realized how little he had learned from Pedro Trujillo. At least there was one small lead. The Sheriff had friends in law enforcement in both Tempe and Phoenix. It was a cold trail, but he might still be able to learn something about Pedro's whereabouts the year Scooter McLeod went missing. He also would attempt to visit Herman Trujillo's widow, Camarilla. Pedro had made one mistake in their talk this afternoon. He had shown himself far too anxious to keep the Sheriff away from his mother.

Luis showed his passport to the border agent and crossed back into Arizona. Every time he made this trip he was struck by the same thought: how vastly different things were on opposite sides of that arbitrary line in the desert.

# Chapter 25

**I**t was well past midnight, but I could not sleep. Maria and I hadn't seen each other or even spoken for two days, not since that awful trip back from Green Valley. I suppose we were playing a game of emotional chicken, and eventually one of us would make a move. What was wrong with me? All she had done was suggest that I get help pulling the jeep out of the mud. I wished she would call, but I pretty much knew it was my mess to clean up.

Two hours later that I finally drifted off into a fitful sleep. I was dreaming about rain and mud. Maria was there, but we weren't in Arizona. There were soldiers around, dressed in desert camouflage. They were milling about as if they were lost, or perhaps waiting for somebody to tell them what to do. The soldiers were mixed in with a herd of goats. Most of the goats were beige, but some were white. The white ones had gaping wounds in their sides, oozing pus and blood. I was trying to get my Humvee started, but it wouldn't move. A telephone rang, but I couldn't find it. Where the hell was it? Where the hell was I?

The ringing finally jolted me awake. I sat up in bed, soaked with sweat, briefly disoriented. Then instinct took over. "Santa Cruz County....Hello?"

"Cal, it's Maria. You've got to come out here right now!"

"What's wrong? Where are you?"

"I just caught some woman in my milking shed, and she's trashed the place. I want you to come out here and take her away. I've got a gun. Please hurry!"

"I'm on my way. Are you hurt? Is she? Should I call the rescue folks? Are your goats all right?"

"Nobody's hurt, but she busted up the milking stands, punched holes in the buckets and cans, and dumped my cheeses all over the floor. It's awful. This woman's crazy. Just get out here before I do something stupid with this shotgun."

It took about five minutes to clear my head, get dressed, and jump in the Blazer. I turned on my flashers but not the siren, and drove off in the dark. The clock on the dashboard glowed green, showing three-fifteen A.M.

After about twenty minutes I pulled up in front of Maria's house, jumped out, and ran inside. Maria was in the middle of her living room, holding a double-barreled shotgun. She had it pointed directly at a woman who was sitting in one of the recliner chairs. It took me a second or two to recognize Muffy Davenport. Boomer was at Maria's side, growling and very alert.

I walked around the chair to face the KELP lady. She was dressed all in black, apparently in honor of the occasion. Her defiant eyes were bloodshot, and she seemed to be having trouble sitting still. "Can you tell that woman to get her gun out of my face? She's creeping me out with that thing. Are you going to, you know, arrest me or something?"

"Good idea. For the moment, you are under arrest for criminal trespass and vandalism. If any of Ms. Obregon's goats are injured, there will be additional charges. And you have the right to remain silent. Anything you say can and will be..."

"Knock it off. I'm familiar with the drill. And if you take the trouble to check, you'll see that none of your girlfriend's precious goats are hurt."

I finished the Miranda warning anyway, and secured her with plastic cuffs.

"Is that necessary?"

"It's routine."

I turned my attention back to Maria, who by now had leaned her shotgun against the wall and moved to the other recliner. I paced back and forth in front of the two women. "Tell me what happened here."

Maria brushed a loose strand of hair out of her face. I noticed her hand was shaking, but her dark eyes held steady. "Boomer woke me up. He started barking and scratching at the door. At first I thought it was just an owl or a coyote or something, but then I heard noises out in the barn. I grabbed the gun and went out there. And she – that woman here – she was just trashing the place. So I marched her back in here, and then I called you."

"All right, I'm gonna call Larry Hernandez now. I want him to take Ms. Davenport down to Nogales and have her booked into the county jail. Then we'll talk."

Larry was not happy to be rousted in the middle of the night, especially because my call had awakened his parents who were asleep in the next room. But he readily agreed to come when I told her what Maria had just been through, and why I needed to stay with her.

I rang off and turned my attention back to Muffy. There were a bunch of things I needed to ask her, but I decided to begin with the fundamentals. "How did you get here tonight?"

She gestured with her head in the direction of Elgin. "My car. It's down the road." She squirmed in her chair in a vain attempt to find a comfortable position to sit with her hands cuffed behind her.

"Okay. Let me have your keys, and I'll see that it is returned to your house later today."

"How the hell am I supposed to, you know, get at my keys with my hands tied up like this?" Muffy Davenport looked up at me, but she seemed to be having trouble focusing, and her breath smelled like marijuana. I'd heard somewhere that being stoned can make you talkative, so this looked like an opportunity.

"We'll deal with your keys later. While we're waiting for your ride, I'm going to ask you some questions. But again, just for the record, you don't have to answer. Do you understand?"

"Sure, ask away. But I'm not saying anything about tonight."

"The sheriff or the DA will get to that soon enough. Let's start with how you decided to come to Arizona."

She seemed to reflect on that a minute, as if I had asked her something profound. Then she started talking. A lot.

"You know, my move to Arizona just seemed like the right thing to do. Things got crazy in California, and maybe a little too hot – not that we ever really did anything of course. But then the cops really got after Skyler, and he split."

"Skyler?"

"Yeah, he was my boyfriend. We met in *KELP*. In most ways he was just my type, and he liked me right off, too. Pretty soon we started living together in the condo I had at Pacific Grove. Some of the other guys in the group were jealous, you know? Skyler was tall and really cute, except for a little skinny maybe. He was a hell of a scuba diver, about the best I've ever seen, and I've known a bunch of them. I'm pretty good myself. And the sex was great. He always knew just what I liked, you know?"

"You know, actually I don't."

"Don't what"

"Know."

If the woman caught my sarcasm, she gave no sign. This was a very different Muffy from the one I had encountered the other day at her place over in Lyle

Canyon. I guessed it must have been the drugs.

"Anyway, the *KELP* group hadn't been my idea exactly, but I heard about it from an old friend at Stanford, and it sounded like fun. Did you know I went to Stanford for a year, Mr. Cop, just like my folks? I might go back some day, who knows? Anyway, I loved the *KELP* plan right off, and it's just as important here in Arizona as it was in California. Because of, you know, all the livestock eating up the range. So I packed up and came here, put part of my money in that dinky little bank at Sonoita, and bought the old Wahlberg place. That took a couple months. I had to remodel it and get some decent furniture. The inside of that place was a dump when I first moved in."

"Is anybody else around here involved in *KELP*?"

"Not exactly. But I've got a new boyfriend. A really cute guy. He's younger than me. He helped some with the flyers."

"Would you mind telling me his name?"

"No, I suppose not. It's Oscar."

"Oscar what?"

"I'm not sure."

"Does he drive a green and white pickup?"

"Yeah, as a matter of fact he does. But I don't see what this has to do with *KELP*, which is what you wanted to hear about, right?"

Muffy Davenport seemed anxious to get on with her story, and that was fine with me.

"So anyway, once I was all settled-in, I decided it was time to get *KELP* busy again. First, I sent out the newsletter. Your girlfriend here, she got one. But nobody paid much attention. Most of these local ranchers seemed to think it was some sort of a joke. Hell, even you stayed pretty calm about the whole thing.

"So now, you know, I decided to stir things up a little.

They say the only way to build a new world is to tear down the old one, which in this case means driving all the ranchers out of the valley. I figured I'd start with the local law's sweetie and her goats, and move on to cattle after that."

So much for not talking about tonight. "Surely you can imagine how people around here will react to someone harming their livestock. You could have gotten yourself shot tonight. And you didn't really start with Ms. Obregon, did you? You started by killing Ollie Swade's cow."

At that point, Muffy Davenport apparently decided to clam up. But it definitely had been useful. For one thing, I now had a solid lead on the green and white pickup I'd encountered five days earlier over in the San Carlos Wash.

~ ~ ~

Larry departed with Muffy Davenport, with orders to have her booked into the county jail and to file a report on the arrest. Once we were alone, I turned my attention back to Maria, who'd been unusually quiet ever since I arrived. "Are you sure you're okay?"

We were seated together on a couch along the west wall of the living room. She seemed to be having trouble meeting my gaze. "Yeah, I guess so. The shed's a real mess, and it's going to cost me a lot to replace the milking stands and the buckets. And then there's my cheese. It's all ruined. But actually I'm okay about that part."

"You sure?"

"Yeah, but the part I'm not okay with is ... about last Friday."

I was relieved she brought it up. "I know, me neither. I'm sorry, Maria. Really sorry."

"What happened? Why did you just drive away the other night? Why didn't you call me?"

It was time to fess up. "Because I was ashamed of myself, if you want to know the truth."

"Ashamed about what?"

"You got any coffee? This could take a while."

Ten minutes later we had moved to the kitchen table, our mugs of steaming black coffee in hand. Maria looked at me expectantly. At least we were making eye contact.

"So here's the deal. It's ... about how I acted the other day. There's something you need to know about me, Maria. I'm not sure you'll understand, and even if you do then maybe you won't want to ... be with me any more."

"What is it? It can't be *that* bad."

"Okay then, here goes." I paused, swallowed some coffee, then plunged in. "See, the problem I have is, I need to be in charge. Not so much of other people, but of my own life and what I do and what happens to me. I think I've always been that way, but Afghanistan made it a whole lot worse, probably because things over there seemed so out of control."

Maria looked puzzled. "So what did that have to do with last Friday?"

"Well that was just the perfect storm. First I got stuck and was afraid I couldn't get out. Then that thunder and lightning closed in on us, and it brought back memories of night operations in the Afghan desert, where some bad things happened. The doctors said this would keep happening. They call it flashbacks or something, and I just can't seem to shake it."

"What sort of bad things? And why didn't you tell me about this before?"

"I'm not going to tell you what happened over there. I can't, really. Let's just say that some people died, and I didn't. Sometimes I wish I had."

Maria got red-faced, and then she banged her empty coffee cup on the table. "Don't be stupid! You know you don't mean that. And besides, did the army say it was your fault some people died?"

*151*

I shrugged my shoulders. "No, they didn't say that."

"Okay, so let's not hear any more of this crap about dying then!" Maria took a deep breath and seemed to get herself calmer. "Instead, let's talk about last Friday." She reached across the table and put her hand on my shoulder. I could see the pain and concern in her eyes. "Did I make it worse over there in the canyon?"

"Sort of. Not because of anything you did, but just because you were there to watch. To see me fail."

"Well, I'm not sure I understand that, because to me you're anything but a failure. To me, you're a good guy. The people in this valley respect and admire you, and that's not always true about somebody that represents the law. They're glad you're here, on the job. You make them feel safe. You make *me* feel safe."

"You seem pretty self-assured, Maria. And independent, too."

"I can be tough, I really can, but it's better when you're here. After Tony died I told myself I'd never feel that needy again. But I was wrong. The last two days have shown me that."

Was this an invitation? I decided to take the chance. "If I move in here full-time the whole world is going to find out, because people need to be able to reach me at all hours. I'll probably have to give them your land line number, in case my cell goes on the blink."

"That's fine. Just please come back. I need you to be with me."

I noticed a single tear that had made its way down Maria's left cheek, but I was the one doing the blinking. Must have been something in my eye.

# Chapter 26

**W**hen I walked into the office on Monday morning Larry was already there, fixing a pot of coffee. I was curious how his trip to Nogales had worked out.

"How did it go last night?"

"You mean with that Davenport woman? She's a real nut case, that's for sure. The whole way down, I didn't think she was ever going to stop talking."

"Did you learn anything useful?"

"Not much. Mostly she seemed to want to talk about various boyfriends, mainly ones from back in California as far as I could tell. It was all a little vague. I asked her once about that group of hers, *KELP* or something? But that was the only time she clammed up. Said she'd already told you everything there was to say. Except then she started blabbing on about the evils of grazing, how ranchers were the villains in this valley, stuff like that."

"Did she mention somebody named Oscar?"

"I don't think so. Why?"

"He's the current boyfriend, apparently. And he drives a green and white pickup, according to her."

"Like the one you saw in the San Carlos Wash the other day?"

"Maybe. It also could be that he's Angel Corona's grandson. Listen, I've got to go down to Nogales for a meeting with the sheriff. We need to get caught up on the McLeod case, among other things. In the mean time, do me a favor, will you? Find out if an Oscar Corona owns a green and white pickup, and if he lives in Patagonia. We may need to pay him a visit."

"Want me to do it? Go see him, I mean?"

I thought about it. Maybe it was time to give Larry Hernandez more responsibilities than just traffic patrol.

"Sure. But only ask him about Muffy Davenport. I want to have a look at that truck myself before we ask him what he was doing down in the wash. I may call you before I head back up from Nogales, to see what you found out."

"Okay, boss. Give my best to all the boys down at headquarters."

"And the girls too?"

"Oops. Yeah, of course, them too."

~ ~ ~

I enjoyed the drive along Highway 83 to Nogales. It was a bright and clear morning. The live oaks were in full leaf, and the grasses were beginning to show green, both a result of the recent rains. I rolled down the window and let the clean fresh air blow away some of the cobwebs left over from the previous night. In about 12 miles I came to the town of Patagonia, a small community populated by a kaleidoscopic mix of Hispanic, New Age, old hippie, rural redneck, and folks dressed up like cowboys who may or may not have been the real thing. Some artists lived there, along with various escapees from white-collar urban America. I was pretty sure the Trujillos had a home here, some place back in the hills above town.

Continuing south I passed the diminutive but grandly named Nogales International Airport. Then I was in Nogales proper, driving through the newer subdivisions on the Arizona side of the border. I could see Nogales, Sonora, on the hillsides to the south. There was a breeze from that direction, and even in the heat of summer my nostrils picked up the scent of charcoal mixed with kerosene.

I parked the Blazer in front of the Sheriff's Department headquarters, which was part of a sprawling municipal compound near the interstate. I got out, entered the double doors, and nodded to the desk sergeant on duty. He buzzed me through, and I walked down the familiar hallway leading to the sheriff's personal office.

Mary Gonzales sat behind a wide desk, guarding his inner sanctuary just as she had been for as long as he'd held the job. "Good morning, Deputy".

"Good morning, Mary. Is he in?"

"He's expecting you. Coffee?"

"That would be great, thanks."

I knocked but did not wait for a response before entering. It was a spacious office, sparsely but elegantly furnished in leather and mahogany. The sheriff was sitting behind his desk, a heavy affair with a highly polished surface virtually devoid of clutter. Sort of like the sheriff himself. Today he was dressed in an immaculate gray suit, white shirt, and a silver bolo tie with a large turquoise stone in the center.

After we both had our black coffee, the sheriff opened the conversation by asking about Maria Obregon. "I read the report that Larry filed last night when he brought in that Davenport woman. Is Maria okay? She's a fine young lady who's come through some hard times. Our families go way back, you know, from our days in Patagonia."

"She seems pretty good under the circumstances. But you can imagine what it was like finding the Davenport woman in the milking shed, and with all the damage to her equipment and products."

"Ah yes, those goats of hers. Not my idea of fun, but her papa says she's all wrapped up in those animals and even starting to make a little money selling milk, cheese, and cream soap. Did you know her father married my sister? I see Maria at family reunions and such. Good family! My wife is her *madrina* (godmother), you know. What she needs now is a nice boyfriend to take her out

*155*

dancing once in a while. That young lady doesn't smile enough since she lost her husband."

I wondered how much the sheriff knew about my relationship with Maria. Probably a whole lot. I decided to change the subject. "Where do we stand on the Davenport arrest?"

"Well now, that's interesting. That woman must really be connected. A high-priced lawyer with a fancy reputation showed up at the jail first thing this morning. Apparently he'd just flown in from California on a private jet. Then we get a call from the courthouse that an arraignment had been set for 9 AM. You've gotta have some serious clout to get a judge and the DA's office moving that early."

I put down my coffee cup and glanced briefly out the window at the heavy traffic moving along I-19 toward Tucson. The day was heating up, and the air around Nogales was starting to look stale. "So what happened?"

"She's been charged with criminal trespass and vandalism of private property. We argued for no bail until we could figure out whether she made a threat to livestock. But the fancy lawyer argued, successfully, that there was no evidence of intent to harm Maria's goats. And, I don't know if I told you, but we found no forensic evidence indicating that she had anything to do with the dead cow at that other guy's place, or that she'd even been there for that matter. The footprints were too loose, from all the mud I suppose, and there were no prints on the knife or the flyer. What was that rancher's name?"

"Ollie Swade. But I wouldn't really call him a rancher. He's retired from the railroad. He runs about a dozen mother cows is all. Is Ms. Davenport still in custody?"

"Nope. The judge set bail at $50,000. That's high for trespassing and vandalism. But nobody objected, the bond was made, and she's already back on the street. Frankly, I hope she skips and goes back to California. It would save us some money and time. What do you think?"

"I disagree. We need to consider the damage to the dairy operation. I don't think Maria has insurance to cover it. Given that Ms. Davenport obviously is well-fixed, I hope a part of resolution of this case could be restitution."

"Good point. I hadn't thought of that."

"Anyway, Larry and I will keep an eye on Maria's place, and I'll let you know if we see anything of Ms. Davenport. And thanks, by the way, for lending Larry to me. You were right. It is getting busy up my way, and he's a good man. We'd be tripping over each other in my office, except that neither of us is there all that much."

"Speaking of your office, I was talking with Sandy McLeod the other day and he asked whether the department might want to lease a bigger space in his new mall. What do you think about that?"

This news was not unexpected, but neither was it especially welcome. "Oh, I don't know. I kind of like it where we are now."

"Why? You've got to admit that place is anything but first-rate. And you said yourself it's too crowded now that we have two people using it. I think it makes a poor impression on the citizens, especially those rich retirees that are moving into your part of the county. It might be good for us to look a little more professional up Sonoita way. So I want you to choose one of those little offices in McLeod's place, and I'll negotiate with him. Do it soon, okay?"

I put down my coffee cup. "All right, if that's what you want. I'm not surprised Sandy wants to rent us some space in his little *villa*. I think he's having trouble filling up the place, given the current downturn in the economy in general and real estate in particular. I think maybe he's in a financial bind."

The sheriff frowned, shifted in his chair, and drained

the last of his coffee. "I hadn't heard that. By the way, the coroner's finished with his report on that body you found in the pickup. He's ruled that it is Sandy's brother, based on dental records and the belt buckle. So, you can tell Sandy it's official."

"What about cause of death?"

"Well, it's hard to be absolutely sure after all these years. But the coroner has decided to call it murder, based on the hole in the skull and the fact that there were traces of blood on the rock hammer.

"You ready for some lunch? We can talk about the McLeod case while we eat. I'll have Mary get us something. *Chiles rellenos* sound good?"

Before I left the sheriff's office, overfilled with chilies and cheese, I asked Luis a procedural question. When I talked to the various 'persons of interest' in the case, should I give them the Miranda warning?

"Good question." The sheriff was silent for the better part of a minute, then apparently made up his mind. "Let's not Mirandize for now, while we're still at the initial fact-finding stage of the investigation. If and when we come up with a likely suspect, then you need to do that for sure. Let's just hope it gets that far."

# Chapter 27

As soon as I left headquarters, I phoned Sonoita and brought Larry up to speed. "I'm finished meeting with the sheriff, and I'm heading back up to Patagonia. Any luck on that truck?"

"Some. Records show a 1992 green and white Chevy one-ton, first registered to an Oscar Corona in 2003. His current address is in Patagonia all right - 850 Alamos Avenue. So I drove down there. It's an old doublewide mobile home. But there was no sign of the truck or Oscar. You gonna check it out?"

"Yep. Might as well since I'll be going right by there. Talk to you when I get back."

Driving north out of Nogales, I reviewed the plan that the sheriff and I had developed for tackling what was now officially a murder investigation into the death of Scooter McLeod. We agreed it was going to be tough. The case was cold, with no hard evidence pointing to anybody in particular. But still, there were several possibilities.

At the top of the list were the Trujillos. The family had a reputation for violence, and they had a strong and clear motive – revenge for Scooter getting Paco sent to jail. The sheriff had told me about his meeting with Pedro Trujillo down in Nogales, Sonora, insisting once again that he personally would pursue that angle. It was my responsibility to learn more about other individuals who were involved with Scooter at or near the time of his disappearance. Not all were suspects necessarily, but they all might have information useful to the investigation.

Barton Hampstead was on the list because he'd been living with Scooter on the Rocking M the summer the man went missing. From what I had seen for myself, and then heard from Dr. Rincon at the State Museum, Hampstead was a very peculiar guy.

I was particularly anxious to talk with Angela Salerno, if I could find her. We needed to learn more about her romantic relationship with the victim, including how and when it might have ended. There was something strange about the way her parents had reacted to the news about Scooter when I had talked to them at their home in Green Valley.

And then there was Oscar Corona, assuming he was behind the wheel of that green and white pickup I had seen at the McLeod crime scene. What was he doing there, and what possible connection could he have with a murder that had taken place before he was born? And what was his relationship with Muffy Davenport? I would try to find Oscar in Patagonia and have a talk, maybe today if he was home.

Ollie Swade also was on my list. There was no obvious connection with the case, but Ollie had said something odd and vaguely threatening about how the McLeods had wanted to buy his land. I needed to go see Ollie in any event, to bring him up to speed on the arrest of Muffy Davenport, and also to let him know there was no evidence that she actually had killed his cow.

Finally, there was Sandy McLeod. Why did he seem so detached, uninterested almost, about anything concerning his late brother? From the telephone conversation I'd overheard coming from Sandy's office in the new mall, it sounded like the developer's enterprises might be in financial trouble. What was the state of those business affairs, and what, if anything, could it have to do with Scooter? I couldn't see any obvious connection.

~ ~ ~

I arrived in Patagonia and turned west into a

160

backstreet neighborhood down along Sonoita Creek, hoping to find Oscar Corona at home.

I got lucky. The truck was parked in front of the mobile home, and it was very familiar. A young man came out into the yard as I pulled up. He was short, heavy-set, with a burr haircut, and wearing a sleeveless orange t-shirt that revealed numerous tattoos on his biceps and forearms.

I stopped and leaned out the window. "Mr. Corona?"

"Yeah?"

"Deputy Creede from the Sonoita Station. I'd like to ask you a few questions."

"What about? I ain't done nothin' wrong."

"I'm not saying you have. I wanted to ask you about a woman named Muffy Davenport."

"Who? What about her?"

"She says you're her boyfriend. Is she right?"

The young man looked down at the ground, scraped the toe of his right boot in the dirt, and looked back up with an unpleasant grin on his face. "That she's my girlfriend? You need to take a closer look. Who needs anybody that ugly? There's all kinds of babes around here better lookin' than her."

"And I'll bet they're chasing you all over the county, you're such a charmer."

Apparently this puzzled Oscar Corona. "Huh?"

"Never mind. Just tell me whether or not you know Muffy Davenport."

"Yeah, I know her. So what?"

At this point I cut the engine and stepped out of the Blazer. It was time to continue this conversation on a more personal level. We stood facing each other in the man's driveway. "Do you know anything about a group she's involved with called *KELP*?"

"Never heard of it."

"So you haven't helped her distribute some flyers around the county? They have to do with grazing."

"I don't know what you're talking about."

"Then just what *is* your relationship with Ms. Davenport?"

This seemed to have Oscar temporarily stumped. "I ... do favors for her once in a while."

"What sort of favors?"

"Just things she needs help with, like fixin' up her place. Getting her some things. She pays me sometimes."

"Are you in the firewood business, Mr. Corona?"

"Sometimes. Why?"

"Did you ever get firewood for Muffy Davenport?"

"Maybe once. I can't remember for sure."

"Are you in the drug business?"

"What? No way. I don't do nothin' illegal."

"What do you do for a living? Besides firewood that is."

Oscar Corona hesitated again. "I haul things for people. In my truck. But why is that any of your business, Sheriff?"

"I'm not the sheriff. I'm a deputy. Have you ever hauled anything for anybody in the San Carlos Wash?"

"Where's that?"

"It's on the ranch where your grandfather is foreman, over near Elgin. I think you know that."

"I never heard of it, that wash you mentioned."

"Do you ever work for your grandfather?"

"No. Him and me don't get along."

"Do you know any of the McLeods?"

"Who're they?"

This was beginning to get boring. "They own the ranch where your grandfather works."

"Maybe I heard of 'em, but I don't know any of 'em. Like I said, I don't get on with my grandfather. I don't go over there."

~ ~ ~

The conversation with Oscar Corona had been mostly a waste of time, but the man's pickup definitely was the one I had seen that day in the San Carlo wash. Which meant that Oscar was lying. But why, and about what? I wished I had something solid to go on.

I was anxious to get back to Sonoita, but there was one more stop to make at Patagonia High School, my old alma mater.

The assistant principal thought it was an unusual request, but he could see no harm. It took about 30 minutes before I was back on the road driving north out of town. Beside me on the front seat was a photocopy of one particular page from the 1990 school yearbook.

The halls of Patagonia High were a reminder, mostly unbidden and unwelcome, of how it was that Maria and I used to be married to different people. She and Tony Obregon and I had been schoolmates from kindergarten clear through high school. He and I played basketball for the *Lobos*. We both thought Maria should have gone out for cheerleader, given her looks and personality. She refused, but she did come to most of our games.

I was good enough to be a small-town starter, but Tony was something else – tall and quick, with a dead-eye jump shot from anywhere inside the paint. I don't know if basketball had anything to do with Maria falling in love with Tony, but that's what happened. By the end of our sophomore year it was obvious I'd become the odd man out. Maria and I were still friends, but she was spending most of her spare time with him.

Then, when we were juniors, Martha Lancaster came to town. She was a rich blue-eyed blond whose father was high up the chain of command in a big defense contracting firm in southeast Tucson. The family lived on a ranchette in the oaks north of Sonoita. Martha was a city kid at heart, but she had a horse that she liked to ride. That was how we first got acquainted. Pretty soon the two of us were having double dates with Maria and Tony.

I should have known that something was wrong from the start, because it was Maria I always sought out whenever I had a problem or needed advice. But that got lost in the fog and passion of a serious romance with Martha that developed the last year of high school and continued after graduation, when all four of us enrolled at the University of Arizona.

Tony Obregon had a full athletic scholarship to play basketball. He and Maria got married in the summer after their freshman year. They moved into the old Obregon homestead, and started commuting up to Tucson for classes. One winter night in our senior year Tony was hurrying home from a late basketball practice when his motorcycle hit an icy spot on route 83, just where it came up over the divide. He was killed instantly. I was devastated by the loss of my best friend. Maria was still around of course, but by that time Martha and I were engaged to be married, which happened right after graduation the following spring.

It hadn't taken very long for things to start going downhill for Martha and me, and it got really bad the day she found me over at Maria's place. We were only talking about Tony and about the goat dairy that she was trying to get started. But it looked wrong for sure, and Martha threw me out of the guesthouse we had been sharing at her parent's place. I moved back home to the Pitchfork Ranch, and, probably on the rebound, decided to join the army and volunteer for Afghanistan.

Three years later I was back, but by then it seemed like Martha had slept with half the men in the valley. Decompressing from my war experiences had been hard enough without the added humiliation. Martha and I quickly divorced. In retrospect, I don't think I ever really knew her at all. If there was anything of substance behind her good looks and the glamour of a privileged life, I never came close to figuring it out.

~ ~ ~

All of these memories were tucked safely back into their usual remote places by the time I had completed the short drive back to Sonoita. It was late afternoon on a Monday, and I remembered that two-fers night was coming up. Fortunately, Larry Hernandez was in the office. I brought him up to speed on my conversation with Oscar Corona. "Thanks for tracking him down. I didn't learn much, but for sure that was his truck I saw the other day in the San Carlos Wash. By the way, any chance you're up for some local night life?"

Larry frowned. "Sure, I suppose so. Why?"

"It's Monday, when a departmental presence is required at the Santa Rita Saloon."

"Oh yeah, I think I heard about that. What are we supposed to do?"

"Just show up in civvies, keep your badge out of sight, and use your eyes and ears. Usually nothing happens, but the idea is to stop trouble before it starts. Actually, I'm pretty beat and I was hoping you might be able to handle it alone. There's a steak dinner in it for you, covered by the sheriff. Okay?"

"Sure."

"Good. And thanks. I'll let Frenchy Vullmers know you're coming. He's the owner. You don't need to show up until about 7:30. And if anything happens, I'm available for backup if you need it."

"Where will you be?"

"I'll have my cell phone on."

"Well, have a good time."

Maybe I had that coming, but it was time to get things cleared up with my new assistant. "Listen, Larry, there's something you need to know. Maria and I ... that is, we're engaged – sort of. I think. Sometimes I spend the night at her place. But I've always got my phone with me, and she gets good reception out there." I jotted down her landline on a piece of paper and handed it to him. "And here's her home number, just in case."

"Sure, boss, that's fine. I wish you both all the best. And just for the record, your relationship with Maria might be the worst kept secret in the county."

"Oh?"

I couldn't think of anything else to say.

# Chapter 28

**E**vidently it had been a quiet Monday at the Santa Rita Saloon because nobody called. Larry had just gotten in from an early patrol when I arrived at the office the next morning. I decided to ask anyway. "So, how'd it go last night? Any big dust-ups?"

"Nope. The food was good, like you said, and the man running the place wouldn't let me pay for my dinner. I wouldn't mind doing that again some time." Larry was headed out the door when he snapped his fingers and turned back. "Oh, I almost forgot. Last night there was a woman at the bar, real classy-looking. She kept eyeing me, and then finally she walked over and introduced herself. She sat down and we made small talk for a while, I think until she figured out just who I was. Then she asked if you'd give her a call. Her name was Sally something."

"Sally Benton?"

"Yep, that's her."

"Did she say what it was about?"

"No, but she acted like it was important."

As things turned out it was very important, but in ways neither Sally nor I would have guessed at the time.

I hadn't had any interactions with Sally Benton outside our weekly meetings at the Santa Rita, where she was one of the most loyal and generous of The Regulars. I found her number in the local directory. She answered on the first ring.

"Good morning, Ms. Benton, this is Deputy Calvin Creede. I had a message from Deputy Hernandez that you wanted to speak with me?"

"Please call me Sally."

"Yes ma'am. How can I help you?"

"My prize Hereford bull has gone missing, and I think I may need your help."

"Was he branded?"

"Oh indeed he was, and my foreman has called the brand inspector in case the animal turns up someplace."

"I assume you've searched your own property?"

"Of course we have."

For sure I had that coming, but she went on without giving me a chance to apologize.

"There's just no sign of him. Normally, I wouldn't bother law enforcement about something like this, but I came across a situation on my range that I think you should see. Could you come out some time and take a look? I'm really worried about this. We'll be doing some riding."

"I can come right now if that's convenient. Should I bring a horse?"

"No need for that. I'll have one of my cowboys saddle up a pair of mounts for us."

~ ~ ~

Sally Benton's V-9 Ranch lay along the western foothills of the Huachuca Mountains. It was mostly mesquite country except for the lower reach of Lyle Creek. Heavy livestock activity sometimes encouraged the spread of mesquite. But the trees on the V-9 were well scattered, with an excellent grassy understory. It was a sure sign of careful and moderate grazing.

Sally lived in a large one-level house with a red Spanish tile roof. There were lots of porches and patios, along with an oval-shaped swimming pool. I pulled up on front of a pair of innately carved oak doors, got out, and rang the bell. Evidently she had heard me coming, because she came right out, already dressed for riding. I gathered we weren't going to waste time sitting around in her living room discussing the weather. Apparently Sally was all business.

We rode down the Lyle wash from ranch headquarters for about a mile, in the shade of cottonwoods and sycamores, skirting the edge of a continuous stand of tall *sacaton* grass, until we came to a boundary fence.

Sally explained where we were, and what we were going to do. "That's the Rocking M over there. We'll ride west, along the boundary fenceline. What I want to show you is up on the second mesa."

I noticed an old one-room adobe cabin about 100 yards onto McLeod land. It looked abandoned. The windows no longer had glass, but the wooden door and a tin roof were intact. An old outhouse stood about 30 yards to the east, testimony to the lack of indoor plumbing. I had a thought. Could this be the line shack where Scooter McLeod and Barton Hampstead had spent their summers back in 1990s?

I pointed to the cabin and asked Sally about it. "Does anybody ever stay there?"

"Not that I've ever seen. I don't get down this way all that often, but you can see this place from my house and there's never been a light on. Why?"

"Just curious."

Sally Benton looked skeptical, but she said nothing. We rode up a gentle slope, following the fenceline to the first low bench adjacent to the wash, and then on to a second higher and much larger upland. From there we had a clear view west across the whole valley. I could see Maria's place. Ollie Swade's homestead stood out as a relatively brown patch in a landscape that otherwise was well on its way to becoming a rich green carpet. A few promising clouds were building over the Santa Ritas and the Canelo Hills.

Sally Benton led me to a disturbance in the grass.

"Here is what I wanted you to see."

There were tire tracks, and they went right through the fence. I could see where the barbed wire had been cut and then strung back together. Whoever had driven here had done so recently, because the grass still lay flat. A week or two in a wet summer like this and it would already be standing up again.

I pointed across the fence. "That's still Rocking M land over there, right?"

"Yep. Of course anybody could have come out here and done this. Maybe it was something to do with illegals or drug smugglers. But with my bull gone ..."

"You're thinking maybe rustlers?"

"Maybe. That bull was worth a great deal. And let me show you the place where these tire tracks stop."

We rode across the mesa, following the tracks. At one point the trail led down a south-facing slope where the soil was gray instead of the usual reddish brown. There was a dense stand of relatively tall bunchgrass on the slope, of a kind that I had never seen before. Each individual plant was adorned with long silvery seedheads that glistened in the morning sun.

We got down off our mounts for a closer look. I wondered how much Sally knew about range grasses, and decided to find out. I pointed to the grass growing at our feet. "What is this variety? I don't remember seeing it anywhere around here."

"You've got good eyes, Deputy. That's called New Mexico feather grass. It's pretty uncommon in this part of the world. I had a fellow out here from the University to look at it one time. He said he'd never seen a stand this large anywhere else in Arizona."

The tire tracks ended right in the middle of the patch of feather grass. It was obvious that a vehicle had turned around here, and there was abundant sign of both cattle and horse activity. Had the vehicle towed a livestock trailer? It seemed likely. I scoured the area looking for anything the rustlers, or whoever they were, might have left behind. I found nothing except signs of a prolonged disturbance.

"Well, what do you think?"

"I think I'll go talk to Angel Corona – he's the Rocking M foreman – and see if he knows anything. And maybe Sandy McLeod."

Sally seemed relieved. "Thank you. Of course I called the McLeods and all my other neighbors when our bull disappeared. Nobody knew anything."

"But that was before you found all this disturbance?"

"Exactly. And you can see why it ... I mean, why I was a little reluctant to bother them again."

"I'm not sure I understand. Don't you suppose the McLeods would want to know about this?"

Sally hesitated. "They're my neighbors, and pretty good ones, too. Angel Corona is a great guy. He always helps with the fences, especially the water gap in Lyle Canyon that seems to blow out every time the wash runs. And I like Janet McLeod. But Sandy - sometimes I wonder about him."

This got my attention, and I wanted to know more. "What about Sandy?"

"For one thing, all he wants to talk about are his housing developments and his silly shopping mall, or whatever it's going to be. Sorry about that, but I don't like what's happening in this valley. It's getting too goddamned crowded, pardon my French. Arthur and I moved out here for the wide open spaces and the views."

"I'm with you on that one."

"I've tried talking with Sandy about cattle or ranching, but he just doesn't seem interested. And when I called him about my bull, he acted almost like it was some sort of

*171*

intrusion. The man makes me uncomfortable, Cal. I just don't know how else to put it."

There didn't seem to be anything more to say. Rather than make small talk, we rode in silence back across the mesa, enjoying the view and the late morning air.

~ ~ ~

I drove straight to Rocking M headquarters from the Benton ranch. Angel Corona was glad to see me, and he seemed genuinely sorry to hear that Sally's bull hadn't turned up. I told him about the place where the fence had been cut along the V-9 boundary. He promised to check it out right away and get back in touch with Sally. He claimed not to have seen or heard any unusual activity that might be related to the incident. I thought the man looked worried, but it was the sort of worry you might have for a neighbor in trouble, not an expression of guilt.

Sandy McLeod was in his real estate office when I got back to Sonoita. His face lit up when I came in.

"Morning, Cal! I hope you're here about that new suite we're holding for you. No time to waste, you know. They're going fast!"

I didn't see much sign of life, and most of the suites were empty as far as I could tell. "Actually, I'm here about Sally Benton's Hereford."

The developer's face fell. "What about it? I already told her I hadn't seen it, and she should talk to Angel. Why such a big deal anyway? I'm sure it's just wandering around on her place somewhere. The V-9 is a big spread – not as big as the Rocking M of course - but still there's plenty of room to lose one cow."

"It isn't a cow, Sandy, it's a bull. And from what she says it's a famous one at that. But the point is that it looks like somebody stole it and then drove out through your ranch. So I wondered if you knew anything about that."

"Not a thing." Sandy McLeod turned his attention

back to a stack of papers on his desk.

~ ~ ~

I visited my grandfather once when I was a boy. He was retired from the Navy and lived in San Francisco. I remember trying to describe to him the way lightning looked coming from inside a monsoon thundercloud, because my grandfather said they didn't have that sort of thing in California. I failed to capture the image with words on that occasion, and every time subsequently. Lightning-filled thunderclouds are the very essence of the monsoon, but they seem beyond the reach of words, or at least any within my command. The closest I had ever gotten was that an active monsoon thunderhead resembled an enormous flickering light bulb, but that wasn't quite right because light bulbs stayed the same shape and thunderheads kept changing. Eventually I decided it was something you just had to experience for yourself to appreciate.

Maria and I experienced it in abundance that night in the Sonoita Valley, as we enjoyed one another's company, along with the rain and the thunder and the light show outside her bedroom window.

# Chapter 29

**T**here didn't seem to be any leads to follow on Sally Benton's bull until the animal turned up someplace. I called the brand inspector the next morning, just to touch base. She had nothing to report, but we agreed it could have been a theft, and she promised to stay in touch.

I turned my attention back to the cases of Muffy Davenport and Scooter McLeod. I had set myself two goals for the day. One was to visit Ollie Swade and catch him up on what we had learned about his dead cow. But first I wanted to locate Scooter's old girlfriend, Angela Salerno, or at least start trying. I might get what I needed over the phone, but I wasn't ruling out the possibility of a visit to Colorado, if that's where she was living.

She proved hard to find. The department had electronic access to all the phone directories for Colorado, including unlisted numbers, but there was nobody by the name of Salerno in Fort Collins or anywhere else in the state. I expanded my search to include New Mexico, Wyoming, Nebraska, Utah, and Kansas. There was an Angela Salerno listed for Española, New Mexico, but she turned out to be a 76 year-old grandmother.

I decided to put in a call to the Fort Collins Police Department, and after several steps I got handed over to a Sergeant Charles Graebner. I explained the reason for my call.

"So all you have to go on is a two-year old Christmas card, and the possibility that some woman named Angela is a school teacher?"

"That's it. That and the fact that she's probably in her

mid-forties."

"And this is really important to your case?"

"I won't know that 'til I talk to her, Sergeant. But this is a murder investigation into a cold case, and she's one of a very few leads we have. She and the victim may have been lovers."

"Any reason to suspect she was the perp?"

"Only that she disappeared around the time the victim was killed. And her parents, who still live in Arizona, had a peculiar reaction when I told them we had found the man's body."

Graebner wanted to know more. "What do you mean by 'peculiar'?"

"Her father acted like he wasn't interested, and her mother started to cry."

"Huh."

"Anyway, I'd appreciate anything you can do. She could be using a married name, but I have no idea what it might be."

"You're not making this very easy for me."

"Like I said, this could be important, and it's about all we have to go on."

"Sure, okay. The only thing I can think of is to get in touch with the school districts in our area. Maybe they'll have a teacher named Angela about that age."

"That would be a big help."

"This may take a while. I'll get back to you if and when I have something."

"Thanks. I really appreciate this."

~ ~ ~

There was just a hint of green in the pastures around Ollie Swade's homestead, testimony to the recent rains. In fact, most of the Sonoita Valley was showing lots of new growth. If this kept up it would be a good summer for the grass and for all the creatures that depended upon it. All except for Ollie's cows, that is. They obviously were eating every new sprout down to the ground as soon as it appeared, and they still looked gaunt. On the other hand, they looked great compared to the carcass that Ollie Swade had not bothered to remove from where it lay out by his fence. It was little more than hide and bones by now, surrounded by a puddle of foul fluid seeping slowly into the ground. Even the vultures were gone.

Ollie was slouched as usual in one of the wicker chairs on his porch. He held a blue and white porcelain coffee mug in his left hand, and he took a long drink from it as I pulled to a stop in his barren yard and got out of the Blazer.

"Morning, Ollie. How's it going?"

"About like usual I suppose. Gonna be a hot one I think, and a little humid from the rain. I hope you're here with some news about who killed my cow."

"Yes and no. Why don't we go inside and talk?"

"Might as well." Ollie grunted, rising unsteadily to his feet. "It's too damned hot out here anyway. Coffee? There's still some on the stove."

"That'd be good." I followed the old man inside. "You really ought to have that carcass hauled away before it gets even muddier out there."

Ollie just grunted.

A swamp cooler blew damp and musty air across the darkened interior of a central room in the house that served as a combination kitchen, eating, and living area. There was an open doorway in the back, leading to a small bedroom. A rumpled single bed was partly covered by a patterned Mexican blanket, and beyond it was another door that probably led to a bathroom.

Each of the four corners of the main room was given to a different purpose. To the right in the back was a sink, stacked with unwashed dishes. Next to the sink were a refrigerator and a corroded two-burner gas range. Left of the bedroom door was a pot-bellied wood stove. The maze of spider webs attached to the stove testified to its inactivity since the weather had turned warm.

To the right of the front door was an open stairway leading down to what I assumed was a cellar. Hanging on one wall of the stairway was a collection of photographs. All the pictures were dusty. The most faded ones were of Ollie and a woman that presumably had been his wife. Beside these were several photos of unsmiling men posed rigidly in front of steam locomotives. Two relatively recent shots were of Ollie the rancher. One was of the old man on horseback. In the other, he was holding a dead coyote by its hind legs. A lever-action rifle lay crooked in his arm.

What particularly caught my eye were objects displayed on a shelf attached to the opposite wall in the stairwell. There were two rusted axe blades, some purple glass, and an assortment of arrowheads, most of them broken. There also was a large clay pot with one side crushed in.

Ollie brought my coffee - no cream, no sugar, and no offer of either. I took a sip and winced. It was strong, bitter, and very hot. Not bad, really. Ollie pointed to a pair of lumpy overstuffed chairs that occupied the living quarters of the main room. We sat, and I proceeded to tell him about Muffy Davenport, and about how she had vandalized Maria's dairy.

"So, you gonna charge her with killing my cow? How about getting her to pay me what it was worth?"

"No can do, Ollie. First of all, we can't really prove she did it. And like I told you before, that cow was already dead when somebody – and it probably was the Davenport woman – stuck that little knife in it. So the most we could charge her with, even if we could prove it, would be trespassing and vandalism. And that's what she's charged with now, for what she did for sure over at Maria Obregon's place. I don't think she'll be bothering you again."

"So that's it? That's all you're gonna do?"

"That's about all we can do, Ollie."

"Are you finished with that coffee?" The old man rose from his chair. "Because if you are, then I guess we're about done here."

"The coffee was good. Thanks. But before I go I was wondering what you could tell me about those things in your stairwell."

"They're just some old pictures and stuff. Why?"

"I don't mean the pictures. I'm interested in your collection of artifacts."

"Those are some things I found around here. Mostly junk, I suppose."

"Where did you find them?"

"Right here on my place." There was a pause. "Oh, I see what you're getting at. I know the laws about that. They all came from right here on my place, on private property. It's all legal."

"Do you know a man named Barton Hampstead?"

"Who's he? Anyway, it doesn't matter because I never heard of him."

I wondered about that while I was driving back to Sonoita. I'd been so distracted by Ollie's collection that I'd forgotten to ask the old man about his dealings with the McLeods.

~ ~ ~

When I got back to the office I had a phone message to please call Sergeant Graebner up in Fort Collins, that maybe he'd found something. The detective picked up on the first ring.

"Police department, this is Graebner."

"Hello Sergeant, this is Deputy Creede in Arizona

179

returning your call?"

"Yeah. Listen, this took some doing, but I found three teachers around here named Angela. As far as I can determine there's only one that fits your general description. She's at the Sunrise Charter School over in Greeley. That's about twenty-five miles southeast of here. So just in case, I got her driver's license info from the Department of Motor Vehicles, including a jpeg of the photo ID. She looks to be about the right age, but the last name is Jordan. You want me to e-mail the photo to you, along with her address?"

"That would be great. And thanks for doing this. I really appreciate it."

"You want me to contact her?"

"No, please don't do that. I'll check the photo and see if it matches an earlier one I have of Angela Salerno. Of course it's been a lot of years, so that may be a problem. How did you get the information? Has anybody at the school been alerted that the police are making inquiries? Do you think she might know about it?"

"I didn't deal directly with the school, only the district office over in Weld County. I said it was just a routine investigation. They pushed a little bit, but I couldn't really think of anything more to say. There's no guarantee she hasn't been contacted. Why?"

"If it is the Salerno woman, she might take off, depending on what happened all those years ago. For sure she doesn't want her parents to know where she is, and it stands to reason she might not want the law to find out either."

"Okay, I'll sit tight. Just give me your e-mail address and I'll send along the driver's license info."

In about fifteen minutes I was looking at a head shot of a woman identified on a Colorado driver's license as Angela Jordan. She had blond curly hair and a narrow face with prominent cheekbones. There was a strong resemblance to the high school graduation photo of Angela Salerno I'd picked up the other day in Patagonia. The license showed her as 5' 10" and 145 pounds. That was tall for a woman, just like her mother. My hopes rose.

# Chapter 30

"What's that you're looking at?" Maria had just come into the office, having finished her morning mail deliveries and hoping to join me for lunch before heading back out for the afternoon run.

"It's a copy of the Colorado driver's license for a woman named Angela Jordan. I just got it from a police detective up there."

"Why?"

"The last time Ray and Vicki Salerno heard from their daughter they thought she was teaching school someplace in Colorado. So I followed that lead. It may have paid off."

Maria turned the document over in her hands. "But this says Angela Jordan. How do you know it's the Angela you're looking for? And why do you want to talk to her in the first place? What's for lunch?"

"Well now, which of those three questions would you like me to answer first?"

"The last one. I'm hungry. I saw you loading up those leftover beans and flour tortillas this morning as I was going out to milk the goats."

"You don't miss a trick, *querida*. Sometimes I think you'd make a good detective."

I put the food on a paper plate, covered it with waxed paper, and put it in the microwave. "Should be enough here for two. How about some coffee?"

"That would be great, thanks. And now you can tell me about this Angela person."

I told her what I knew and suspected, then laid the high school photo of Angela Salerno next to the driver's license image of Angela Jordan. "What do you think?"

"Seems pretty close, but a lot of years have passed. Why don't you show it to her parents?"

I shook my head. "I don't want to get their hopes up, especially her mother. She was really upset when I talked to her the other day over in Green Valley. But there's more to it than that. I'm pretty sure there's a dark side to the history between Scooter McLeod and Angela's parents. I don't want to go blundering into something before I've got my facts straight."

Maria filled one of the warm tortillas with a steaming spoonful of beans. "And you're hoping this Angela person up in Colorado can fill you in on that history?"

"Something like that, I suppose."

Maria glanced up between bites. "You gonna go up there?"

"If I can get the green light from Luis."

"I expect he'll go for it." She rose and stretched, gulped two last swallows of coffee, and tossed her napkin and paper plate into the wastebasket. "Well, I gotta get back to work. See you tonight."

Just then Larry came in, passing Maria at the door. "Smells good in here."

"Help yourself. There's a tortilla left, and enough beans to fill it. What's new out there?"

"Not much this morning. But I did run into something interesting on the way home last night."

"Oh yeah?"

"I was headed east on 82 toward my folks place, when I caught up with a Chevy pickup moving real slow in the same direction. I got close enough to read the plate, and I'm pretty sure it matches the one registered to Oscar Corona."

"Was it green and white?"

"Yep. And here's something odd. The bed was filled with mesquite logs, piled up almost as high as the cab."

"Where did the truck go?"

"Don't know. I followed it east as far as the county line. But the tag was current and the driver was staying well under the speed limit, so I couldn't think of any legitimate reason to pull him over. I hope I did right."

"You did. But it sure sounds like Oscar."

"Is he in the firewood business? It's a strange time of year for that."

"I asked him about that when we had our little chat in Patagonia. He said he hauled things for people."

"Like what?"

"Good question. He did say he might have brought some firewood to Muffy Davenport, and his pickup was full of mesquite that day I saw him over in the San Carlos Wash. Still, there's something odd about this whole thing. Keep your eyes out for that truck. We need to get to the bottom of this."

"Will do, boss. And thanks for the lunch."

# Chapter 31

Less than twenty four hours later I was on a Frontier Airlines jet circling in for a landing at Denver International Airport. It was a fine clear day and I could see the distinctive white domes of the main terminal as the plane banked for its final approach. I'd read someplace that particular roofline was supposed to make the building look like the snow-capped Rocky Mountains. Personally, I thought it looked more like something put up by the Ringling Brothers.

I picked up a rental car and headed north, driving through a mixture of open prairie, fields of winter wheat, and the bedroom as well as farming communities between Denver and Greeley. Oil and gas wells were everywhere, testimony to an ongoing energy boom. No trace of snow remained on the crest of the Rocky Mountain Front Range off to the west.

My first stop would be the Weld County Sheriff's Department, because it turned out that Angela Jordan lived east of Greeley and beyond the jurisdiction of the city police. I had an appointment with a detective named Delbert Blevins. Sergeant Graebner of the Fort Collins police had helped set up the meeting the previous afternoon, once Luis Mendoza had given me the green light for the trip.

Deputy Blevins ("call me Del") resembled one of those cop characters from a 1950s gangster movie I'd seen once on late-night TV. He was a chain smoker, overweight, with a really bad comb-over. He was dressed in a rumpled blue suit, an off-white shirt, and multicolored tie. There was a brown food stain on the tie. It was the only thing that matched his shoes. His eyes reflected the boredom and cynicism of a cop on the final glide path to a much-anticipated and obviously overdue retirement.

We were seated on opposite sides of a battered metal desk in a cubicle that served as his semi-private office. Blevins offered me a cup of stale-looking coffee. I declined. "So what is this Jordan woman supposed to have done? I did a background check after Chuck Graebner called. She's squeaky clean as far as we're concerned. Not even a traffic ticket."

"She may know something about a murder that happened in my county 20 years ago. We just want to talk to her."

"Why now? I mean why did this just come up?"

I explained just enough about the case to persuade Blevins to accompany me on a visit to the woman's home. His presence would make it official, in case anything she said turned out to be evidence.

Del Blevins sighed conspicuously, heaved his substantial girth upright, and stubbed out his cigarette in an ashtray already filled to overflowing. "All right then, let's go. The sooner we get this over with, the sooner I can log out. It's been a long damn day. You going back to Arizona tonight?"

"Maybe. We'll see how it goes."

~ ~ ~

Angela Jordan lived in a small frame house at the edge of a cornfield, not far from the South Platte River. Two enormous cottonwoods grew in the front yard, most likely planted by some long-ago farmer trying to get a little shade against the heat of the Colorado High Plains. There was no garage and no sign of a vehicle. We pulled into the gravel drive, got out, and went to the door. I knocked, but there was no answer. Blevins decided maybe nobody was home. "You want to wait, or come back tomorrow?"

"Lets park down the road and wait a while."

The wait lasted about an hour. The woman was driving a Subaru wagon, maybe ten years old. She stopped to collect mail from a battered old box on a post at the end of her driveway, then pulled up beside the house. She carried her mail and two bags of groceries inside. If she had seen Del Blevins' unmarked cruiser coming down the road she gave no indication.

This time Del knocked and again we waited.

Nothing.

He knocked a second time and identified himself as a deputy sheriff. It took a while, but eventually we heard the sounds of movement somewhere inside. A voice came from behind the door, which remained closed. "Yes? What do you want?"

"I'm with the sheriff's department. We'd like to talk to you ma'am. Could you open the door please?"

"I need to see your badge and an ID. Please hold them up to the glass."

Del Blevins did as he was told. Eventually the door opened, and I had my first look at the person who might once have been Angela Salerno. She was tall and lanky, except for a slightly pear-shaped mid-section. Her face was more pinched than it had appeared on her driver's license. But it was Angela all right.

"Good afternoon, ma'am. I'm Deputy Calvin Creede from the Santa Cruz County Sheriff's Department in Arizona. Are you Angela Salerno? Or was that your maiden name?"

A look of wariness mixed with fear came over the woman's face. "I used to be Angela Salerno, but now my name is Jordan. What do you want?"

"May we come in, please? This may take a while."

At this point Del Blevins decided to insert himself into the conversation. "Ma'am, we're here on official business.

Please let us in. Now."

Great technique.

Suddenly Angela put her hands up to her mouth, and for the first time looked directly into my eyes. "Is it my mother? Has something happened to my mother?"

"No ma'am, your parents are fine. I saw them just last week."

"Well then, what do you want?"

"I need to talk to you about a man named Jeremiah McLeod. You may have know him as Scooter."

She froze, still blocking the door. "I don't want to talk about him. Please go away."

"I really can't do that, ma'am."

It took a while, but eventually all three of us were seated in Angela Jordan's sparsely furnished living room. I asked the first question. "You did know Scooter McLeod, is that correct?"

Del Blevins had taken a small spiral bound notebook out of his shirt pocket and was conspicuously jotting things down in it. Angela Jordan noticed. Clearly, she was less than pleased. After a significant pause, she responded.

"Yes, I knew Scooter McLeod. We went to high school together, along with a whole lot of other kids. But that was years ago. I haven't seen Scooter since."

"Since when?"

"Since I left Arizona."

"And when was that?"

"It was in 1995."

"And you never even talked to him after that?"

"That's right. But listen, just what is this all about? Did something happen to him?"

Once again, Del Blevins decided to get himself involved. "Oh, something happened to him all right."

I realized I needed to take complete charge of this interview, before the Colorado detective did any more damage.

"Once again, Ms. Jordan, it would be a big help if you could tell me about the last time you saw Scooter McLeod, and under what circumstances."

"It was a long time ago. I don't really remember the circumstances."

"Mr. McLeod disappeared in the summer of 1995, the same year you claim to have left Arizona. We recently determined that he was murdered. Naturally, we're anxious to talk with anyone who saw him alive around that time. I believe you and Mr. McLeod were involved. Romantically, I mean. Can you confirm that?"

Angela Jordan began to tremble, and tears welled-up. But it was over quickly, and pretty soon the old Angela was back – angry and afraid, perhaps, but more resolved than upset. Odd, it seemed to me, if she and Scooter had been lovers.

"I'm sorry he's dead, really I am. But I never saw him that summer. I just told you that I was gone from Arizona by 1995. So I don't see how I can help you. Now if you will excuse me, I have some papers to grade. I'm a teacher here in Greeley, and I have a summer school class for students with reading disabilities. They're good kids for the most part, and I take my responsibilities seriously."

I decided to try a different approach. "Detective, would you excuse us for a while? I would like to talk to Ms. Jordan alone."

Del Blevins shrugged. It wasn't exactly procedure, but apparently he really didn't care. "Sure. I'll be out in the car. Don't make it too long, okay?"

# Chapter 32

After Del Blevins had waddled back outside to his cruiser, I continued my interrogation of Angela Jordan. "I know this is difficult, but we've got a murder on our hands here, and I really need to ask you more about your relationship with Scooter McLeod."

"What about it?"

"You were lovers, isn't that right?"

She hesitated, but only briefly. "All right. Yes, Scooter was my boyfriend. But I had nothing to do with his ... disappearance. How many times do I have to tell you? I was gone from Arizona by that summer."

"So you were no longer involved with him in 1995? When did you last see him?"

"I saw him at Christmas, in 1994, when he and I were home from college. That was the last time, I swear."

"I understand he went to Yale? Were you there as well?"

"Oh no, I wasn't good enough to get into a place like that. I was at Northern Arizona University, up in Flagstaff. I was studying art." She paused and looked out the window. "I wanted to be a painter."

"What can you tell me about Scooter's drug arrest? Were you with him when that happened?"

"No. I mean I didn't have anything to do with that. But I was shocked when I found out about it. We never did drugs. I wouldn't stand for it."

"So the first thing you knew he'd been arrested? Did your parents find out?"

"Sure they did. It was all over the valley, including the local paper. My father told me never to have anything to do with Scooter again. But I did anyway."

"And what year was that?"

"I think it was in the summer of 1993."

"But the last time you saw Scooter was the following year, at Christmas time, in 1994?"

"That's right, yes."

"Why didn't you see him after that? Why didn't you see him the following spring break, or the next summer?"

"He didn't come home for spring break."

"Did you?"

"Yes."

"And what about the summer?"

"I wasn't at home then. I keep telling you that."

"Why not? Had you graduated? What were you doing that summer, Ms. Jordan?"

I was pushing hard now, perhaps too hard, and I wasn't surprised when Angela resisted.

"You can't make me answer that. I don't think I want to talk to you any more."

"You have the right not to answer my questions. But I'm sure we could get a judge to require your testimony under oath down in Arizona. And that's what I'll do if you force me."

"Then you go ahead, because there's nothing more I want to say. My relationship with Scooter McLeod is in the distant past. I have a new life now."

I decided it was time to play my trump card. I reached in my pocket and extracted the holy medal we had found around Scooter McLeod's neck. She took it from me, turned it over in her hands several times, and then frowned. "Where did you get this?"

"We found it on Scooter McLeod's body. Is it yours?"

Angela Jordan did not reply. Instead, she dropped the medal on the table beside her, covered her face with her hands, and began to cry. At first there was no sound, just tears. But then the dam broke, and the whole thing quickly escalated into noisy, heart-wrenching, convulsive sobs. It seemed like an eternity, but probably only five minutes passed before she regained at least some control of herself, to the point where I thought we might continue.

"I'm sorry. I can see this is very difficult for you. But please consider my position here. If you can just tell me what you know about Scooter McLeod's activities in that last year of his life, and assuming you had nothing to do with his disappearance or death, then perhaps I can leave you in peace. But you need to tell me everything. Okay?"

Angela Jordan gave that prospect some serious thought before she responded. "All right, I'll tell you what you want to know. But only on one condition, and you have to promise."

"I can't make promises about anything involving criminal activity, Ms. Jordan. I'm sure you know that. What's the condition?"

"You have to promise not to tell my parents where I am."

I wasn't surprised, and it was a promise I could keep, up to a point.

"You have my word. Of course it may become necessary for us to bring you to down to Arizona, in which case they're likely to find you in any event. And I'm just speaking personally now, but it seems to me that your parents really would like to see you. Especially your mother."

"It's not my mother so much as my father. He's the reason my life turned out the way it did. I don't think I'll ever be able to forgive him. My mother went along, because she's weak when it comes to him. So she's partly to blame, too."

"Blame for what? And what does this have to do with Scooter McLeod?"

195

She took a deep breath, and began. "Scooter and I were lovers, Mr. Creede. You're right about that. It started in high school and continued when we both went off to college, even though we only saw each other in the summers and when we were home for holidays. And we were always careful, you know, about my getting pregnant. Because we both had plans that required completing our educations."

"Did something change?"

"Two things changed. First, Scooter brought a young man with him to Arizona for the summer of 1994. He was a college roommate, I think. Anyway, they both got so involved with exploring on the McLeod ranch that I began to feel like an intruder."

"Exploring for what?"

"Artifacts. You know, arrowheads, bits of pottery, that sort of thing. I didn't have any problem with that, but Scooter just seemed to get more distant as the summer went on. All he did was hang around with this roommate."

"Was the roommate called Barton Hampstead?"

"Yes. How did you know that?"

"You said two things changed. What was the other?"

"It was when we both came back home for Christmas that year. We began seeing each other again. It seemed like things were getting back to normal. But then one night we were out for dinner at the Santa Rita, and we had a terrible fight."

"What about?"

"Scooter accused me of being jealous."

"Jealous of who?"

"Bartie Hampstead."

"Were you?"

"I don't know, maybe a little. We were both pretty drunk. He asked why I didn't want him to spend time with anybody but me. I said if that's the way he felt, then he could spend all his time with that man for all I cared. Then I walked out. And that's the last time I ever saw him. So you can see that I don't know anything about what happened to him that next summer."

Angela began to cry again. But I wasn't finished. Something still didn't make sense. "Why did you break up with your parents? Did it have something to do with Scooter?"

"I really don't want to talk about that."

This was getting redundant. "Then we don't have a deal, and you can expect a subpoena from Arizona. You agreed to tell me everything."

She thought about that and finally gave a brief nod. "What I'm about to tell you must remain confidential. Nobody in Colorado knows about it. Can you do that?"

"If it proves to have nothing to do with the case, yes."

"All right then, I'll tell you. The thing is, I got pregnant, from when Scooter and I were together that Christmas. I didn't find out for sure until I'd gone back to Flagstaff. It was just before spring break. I came home and told my mother I wanted an abortion. Scooter and I had broken up, and I didn't want the baby. I made her promise not to tell my father, but she broke her promise."

"Then what happened?" The possibilities were ominous.

"My father was furious when he found out. He was shaking with rage. And he told me what to do. It wasn't even a conversation, really, just him telling me how things were going to go."

"How was that?"

"First he said that Scooter and I would get married. I told him we'd broken up, and that wasn't possible. So then he decided I would drop out of school and go back to New Jersey. That's where the rest of the family lives. I'd have the baby and put it up for adoption."

"Is that what you did?"

"No. I didn't want to drop out. I only had a year and a half to go for my art degree. So I found out about a place across the border in Nogales where they did abortions, and I went down there. I figured once that was over there would be nothing my parents could do, so they would let me go back to school. But it didn't work out that way."

"Why not?"

"I got back home from ... from Mexico, and everything seemed fine for a while. But then I started to bleed, and I couldn't stop it, and I tried to run away but my father caught me and he saw all the blood, and ..."

She started to cry again. Just then Del Blevins came in the front door. The guy's timing was incredible. "How much longer is this going to take?"

"Just give as a few more minutes here, please."

"I'll give you five, then we're oughta' here. It's late and I've already used up my overtime for this month. You can always come back afterwards, by yourself."

I turned my attention back to Angela. "I'm sorry about that. Please go on."

"They flew me by helicopter to the hospital in Sierra Vista. They say I almost died from loss of blood. But I didn't die, Mr. Creede. The surgery saved my life, but now I can't have babies. And so I ran away."

"Where did you go?"

"I went to Chicago, because of the Art Institute."

"Did you tell your parents?"

"No. I didn't want to see them ever again. Or at least not my father. So I stayed in Chicago. It was hard. I got a job as a waitress, and I got married for a while, but that didn't work out. Neither did my attempts to make a living in art. Eventually I got a teaching degree from Northwestern University. That's how I ended up here, in Colorado."

"Do you blame your father for what happened?"

"Wouldn't you?"

I wasn't sure about that, but I was pretty sure about something else. Lifetime estrangement from your only child and no chance for grandchildren just might add up to a motive for murder.

"I have one last question, Ms. Jordan."

"What's that?"

"Did Scooter McLeod know about any of this?"

"You mean about my being pregnant and about the abortion? I don't think so. At least I never told him."

~ ~ ~

I caught the last flight out of Denver, and it was nearly midnight by the time we touched down in Tucson. It had been a bumpy ride. A major monsoon storm had settled over southeastern Arizona that afternoon and the pilot had to negotiate his way around several big thunderheads to get safely on the ground.

I walked out of the terminal to a wet parking lot and the sweet smell of desert rain. It was stormy all the way home, and I drove carefully, watching for slick spots on the highway where my vehicle could easily have spun out of control. Hopefully Maria was still awake, because I was anxious to get her reaction to the story Angela Jordan had told me. Was it plausible? Was it the truth? It all seemed reasonable to me, but a woman's perspective might be different.

# Chapter 33

**M**aria had been dead to the world by the time I got in from Tucson, which meant there were two things that had to wait until morning. We were dealing with the second one over breakfast. I filled her in on details of my conversation with Angela Jordan up in Colorado. "So anyway, she appears to hold her father responsible for making a mess out of her life."

"You mean because of the botched abortion?"

"That, and I assume for the fact that she couldn't have children. Does that make sense to you? It's not like he made her go across the border."

"I think he did. She didn't want the baby, and he wouldn't help her. Neither, apparently, would her mother. So she felt trapped. It's true she made a foolish choice, but she was young and scared and probably didn't know where else to turn. So yes, I think she had plenty of reason to blame both her parents."

"And then not see them for all these years?"

"That's extreme, I'll admit."

"Which makes me wonder if Angela had some other reason to hide. Anyway, I'm definitely going over to Green Valley to see the Salernos again. The case files confirm what Barney Stroud told me. When he asked Ray Salerno where Angela was the summer Scooter disappeared, he told Barney she was traveling in Europe. I need to find out why the man lied."

"So you think he might have had something to do with Scooter's death?"

"That, or maybe he suspected Angela needed an alibi."

Maria nodded. "I hadn't thought of that. What a

201

mess."

~ ~ ~

Larry was having his usual cup of coffee in the office and getting himself organized for the day, when I walked in about 7:30 AM.

"What's new, Deputy?"

"I was going to ask you that. Have a good trip up to Colorado? Was it her? The woman you were searching for, I mean?"

"It was Angela Salerno all right, except now she's called Angela Jordan."

I filled him in on the details. "So I'm gonna go see her parents again. What have you got planned for the day?"

"Nothing much. It's been pretty quiet around here. I'm due to patrol over toward Lyle Canyon today, but it's not an emergency. Is there something else you'd like me to do?"

"No, that's fine. But do me a favor. As long as you're over that way, take a swing by Muffy Davenport's place – that's the old Wahlberg Ranch? Let me know what you see."

"Sure. Are we looking for anything in particular?"

"A couple of things. First, I'm anxious to know if she's still around. Luis thought she might skip and go back to California once she made bail. And I'm interested in keeping tabs on Oscar Corona. I think he hangs around there a lot of the time."

"You want me to knock on the door?"

"No. Just do a drive-by. Let me know what you see – whether the place is occupied, any vehicles around, that sort of thing. Also, keep any eye out for a pile of cut mesquite stems and branches. Last time I was there, it was lying up against the side of her garage."

"Will do, but why are we interested in a bunch of firewood?"

"Because it may have been in Oscar's pickup that day I saw him down in the San Carlos Wash. And it might not really be a load of firewood at all."

"Huh?"

"I'm working on a weird hunch. Just find out if it's there, and let me know."

~ ~ ~

After Larry left on patrol, I phoned the Salerno residence in Green Valley. A man answered and said they had gone to Cancun for a long weekend, that they would be back late Monday.

"Shall I give them a message, sir?"

"No, just tell them Deputy Creede phoned from Sonoita. I'll call back first of the week."

Working my way down a mental to-do list, I next went on line, found a general number for Yale University, and made the call. It took two more steps until I got the connection I was looking for.

"Registrar's Office, this is Jessica. How may I help you?"

"Good morning. My name is Calvin Creede. I am a deputy sheriff in Santa Cruz County, Arizona. We're investigating the death of a former student of yours, Jeremiah McLeod, Jr., and I'm interested in getting a look at his records."

"I'm sorry, but we do not share that kind of information, sir. All of our records are confidential."

"I appreciate that, ma'am, but this is an official murder investigation. I'm sure I can get a subpoena, but I was hoping this might be done more simply. May I speak to the person in charge?"

"One moment, sir."

After about a minute another woman came on the line, a Ms. Charters, who identified herself as the assistant registrar. I explained who I was and why I was calling, that it was a case dating back to 1995, and that the person was deceased. The woman asked for my badge number and contact information, including the name and location of my superiors. She said she would look into it. I thanked the woman and hung up. I wasn't optimistic, but to my surprise Ms. Charters called back in about forty-five minutes. She had good news, maybe.

"Good morning Deputy Creede. We may be able to release certain information about Mr. McLeod, since you appear to have a legitimate need. I've cleared it with legal, and they checked with your sheriff. But first I must ask why you think it would be useful to your case. You say this gentleman, Mr. McLeod, died in Arizona? What can that have to do with any of us back here in New Haven?"

"Perhaps nothing, but this is a very cold case and anything we can learn about the victim might help. I'm interested in what classes he attended, his major field of study, any clubs or activities, that sort of thing."

"I see. Well, it took me a while to search our archives. This was a long time ago."

I could hear the rustling of papers, and then the woman came back on the line.

"Jeremiah McLeod first registered at Yale in the fall of 1992, and he attended classes for three years, until May of 1995. In 1993 he declared a major in anthropology, but with an individually structured minor in environmental conservation. It was an unusual arrangement that had taken special permission from the Deans of both the School of Forestry and Yale College."

"Was he a good student?"

"I'm sorry, but grades are one thing we'd much rather not share, unless it is absolutely necessary."

"No, I don't suppose it is. But can you tell me this - was he in good standing?"

"He was. In terms of grades, that is."

"Was there something else?"

"Well, he was involved in a sit-in."

"What was that about?"

"It was in the spring of 1994. He and a few dozen other students were removed by police from the administration building, after they refused to leave voluntarily. There's a report about it in his file."

"Was he charged with anything? Would there be any records of that?"

More paper rustling by Ms. Charters.

"I see no indication of an arrest. It was before my time, you understand, but I expect the students simply were hauled out of the building and released. That's the way we usually handle such things nowadays."

"Thank you, Ms. Charters. You have been most helpful. I have just one more question, if I may. Do you see any indication of what the sit-in was about?"

"No I don't. But I have a date. It was April 22, 1994. Maybe there would be something in the local paper, the New Haven *Register*. You might check their archives."

"Well, thanks again. I may be back in touch if anything else comes up."

I was about to get back on the computer when I remembered something important. April 22 was Earth Day. It couldn't be a coincidence. Scooter McLeod was studying environmental conservation, and he'd been involved in an Earth Day sit-in. I wondered how his father the rancher had reacted. Or better yet, what about his younger brother, the aspiring developer? Maybe it was time for another visit with Barton Hampstead, who probably would know something about his friend's environmental activities and opinions.

*205*

# Chapter 34

## Sheriff Luis Mendoza

**S**omething about the Trujillos and Scooter McLeod's murder just wasn't adding up. The Sheriff had come to that conclusion four days earlier, after he had checked some case files and court records. Scooter had indeed turned state's evidence against Paco Trujillo, and Paco had died shortly thereafter in the Santa Cruz County jail, where he was being held awaiting trial on drug charges. This gave his brother Pedro and their father Herman plenty of reason to have it in for Scooter, and Luis had no doubt that they or one of their many operatives were more than capable of killing.

The problem was with the timing. Scooter McLeod had died in 1995, nearly two years after Paco's arrest. If the Trujillos were responsible for Scooter's death, why had they waited so long to exact their revenge? It didn't necessarily rule them out as suspects, but if they were responsible there had to be more to the story. There must be a piece to the puzzle that neither he nor his deputies had yet discovered. The Sheriff realized he needed to find that missing piece, and he decided the way to start was by having a talk with Camarilla Trujillo. Pedro had told Luis not to bother his mother, but that was all the more reason to try. What might Pedro be hiding?

It had not been easy to arrange. Luis wanted to make sure Pedro was elsewhere when he visited the recently widowed Senora Trujillo at their home in the hills above Patagonia. This meant he needed solid information on Pedro's whereabouts, and it all had to be set up at the last minute so the man would not get word in time. The Sheriff had contacts in Mexico who could let him know when Pedro was at his restaurant. Then he would take a chance Camarilla would be at home and that she would let him in when he showed up unexpectedly at her door. Two things worked in his favor – a strong tradition of Mexican hospitality (did it apply to drug families?), and the fact that she might remember him as an old high school friend of Pedro's. It was shameless, he knew, but he also would play the grief card. He was not visiting as sheriff but as an old family acquaintance coming to express his sympathies for her husband's recent demise.

~ ~ ~

The term 'sprawling compound' was an overworked cliché, but Luis could think of no other way to describe the Trujillo estate. He had been there before, years earlier, when the family had hosted the high school football team for an end-of-season party. It still looked much the same. A white adobe wall surrounded a large plot of level ground at the base of Red Mountain. The wall was low, less than four feet, except at that point where it arched up over the entrance drive. A steel gate blocked the road, and there was a guardhouse with somebody in it. The large mesquite trees inside the wall had been trimmed of their low-hanging branches, and the grasses were unusually lush even for the monsoon season. He could see multiple structures beyond the gate. Each was painted white and had a red tile roof.

He pulled up to the guardhouse and identified himself by name but not by profession, and asked if he could speak to Mrs. Trujillo. He drove an unmarked car, and he was not in uniform. A bouquet of red roses lay on the front seat, along with a small cake that his wife had baked the night before. They were conspicuously displayed. He hoped it worked.

The guard stayed on the telephone for about a minute, and then turned his attention back to the Sheriff. "Mrs. Trujillo would like to know the purpose of your visit."

"I am here to express my condolences for the loss of her husband. I am a family friend." Not exactly true, but close if you went back far enough.

The guard went back on the phone. Another five minutes passed. Was it enough time for somebody in the house to have made a call across the border?

Finally, the guard gave Luis a nod and raised the gate. "Mrs. Trujillo will see you." He pointed toward a one-story hacienda style home built in a U-shape around a large central courtyard. Other buildings in the compound included a barn, a multi-car garage, and two smaller homes that the Sheriff guessed might be for servants or overnight visitors. He pulled up in front of the main house, got out of his car, and followed the gravel path up to a massive oak gate built into the wall that framed the fourth side of courtyard. A heavy iron hoop was attached by a hinge to the middle of the gate. He swung it against a striking plate three times, and a young woman came. She said nothing, but indicated by a gesture that he was to follow her inside.

The matriarch of the Trujillo family was seated alone at a white table beside a marble fountain in the middle of the courtyard. The spreading branches of an enormous mesquite provided ample shade. Camarilla Trujillo rose as Luis approached. She was in her mid-seventies, dressed entirely in black. She wore no jewelry except a simple wedding band, but she was carefully made-up and her silver hair was immaculately groomed.

"Señor Mendoza? To what do I owe the pleasure of your visit?"

"I am here to personally express my condolences for your recent loss, Señora Trujillo." Luis handed her the dozen red roses he was carrying. "And my wife Serena asks me to express hers as well. She prepared this small cake, which she hopes that you will enjoy."

"Thank you. It has been very difficult. Herman and I were married for 55 years. Still, he had been ill for so long and he suffered so much, it is some consolation to know that he now is at peace. And your family? I trust they are well?"

"They are."

Camarilla Trujillo pointed to a chair and was about to invite Luis to be seated when another woman emerged from somewhere inside the house. She made a striking figure, dressed in a white nun's habit. A nurse perhaps?

"Ah Lucinda my dear, do come and join us. This is Luis Mendoza. You may remember him from high school. He played football with your brother. Now he is the Sheriff of our county."

Camarilla turned to Luis and continued with the introduction.

"You may remember my daughter Lucinda? Today she is Sister Magdalena, who lives at the Santa Rita Abbey. They have granted her a three-month leave since her father passed. It is wonderful to have her with us, even for just a short while."

"Sister," he said, nodding to the woman, "it has been many years."

The woman nodded back and smiled briefly, but she did not speak. He wondered if her order was one that observed a vow of silence. He would have to ask Serena, who had been to Mass at the Santa Rita Abbey on several occasions.

Camarilla Trujillo gestured toward the table. "Please, let us sit down. And tell me, Señor Mendoza, do you often see my son Pedro? I know you once were close, at least back in high school. But I am thinking perhaps that is no longer the case, now that you and he have such, well, *different* lives."

Was there a twinkle in her eye? Was he being teased? Luis could not be sure. But he recognized an opportunity when it was handed to him.

"In fact I saw Pedro just last week, at his restaurant."

"Really? I hope you had a meal. I understand the food is excellent, though I have not been there in many years."

"Yes, Pedro and I ate together, and you are right about the food. But I also was there on business. I know this is an awkward time for you, Señora, and the last thing I wish to do is bring back unpleasant memories, but it is necessary for me to discuss this particular business with you as well."

Both women eyed him warily. "And what business might that be?" asked Camarilla Trujillo.

"It involves your late son, Paco."

A long and stony silence followed. He waited what he judged to be an appropriate amount of time, and then proceeded with the real purpose of his visit.

"About two weeks ago one of my deputies discovered the body of a man named Jeremiah McLeod, Jr., up near Elgin. He disappeared over 20 years ago. The evidence shows he was murdered. We are trying to trace his movements and activities around the time of his death."

"And what could this possibly have to do with me or my family?" asked Camarilla Trujillo. Sister Magdalena remained silent, but she bore a new expression that Luis could not interpret.

"Once again, forgive me Señora, but we know that Jeremiah McLeod – you may have known him as Scooter – was involved with your son prior to both of their deaths. I am trying to determine if there was any connection. I was wondering ..."

Camarilla Trujillo cut him short. "Sir, I welcomed you to my home out of respect for your family, and in return you have chosen to insult me. Do you take me for a fool? You are no longer welcome here. Please leave."

The woman rose stiffly, turned her back to the sheriff, and began to walk away. Her daughter followed in silence.

Luis Mendoza had been on a fishing expedition. He was not in the least surprised at the reaction he had gotten from the mother of Paco Trujillo. In fact, he had been counting on it. The whole plan was to get a rise out of Pedro. His mother would no doubt tell him that the Sheriff had visited and what he had said. Then, just maybe, Pedro would make a mistake. It was a long shot, he knew, but sometimes you got lucky.

He didn't realize just how lucky until he was leaving the Trujillo compound. He was about to get in his car and drive away when Lucinda Trujillo came out a side door to the house and quickly approached. Her white habit flowed behind her, and she glanced back over her shoulder as she walked. She silently handed him a note, and quickly retreated back inside. Luis recognized the same peculiar look on her face as before. Whatever it was, it didn't belong on a nun.

He opened the note and read two short lines: "Talk to a man named Hector Morales. He lives in Nogales, on the Mexico side."

It came to the Sheriff on his drive back to headquarters. The look on Sister Magdalena's face had been one of pure hatred.

# Chapter 35

I was on the phone with somebody from the New Haven *Register*, trying to get information about an Earth Day sit-in on the Yale campus in 1994, when a call came in on the radio.

"Sonoita headquarters, this is Patrol One. I've got an emergency situation out here. Come in, please. Over."

It was Larry, using the identifiers that we had agreed upon for our radio communications. From the tone of his voice, it sounded like trouble. I quickly extracted a promise from the woman at the *Register* to dig into their archives. Then I hung up and walked over to the radio.

"This is Sonoita headquarters. What's the situation? Over."

"There's a vehicle run off the road. It's clear down at the bottom of the canyon, all smashed up but on its wheels. It must have rolled a bunch of times. From the debris scattered around I'm guessing we've got an illegal transport situation on our hands. You'd better get the Border Patrol and emergency services out here."

"Where are you?"

"On 83, about five miles south of the Canelo Ranger Station."

"I'm on my way."

"I'm going down there to take a look."

"Shouldn't you wait for some backup?"

"Don't think so. There might be survivors. I think maybe I can see somebody moving around next to the vehicle."

"So when do you think this happened?"

"No way to tell until I get down there and check the

condition of the passengers."

"Okay, but take your phone and radio with you, and keep in touch."

Then I had a hunch. "What can you tell me about that pickup?"

He must have already disconnected, because there was no reply. I tried three more times on my drive out to Lyle Canyon, on both the phone and radio, but he still didn't answer.

~ ~ ~

Everybody arrived about the same time at the place where Larry had parked his Jeep. I got out and peered over the side. Three bodies were scattered on the slope leading down to where the remains of an all-too-familiar green and white Chevy pickup had come to rest in the Lyle Canyon creek bed.

There was no sign of Larry, and nobody answered when I called out. I tried his radio one more time, but got only silence in return. The cell signal was weak, but I dialed anyway. To my surprise the call went out, but nobody picked up. I was about to start climbing down to the wreck, when one of the Border Patrol agents tapped me on the shoulder.

"Did you just try to call your partner?"

"Yeah, why?"

"Because I heard a phone ringing somewhere down the there."

Jesus.

The five of us – two each from Border Patrol and the ambulance crew, plus me - scrambled down the steep bank. It was obvious to everyone what had happened, because we had seen it before. In recent years the bloodiest accidents in Santa Cruz County all had involved carloads of border crossers. If this incident had followed the usual pattern, the driver of the Chevy pickup had spotted a Border Patrol vehicle somewhere, and was speeding to avoid capture. He'd missed a curve and run off the road.

We all got busy. The Border Patrol agents searched the area for signs of other passengers, while the techs from the ambulance went to work on the one known survivor, a young woman lying about fifteen feet up the canyon from the pickup. She looked in bad shape, with one side of her skull obviously crushed in. But that was the least of my worries. Where the hell was Larry?

I walked over and looked in the driver's side window of the pickup, half expecting to see Oscar Corona, either dead or alive. There was somebody inside all right, but it wasn't Oscar. It was Muffy Davenport, and she was on the passenger side, crushed between the seatback and the dashboard. I walked around to the other side for a closer look at what was left of her face. The door wouldn't open, but there was no emergency. I could see that she was stone cold dead.

About then a young Border Patrol agent named Fuentes called out to me from 50 yards down the canyon. "Deputy Creede, there's something over here I think you should see."

I walked down to where he was standing and followed his eyes to a patch of relatively open sand in the creek bed. In the center of the clearing lay a standard issue Sheriff's Department radio, along with a cell phone. Leading downstream was a trail of blood. My gut seized up. One more time I yelled for Larry, but still got no response.

~ ~ ~

Agent Fuentes and I started walking down Lyle Canyon, and I kept calling Larry's name. At least one person was losing a lot of blood. It made the trail easy to follow, but it certainly did nothing positive for my spirits. We probably walked for about thirty minutes, but it sure

*215*

seemed longer. Then, just when I was about to go into full panic mode, somebody came out from behind a big sycamore trunk. It was Larry, making his way slowly and unsteadily upstream. He was holding his head, and apparently didn't see us at first. I felt relieved and anxious at the same time, as I ran down and looked into his eyes.

"You okay? What the hell happened?"

He blinked a couple of times, then shook his head as if to clear some fog. I couldn't see any blood. "Yeah, I think so."

I pointed to a sofa-sized boulder next to the creek, and suggested we sit down. He readily complied. "So again, just what happened here? How did you lose your radio?"

"It was the guy driving the truck, I think."

"You mean Oscar Corona?"

"I suppose so. Anyway, I found him lying beside the driver's side door. The front of his shirt was all bloody. I thought at first he was dead, but he must have been playing possum. When I bent over to check, he reached up and grabbed my gun. Then he made me walk down the canyon."

"You had your gun out? Why? Did he try to shoot you?"

"No, he ... hell, Cal, I don't know what he had in mind. Maybe he thought he could use me as a hostage. All I know is I screwed up big time."

I almost said something like 'no kidding,' then thought better of it. It looked like Larry had messed up for sure, but I wasn't about to make an issue out of it under the circumstances. "So where is he?"

"He's downstream, where I left him."

"How do you know he's still there?"

"Because he's dead."

"Dead?"

"Yeah, I think he'd been hurt bad in the wreck. There

was all that blood down the front of his shirt. The farther we walked the worse it got. I think he finally just bled out. I'm surprised he survived as long as he did."

"You feel up to walking back down there?"

"Sure, but I guarantee the guy's a goner."

So we did, and he was.

Larry and I left Agent Fuentes with the corpse of Oscar Corona, and walked back upstream to the scene of the accident. The EMTs checked him out, and he actually seemed to be okay. No doubt his ego had suffered a big bruise, but apparently that was about it.

Border Patrol was busy collecting the bodies. Larry looked puzzled about something. "How did he expect to smuggle all those people in an open pickup without getting caught, especially in the daytime?"

I was pretty sure I knew the answer. "You remember that load of mesquite I was telling you about? Well, it was a fake, all hollowed out underneath and shaped to fit in the bed of his truck."

"You mean that's where he stashed his passengers?"

"Yep, in the bed under that false load of wood. Look up the slope, about half way. It's there, upside down."

Larry glanced up the hill. "I'll be damned. So those poor souls inside didn't have a chance when Oscar went over the edge. And how many were there, maybe four or five of them crammed in that little space?"

One thing still puzzled me. "What I don't understand is why in hell you had your gun out."

"I thought there might be somebody still alive down here, like for instance the smuggler. Some of them can be really bad dudes."

That sounded reasonable, so I let it go.

One of the EMTs approached and said they were going to evacuate the injured woman. There was no good place for a helicopter to land at the site, so they would transport her in the ambulance back to Sonoita and wait for a flight from there.

I walked over to the closest of three Border Patrol Agents at the scene. "Any other survivors?"

"Not that we can find. But there are two more bodies out there in the brush, besides the three on the slope and the guy down the canyon. It must have been awful. I wonder how long they were down there, and why nobody spotted them sooner."

Larry joined us, and offered his opinion. "It's pretty much out of sight from up on the road. The only thing gave it away were two skid marks in the gravel, and they weren't very obvious. I almost didn't stop."

The Border Patrol would take responsibility for removing the bodies of the crossers from the site. They also would attempt to identify the victims and notify their families, including that of the woman who had survived. But they would leave Oscar and Muffy for the Sheriff's Department.

I climbed up the slope and got on the radio to Nogales. The desk sergeant said they'd heard the communications, and everybody was wondering when I was going to check in. I asked to be patched through to the sheriff rather than talking to anybody else, following our standard protocol.

"Luis, it's Cal. We've got a situation out here in Lyle Canyon you should know about. There's been an accident involving a pickup full of border crossers. The driver was Oscar Corona, and Muffy Davenport was with him. They're both dead." Then I filled him in on what had happened to Larry.

"I'll be damned. Is Larry okay? Has Border Patrol been there? How many passengers were there, besides Muffy?"

"Yeah, the patrol's here. Looks like there were at least five passengers. Only one person survived the crash, and her maybe not for long. She's on her way to Tucson, probably by helicopter. Patrol's got the dead ones and their belongings. Oscar and Muffy are still here. You probably should send somebody with the equipment to extract Muffy's body from the wreck and then haul both of them off to the morgue. I'm on the Lyle Canyon road, south of the Canelo Ranger Station."

"I'll take care of it. Any idea how the wreck happened?"

"The usual way, I expect. Something scared Oscar and he was driving too fast, missed a curve."

"Was the Border Patrol in pursuit?"

"Apparently not, but Corona must have spotted something."

"Helluva' deal. What about next of kin?"

"Oscar Corona is Angel's grandson. He's the foreman at the Rocking M. But it might be better to start with his parents. I don't know them or where they live, so maybe you could get somebody to check into that. As for Muffy, didn't you tell me her father was head of Davenport Petroleum out in California?"

"Yep. Let me handle the notifications, Cal. You've got enough on your plate. And I'd better let the D.A. know that the Davenport case is now closed. If I can't find Oscar's parents, I'll get in touch with Angel. He and I go way back. *Madre de Dios*, this is going to break his heart. Oh, and you'd better have Larry write up a full report. Sounds like he didn't' handle the situation all that well. About the worst thing that can happen is for an officer to lose his gun to a suspect."

The sheriff was right, of course, but mostly I just felt relief that Larry was in a position to make his report at all.

# Chapter 36

**M**aria had finished milking the goats, and we were having a beer before dinner on her little patio. The limestone cliffs of the Mustang Mountains glowed pale pink, lit by the last rays of the evening sun. There was no breeze. The tranquility of the scene belied the tragic events of the day just ended.

I described what had happened over in Lyle Canyon.

Maria was distraught. "That's awful. Those poor people. All they were trying to do was find a better life for themselves. Were they Mexicans?"

"I don't know who they were, but I'm sure they knew the risks."

"Which tells you a lot about how bad things must be down wherever they came from. I feel sorry for them. Oscar Corona and Muffy Davenport, well, that's another matter. But still, I don't think they deserved to die. Why do you think she was riding with him?"

I sipped my *Bohemia*. "Good question. And by the way, this probably is the end of any chance you'll get reimbursed for the damage she did to your dairy."

"That all seems kind of trivial now, don't you think? Let's change the subject. What's new on the McLeod case?"

"Seems like there's another Tucson to Green Valley run in my future, as soon as I can set up meetings with Barton Hampstead and the Salernos. Want to go along?"

"Not for the next couple of days. I'm behind on some things I need to do with the goats. And – did I tell you? – I had a call from Dr. Rincon at the State Museum. Anyway, he showed that little bell I found to some colleagues, and they want to come down with a metal detector to look for anything else that might be in the area. They're coming Sunday, so I can go out with them. I've cleared it with Janet McLeod."

"Sounds interesting. I'd like to come along, unless that's the day I'm up in town."

"I understand why you want to talk to the Salernos, given what you learned from their daughter up in Colorado. But why do you want to see that Hampstead guy again?"

"I found out something interesting today about Scooter's time at Yale. Turns out he was doing a minor in environmental conservation, and apparently he was active in Earth Day events, including a sit-in. I want to get Hampstead's take on all of that."

"How could that be related to your case?"

"It probably isn't. I'm just trying to put all the pieces together."

"No you aren't, Mr. Deputy. You've got some sort of a theory working around in your head. I know you too well."

"All right, then suppose you tell me. What might that theory be?"

I did not pose the question just to make chitchat. Maria had become an excellent sounding board, and I never had doubted that she would keep things to herself.

She took a sip of her *Pacifico*. "Let's try this. Scooter McLeod comes home from Yale that summer all stirred up about saving the earth and he starts in on his dad and brother about what to do with the Rocking M. He's heard all about the evils of grazing and development, especially development, and he tries to get his family to put the ranch into some sort of a conservation trust. How am I doing so far?"

"Pretty good, but go on with your theory."

"Okay. So Sandy in particular goes ballistic. He's up at

the U of A in Tucson majoring in business, and he's got these enormous dollar signs in his eyes. And suddenly one of the two people due to inherit the ranch has turned into a mushy-headed tree-hugger. Or is there such a thing as a grass-hugger? Anyhow, one thing leads to another, and ..."

Maria stopped talking and shrugged.

"Lady, you're about half smart. You know that?"

Just then the evening calm was broken by a noisy commotion coming from the direction of the goat barn. Maria jumped up. "Here we go again. I'll be right back. That new buck I bought last week is having trouble settling in. I think the other billy boy is jealous."

She was gone for about five minutes. Things were quiet when she came back, but she was rubbing her backside. "This is going to take a while. I had to put him in a stall farther down the line, away from everybody else. He decided to butt me during the move."

Maria had given me an opening and I decided to take it. "Those goats of yours, you really like them, don't you? And while we're on the subject, why don't they have ears like ordinary goats?"

"They *do* have ears, stupid. They're just small. It's a characteristic of the LaMancha breed. And yes, I like them a lot. They're smart and tough, they can take the climate here, and they produce good, rich milk. Which reminds me. If you go up to Green Valley, I promised your mother some cheese. Don't let me forget to give it to you."

"The reason I asked about the goats is that you've said more than once you might quit the mail job someday and just do the dairy full time. Does it make a profit?"

"Not yet. But I had some good news the other day."

"What was that?"

"A woman called who runs a big health food store up in Tucson. She'd heard about my goats, and she wants to sell my products."

"That's great!"

"So I may have to increase the size of my herd. Either that or stop selling stuff weekends at the farmer's market in Patagonia."

Then she seemed to have a change of heart. "Oh I don't know, maybe it never will make any money. I like the people at the post office just fine, and the benefits are really good."

Our conversation had arrived at the point where I hoped it would go. "You know I have good benefits with the County."

I waited for a reaction, but none came. "And they extend to spouses. So if we got married you could give up the post office and concentrate on the dairy pretty easily."

There was a long pause. Maria's face was soft in the evening light. She looked more beautiful than I could remember. But something was wrong.

"Sure, we could do that. But I don't know if I'm ready."

"You keep saying that. But ready for what? We're already living like we're married. Why not make if official? I know our parents would be pleased."

Maria laughed.

What was so funny?

She must have seen the look on my face. "I'm sorry." Another giggle. "It's just that you're talking like a hopeful bride. It's the would-be groom who's supposed to put on the big stall when it comes to marriage."

I laughed too, but it was just to go along. "Just think about it, okay?"

"Let's eat. I'm starved. But I *have* been thinking about it. And I'll think more, I promise."

# Chapter 37

**B**arton Hampstead opened the door and stood back. He was dripping wet and wearing nothing except a pink thong bikini. "Oh, it's you again. Come inside while I go put something on. Make yourself comfortable."

His absence gave me the opportunity to have a second look at the man's collection of artifacts, but I didn't see anything new. Barton came back in about three minutes, dressed in one of those flowing robes he seemed to favor. The time before it had been solid green. Today's selection was a garish patchwork of red, yellow, and brown, with a big green parrot embroidered on the back.

We sat again in two of his huge leather armchairs.

"What can I do for you, Mr. Creede? Have you figured out yet who killed Scooter?"

"We're still in the early stages of our investigation. I'm hoping you can fill me in on some of the details about Scooter's activities at Yale, and how they might have affected relationships with his family."

"Activities?"

"I believe he may have become involved with environmental groups. What can you tell me about that?"

"Oh, I see what you're getting at. Sure. He majored in anthropology like me, but he was doing a minor in nature conservation or some such. And there was a student club he belonged to. They were pretty active on campus, had some demonstrations, that sort of thing."

"What were the demonstrations about?"

"I really don't remember the details. It was a long time ago. But I think they were trying to get Yale to divest itself of stock they owned in companies that the students thought were damaging the environment."

"What sort of companies?"

"I don't think I ever knew that. It wasn't an issue I cared very much about. I know it's not the politically correct thing to say, but I still don't get much involved in environmental issues."

"Did you and Scooter ever argue about it?"

"About the environment? No, not really. But he sure got into it with his father and Sandy, I remember that."

"What did they talk about?"

"I think I told you that Scooter and I lived in an old place over in Lyle Canyon when we were exploring together those summers on the Rocking M. But we got invited over to the big house for dinner sometimes."

"I recall your saying that, yes. Is that when these arguments happened?"

"At least some of them. But I got the feeling Scooter had been round and round with the family before then."

"What was it all about?"

"Scooter wanted to have the ranch placed in some sort of a trust, so it couldn't ever be sold or split up or turned into housing developments. I think he called it a conservation trust. There wasn't much of that sort of thing going on back then. I think it's pretty common today."

"And the rest of the family didn't like this?"

Hampstead nodded. "Especially Sandy. He was furious. He said he was going to the business school up in Tucson just to learn about development. He said they could all get rich. Then Scooter would say something about protecting the land being more important, and that they already had plenty of money. They'd end up yelling at each other over the dinner table. It was very ugly and it made me uncomfortable."

"How did the parents react?"

"Their mother looked sad and embarrassed. Mr.

McLeod, the father, he tried to get Sandy and Scooter to compromise. He suggested maybe they could develop some of the land and keep the rest as a cattle ranch."

"And how did that go?"

"As I recall it pretty much didn't go anywhere. For one thing, Scooter was almost as negative about ranching as he was about development. He would go on about the evils of grazing. I think if he'd had his way he would have turned all of the Rocking M into a big nature reserve."

But he never got the chance, I thought to myself.

~ ~ ~

I had a good lunch with my parents in Green Valley, and gave my mother the goat cheese from Maria. She seemed genuinely pleased. Then I excused myself and drove over to the home of Ray and Vicki Salerno.

It had taken some heavy lobbying, and the better part of a day, to get them to agree to see me again. They wondered why we couldn't just talk on the phone. But I had some new questions to ask, and I was anxious to see as well as hear their reaction when they found out what I had learned from their daughter.

It was a hot day in the Green Valley desert, but things were decidedly chilly in the Salerno home. I had the feeling I'd interrupted something unpleasant, the way the couple were avoiding eye contact with one another. Unlike my previous visit, this time there were no offers of refreshments, there was no small talk, and we stayed in the living room. Ray and Vicki sat at opposite ends of a large white leather couch, while I was shown to a rather uncomfortable hard-backed chair made out of a dark wood. A glass-topped coffee table separated us. It was cluttered with figurines of dogs and horses.

"Thanks for seeing me again."

Ray spoke first. "That's all right. But really, I thought we'd pretty much covered everything the last time."

"Not quite. In 1995 you were interviewed by a man named Barney Stroud. He was the deputy sheriff in Sonoita who investigated the disappearance of Scooter McLeod. Do you remember that?"

Again, Ray spoke up, while Vicki sat in silence. "Maybe. Why?"

"He claims you told him that your daughter was traveling in Europe that summer. Does that sound familiar?"

"I may have mentioned that. I can't really remember. Why is that important?"

"Because I have spoken with your daughter, and she tells a different story."

Vicki Salerno immediately interrupted. "You talked to Angela? Where? How? Is she all right? How did you find her?"

"She's fine. In fact, I've been to see her."

"Where is she? It was that postcard, wasn't it? You found her in Colorado, didn't you?" Before I had a chance to respond, she turned to her husband and blurted out: "I *told* you we could find her, Ray. Why wouldn't you let me try?"

I needed to regain control of the conversation. "I can't tell you where she is. She made me promise."

"But she's my *daughter*! I have a right to know!"

"I understand your feelings, ma'am. But she's also an adult with her own rights to privacy. On a personal note, I did tell her that I thought you were anxious to see or at least talk to her. But of course I couldn't make her do that. And now – I know this is difficult Mrs. Salerno – but I really do need to get back to my earlier question. Was Angela in Europe in 1995, or is there something else you'd like to tell me about that?"

Ray answered my question with one of his own. "What did she tell you?"

I repeated the story Angela had told me, about the affair with Scooter McLeod, about her botched abortion, and about her time in Chicago. I didn't leave out any details – not because I enjoyed torturing Vicki Salerno, but because I really wanted to get a reaction from her husband.

Mr. Salerno was a cool customer. While Vicki sat there in ashen silence, Ray looked me straight in the eye and spoke simply and directly.

"All right. I made up the story about Europe. Surely you can understand why. But one thing I told that other officer was the truth. Angela was gone from the valley the summer that Scooter disappeared. So you can see that she couldn't have had anything to do with it. With his death, that is. And surely you also can see how hard this is for my wife. So please, sir, just leave us alone now. My daughter is innocent."

It wasn't Angela's innocence that I was wondering about. I was reminded again about how hard it was to solve a cold case. If anybody had actually witnessed the murder of Scooter McLeod, they certainly weren't talking. Unless somebody confessed, I wasn't at all sure there would be a resolution. But there was nothing to do except keep digging and pushing people. Maybe somebody would crack.

# Chapter 38

### Sheriff Luis Mendoza

The San Raphael Valley was the Sheriff's favorite part of Santa Cruz County. Nearly everybody in the department thought of him as an urban man, wise to the ways of the city. They admired his insights into how things worked in a crowded border area with its particular law enforcement subtleties and complications. All of that was true. But what most people did not know was that he had been born and raised on a ranch in the San Raphael. His father had been a cowboy, and as a teenager Luis had learned to ride and then to love the rolling grasslands and oak savannahs of the broad valley floor.

There were good reasons why the San Raphael Valley had so far escaped the attention of those who would gladly and greedily turn it into the next Sun City. In the first place, it was too far from everything. There were no paved roads, no towns, no stores, and no hospitals, just a handful of big, mostly old, ranches. Of course someone or some entity could overcome these obstacles if their pockets were deep enough to build all the amenities up front.

The other problem was more difficult. In fact, it was nearly intractable under present circumstances. The San Raphael Valley sat right on the border.

Luis Mendoza knew firsthand that bad things were happening along the line separating Arizona from Mexico. But the press exaggerated these things in their thirst for something to talk and write about, as did shameless politicians and others who wanted to play the fear card to their advantage. The irony hadn't escaped him. His favorite place survived unspoiled partly because people were afraid to live there. He had read once that some of the best natural areas remaining on earth were places where people could not or would not live, like the demilitarized zone between North and South Korea, and retired nuclear facilities whose natural landscapes lay on top of soil and ground water polluted beyond redemption. The San Raphael Valley was not that bad, of course. Maybe someday it would all change, when things got better and border hysteria calmed to the point of reason. The Sheriff had mixed feelings about that.

~ ~ ~

A call came in to Nogales headquarters from a deputy on patrol down in the San Raphael. There was a body in a ditch beside one of the roads crossing the valley. Border Patrol had responded, but they were pretty sure it wasn't a normal crosser. The body had no identification, but the clothes and the man's physical appearance weren't right. Luis Mendoza decided to check it out personally, mainly because he liked any excuse to drive back home.

The Sheriff and Detective Julie Benevides from the Criminal Investigation Division loaded up his SUV with the things they would need at a crime scene. They drove north on route 82 as far as Patagonia, then turned east on a road that eventually climbed up over Red Mountain Pass and down into the San Raphael Valley.

Luis admired the view as they drove out onto the open savanna. It felt like home. The grasses were tall and green, set in motion by periodic gusts of an otherwise gentle south wind. A few cattle, mostly Herefords, grazed in the scattered shade of widely spaced Emory oaks. There were no clouds. The Huachuca Mountains framed the eastern horizon, clear and crisp.

They found Deputy Alice McKnight and two Border Patrol agents standing together beside a gravel road just north of the relictual border town of Lochiel. The Sheriff pulled to a stop and got out of the Explorer. Detective Benevides joined him, carrying a large backpack loaded with their gear. She was of medium height, with a narrow face made more so by the fact that her red hair was pulled back into a tight ponytail.

They exchanged perfunctory greetings with the other officers, then turned their attention to the matter at hand. The body was face down, clad in the remains of what looked like a flowered Hawaiian shirt. There was a large open wound on the back of the head, just below the hairline. It gaped raw and purple, and there were maggots crawling in and out. Julie Benevides walked over to where the body lay, and bent over for a closer look. She pointed to the corpse and asked the first question. "Have you moved it?"

Deputy McKnight looked worried, and Luis remembered she was a rookie. This might be her first corpse.

"No ma'am."

Benevides took a camera out of her pack. "That's good. I'll get some photos, and then let's roll him over. Anything in the area?"

One of the Border Patrol agents spoke up. "Nothing so far. Looks like a gunshot wound to me, but we haven't found any shell casings. The tire tracks here are pretty fresh, and there are a couple of footprints, but they aren't very clear. I don't think they're gonna be much help."

"Any guess as to how long he's been here?" The Sheriff had some ideas of his own.

Deputy McKnight pointed to the man's legs and shoes. "Probably not more than a couple of days. I lifted one leg, and there's mud underneath. So I think he had to have fallen here since the last rain. And the decomposition's not very far along. But that's not the most interesting thing.

Take a look around the head."

The Sheriff asked what he was supposed to be looking for.

"There's no sign of blood. A wound like that, you'd expect a lot of blood."

"Meaning you think he was killed someplace else and then dumped here?"

"That would be my guess."

Detective Benevides nodded her agreement. "But we need to scour this whole area anyway, before we leave, and collect anything that looks like evidence. Now let's check his face."

The deputy and one of the Border Patrol agents rolled the body. Luis bent down for close. "My god, I think that's Barney Stroud."

"Who's Barney Stroud?" asked McKnight.

"He used to work for the department. He lives in a retirement place over in Sierra Vista. Make that used to live, I guess."

"How in the hell did he get here?" asked one of the agents.

The Sheriff did not respond.

Julie Benevides took more photographs while the rest of the party searched the area for any other clues. Nothing turned up.

An hour later Luis Mendoza instructed that the remains of Barney Stroud, retired deputy for the Santa Cruz County Sheriff's Department, be placed in a body bag for the drive back to Nogales, and then up to Tucson. He'd seen all he needed. The medical examiner could do her work in the morgue.

~ ~ ~

As soon as Luis got back to headquarters he put in a call up to Sonoita. He needed to talk with Cal Creede. Nobody answered in the office, but he got a response on the radio.

"Ten-four. I'm on my way back from Green Valley. What's up?"

The Sheriff told him about finding Barney Stroud's body.

"Jesus! And he's been shot? I wonder how he got way down there. I don't think he drives any more."

"So somebody must have taken him from Sierra Vista, which is why I'm calling. Do you remember the name of the place where he lived?"

"It was something about Coronado, I think. I can check it when I get back to the office if you want."

"No, that'll probably be enough."

Mendoza fired up his computer, Googled 'retirement' and 'Sierra Vista,' and easily found a web site and telephone number for the Coronado Vista Manor. He made the call, and quickly got through to the manager.

Barney Stroud had gone missing three days earlier. The manager had contacted Sierra Vista Police and the Cochise County Sheriff's Department, but he hadn't thought to call anybody in Sonoita or Nogales. Why would he?

The Sheriff wanted more details. "What happened? Did anybody see anything?"

"Not a thing. He didn't show up for dinner one night, but that isn't unusual since residents have small kitchens in their apartments where they can warm a bowl of soup or make a sandwich. And lots of these old folks only eat one or two meals a day. It wasn't until after breakfast the next morning, when we still hadn't seen him, that I checked in his room."

"Is that protocol?"

"What do you mean?"

"I mean, wouldn't you normally check on somebody his age every day?"

"Normally we would, but how well did you know Mr. Stroud?"

"I used to know him back when he worked for the department, but I haven't talked to him in years. Why?"

"Because he was a pretty strange guy, Sheriff."

"Strange how?"

"He liked to be left alone. He rarely socialized with any of our other residents, and he liked to go for walks by himself. A couple of times in the past year, when we hadn't seen him for a while, we checked on his room. Once when he didn't answer I used my master key and went in. He was just sitting in there, staring out the window. And he became very angry. He told me to get the hell out. So yes, I suppose I should have checked his room earlier this time. But then it wouldn't have made any difference, would it?"

"Any sign of disturbance in his apartment? Was anything missing?"

"Nothing seemed out of place. Of course I wasn't sure what to look for. It's not like we keep an inventory of everybody's possessions here. We work hard to provide a safe and pleasant place for our residents to live, but we like for them to have as much personal freedom as possible. I'm sure you understand."

"Did he have any relatives?"

"No, there was nobody, or at least nobody he told us about."

"Okay. I guess we'll handle his funeral arrangements over here. Since he used to be with the department, he's entitled. Before I let you go, is there anything else you can tell me about Mr. Stroud that might help us figure out what went on here, and why? Did anybody see anything, or report anything unusual around the time of his disappearance?"

"We asked around of course, but nobody saw anything. Like I said, Barney was pretty much a loner."

There was a pause, as if the manager of the Coronado Vista Manor was making up his mind about something. "You say Barney had been a deputy sheriff in your department?"

"Yes, that's right. I believe he retired some time in the mid 1990s."

"Had he done something else earlier in his life? Was he in some sort of business?"

"Not that I know of. Why?"

"No reason, I suppose. It's just that, well, of all the retirement places in Sierra Vista, ours is by far the most accommodating. And the most expensive. Plus Barney always seemed to have lots of cash around. You know, to buy extra things. Somebody brought him one of those really big TVs a couple of years ago. It must have cost thousands. The thing barely fit in his room. So, I was just wondering how he could be so well fixed if all he had was the pension your department provides to its former employees. Not that you aren't generous, I'm sure, but still ..."

# Chapter 39

It was a fine Sunday morning in the Sonoita Valley, and I was indulging in some time off. Well, more or less. Larry Hernandez seemed to have pulled himself back together following the unfortunate incident of in Lyle Canyon, and he was somewhere out on patrol. He'd gotten a lecture from the sheriff, but no official reprimand.

The monsoon had retreated back down into Mexico, but the rains already had worked their magic and the grasses were emerald green against a cloudless blue sky. Maria and I, along with Dr. Julio Rincon and two young assistants from the State Museum, were in the San Carlos Wash, walking upstream. The museum director had introduced his team as summer interns - students at the university named Gabrielle Remy and Charles Atwood.

Boomer was in the lead because that's what Labradors did. Maria came next, because she knew our destination – the place where she had found the little bell. Each of the anthropologists carried a metal detector.

I noticed at least two sets of tire tracks in the wash. They were deep but not fresh. I remembered that Angel Corona had driven up this way to check on a fence the day we had first visited the final resting place of the old pickup that had once belonged to Scooter McLeod. But he had been driving an ATV, and these tracks were too wide. Presently we came to a fence crossing the wash, and the tire tracks stopped. We all ducked underneath the loose barbed wire, and Rincon consulted a map.

"This is interesting. If I'm reading things right, we just crossed onto a state lease. We're now on a section of the Rocking M ranch that is public land."

Maria immediately got the point. "So that little bell I picked up was ... oh shit." Then she blushed.

Dr. Rincon quickly came to the rescue, and my opinion of him rose. "I'm sure you didn't know. And besides, you recorded the location and gave us the bell. We won't disturb anything today. But if we get hits, then we might ask permission from both the McLeods and the State to conduct a formal excavation."

We walked on in silence, listening for any sort of squawk from the metal detectors that Rincon and his assistants were sweeping back and forth across the sand.

Maria obviously was fascinated and had a question for the curator. "So what do you suppose might have happened along here?"

He replied cautiously. "Hard to say for sure. That Clarksdale Bell you found definitely suggests a Spanish presence in this area. It could have been a random loss, something that fell off a horse for example. But it also could indicate an old campsite. That's what I hope to determine today."

The group walked for another ten minutes without incident. Then Boomer, who had been circling ahead, suddenly froze in place and growled. He had spotted a very large diamondback rattlesnake warming itself on the sand in the middle of the wash. It was nearly four feet long. We all gave the animal a wide berth. All except Maria, that is. She walked right up and photographed the snake, which neither moved nor rattled once during the whole episode. It gave me the creeps, but apparently it was just another day in the field for her.

Maria continued upstream, and we all followed. Eventually she stopped at a bend in the creek bed next to a large overhanging mesquite, and consulted her GPS. "This is the place where I found the bell. Or at least it was right around here."

Rincon immediately took charge. "Gabrielle, you go downstream in the wash, no more than 300 meters or so, then move up onto that bench on the east side and work your way back to this point. Charlie, you go upstream and then come back down on the same side as Gabrielle. I'll cover the west side. Let's meet back here in about a half hour, unless you find something significant before then, in which case give a holler and we'll all converge on your spot."

I asked Rincon if there was anything Maria and I could do.

"No, just sit tight. These detectors are by far the most efficient way to search an area for anything metallic."

The team from the museum walked away in their respective directions, leaving Maria, Boomer, and me alone in the wash. Suddenly I heard a long drawn-out croak, and a jet black Chihuahuan Raven flew in from the south and circled repeatedly over our heads. I spotted its nest in a nearby mesquite. The bird clearly was agitated by our presence, so we all moved upstream a respectful 50 yards.

It was about twenty minutes later that we heard a woman's voice cry out. "Dr. Rincon! Dr. Rincon! There's something here you should look at!"

Gabrielle was up on the bench and about halfway back to the starting point. The group quickly converged on her position, and it was immediately apparent what she had found, even to my untrained eye. Someone or something had churned up the whole area, and at least some of the digging was fresh.

Rincon asked the Gabrielle if she had any hits on her detector.

"No sir, nothing. Just all this disturbance. How about you Charlie?"

The young man shook his head.

241

Rincon put down his backpack and extracted from it a large camera and a tablet of blank paper. "I'm going to take some photos and make sketches of this area. It appears like something major has happened here. And some of this digging is much older and more regular than the rest."

Maria was curious. "What do you mean?"

Rincon pointed to three rectangular areas in the grass where the ground was depressed, perhaps a foot lower than the surrounding landscape. "Those look like old archeological excavations – not just random digging but a systematic search." Then he turned to me. "I think we need to treat this as a looting site, and I could use your help."

"You mean it looks looted because of the more recent disturbance?"

"Exactly. And there are two people I think could have been responsible. One you know - Barton Hampstead. The other is a guy that may live around here somewhere. His name is Oliver Swade. Do you know him?"

"Sure do. And it's funny you mention it. I was in Ollie's house just a few days ago, and I noticed he had some artifacts. They didn't look like much, and he swore they all came from his property, but I wondered about it at the time. What is your connection with Ollie?"

"He has a history of coming around the museum trying to sell things. Apparently it started a long time ago, before I was on the staff. He's always given us the same story – that it all came off his property."

"Have you ever tried to explore his land?"

"We've asked for permission, but he always refuses. And we've asked him to please stop digging, wherever it is."

"You said you needed my help. What exactly can the Sheriff's Department do for you?"

"Well, first I have a small confession to make. I

suspected we might find something like this today, and I brought a piece of equipment along just in case. It's a motion detector that triggers a video camera."

"So you want to set it up and then have me check it?"

"It's more than that. It sends a signal, good for better than a mile, that you can receive on a remote monitor. I'd like to put the monitor in Ms. Obregon's house, and maybe you can catch this guy in real time. Assuming you're comfortable with this."

Maria readily agreed. "That won't be a problem. But we're both gone a lot. What happens if somebody comes here when we're not watching the monitor?"

"It records things. So we can get visual evidence even if we can't catch him - or I suppose her - in the act. Is it okay if I set this thing up?"

I nodded. "And I think you can regard that permission as officially coming from the Sheriff's Department and not just from me personally. But if I may ask, where did you get such a sophisticated piece of equipment?"

"From the Border Patrol. It's all back in my truck. Let's go get it and you can help."

And so it happened that Maria and I had something to watch in her living room besides each other, the dog, and an old television that only got two and a half channels because she refused to pay for a satellite dish.

# Chapter 40

**I** arrived at the office Monday morning to find Larry typing up a report.

"Glad you're here. A woman called to say that somebody or something was killing her chickens. Her Chihuahua had barked in the middle of the night. I guess when she went out in the morning to feed her flock, she found blood and feathers and a lot fewer chickens than she'd had the day before."

"Was it Gloria Murphy?"

Larry pushed the print button on his computer. "The very one. She wants somebody to come out. I take it this may not be the first time?"

I sighed. "More like the third. You want to handle it, or shall I?"

"Well, I'm supposed to go down to Nogales today for some sort of anti-terrorism training the feds are putting on. You want me to skip it?"

"No, you'd better go. I'll handle the chicken crisis."

Gloria Murphy was a newcomer to the area who was trying to sell eggs from organic free-range chickens to a local health food store. I suspected her problem was a tendency to let the chickens range way too freely after dark. There was a coop, but it had no fence around it, and so her animals were an open invitation to all the coyotes and owls in Santa Cruz County. When she called the time before I had suggested that she shut them in at night, and perhaps get a bigger dog. Apparently she had not taken my advice. Another city kid, I thought. Just like my ex-wife.

Gloria and her chickens lived on a forty-acre ranchette that was part of a small development northwest of Sonoita.

Animal damage complaints technically were the responsibility of the Game and Fish Department rather than the sheriff. But truth be told, I didn't mind the diversion from all the other current problems, and maybe a personal visit would get her attention. I closed up the office, climbed into the Blazer, and headed north out of town on Highway 83. I turned west on a gravel road and drove for about seven miles to Gloria Murphy's modest ranch-style house set among some Arizona white oaks in the foothills of the Santa Rita Range.

The young woman, her Chihuahua dog, and several of the chickens were waiting in the front yard as I pulled up. She was an attractive blue-eyed blond dressed in jeans, leather sandals, and a tank top. She came right over and introduced herself as I was climbing out of his truck.

"Thank you so much for coming. I'm so distressed about my chickens, you know. Before, you said I should keep them shut up at night, but then they wouldn't be free-ranging would they?"

"Well, ma'am, I don't know the rules about that. But they'd still be lots better off than those chickens that spend their whole lives in little cages on the big farms. And during the day they'd get to forage on their own. Wouldn't that satisfy the people who own the store?"

"I suppose so. I guess I could ask."

"I think that's a good idea. And if the predators still give you trouble, the game and fish people would give you permission to set traps for the coyotes and maybe the raccoons that likely are the critters going after your birds."

"Oh absolutely not. I just couldn't bear the thought of trapping anything."

I suggested again that she might want to get a bigger dog, and then I left. On the drive out I remembered spotting a bumper sticker on an old beater in Patagonia that could not possibly have been driven by Gloria

Murphy. It said "Eat Free-Range Roadkill."

~ ~ ~

The rest of the day would have been totally forgettable if it hadn't been for two phone calls that came into the office, one immediately after the other, just before five o'clock.

The first was from Barton Hampstead. "I got to thinking about my last summer on the Rocking M Ranch with Scooter, and I remembered something that might be important. So I thought I'd give you a call."

"I'm glad you did. What is it that you remembered?"

"There was this guy that kept pestering us, especially Scooter. He knew we were interested in archaeology, and he tried to sell us some things he had found."

I was struck by the odd coincidence in light of yesterday's discovery in the San Carlos Wash. Or was it a coincidence? "What sort of things?"

"Oh, various artifacts, mostly junk as I recall. We never bought any of it. But it made Scooter really mad, and that's why I thought it might be important to your investigation."

"Why did it make him mad?"

"Because he thought the man was looting, and maybe on the Rocking M, even though he claimed it all came from his own place."

"Do you remember the man's name?"

"No, I'm afraid not. I was pretty sure you'd want to know, and I've tried to remember, but I just can't. It was too long ago. All I can tell you is that he was somebody who lived in your area. He didn't seem like an educated man, just somebody hoping to make a buck. But the point is that Scooter threatened him – threatened to turn him in for looting. And so I thought maybe he was the one that – you know – might have killed Scooter."

"Thank you very much for this information. And if by

any chance you happen to remember the man's name, please call again."

"I'll do that."

I had scarcely hung up when the phone rang again. I picked up and identified myself.

"Hello Mr. Creede, this is Vicki Salerno."

This was interesting. "Yes ma'am?"

"I have a favor to ask. I ... know what you told us the other day when you were at our house. And a promise is a promise. But you have no idea how *desperate* I am to talk with my daughter. Isn't there any way that something could be arranged? If you could just give me her address, or a phone number, I promise I wouldn't tell her how I got it."

"I'm sorry, but I gave her my word. It's not that I'm unsympathetic to your situation, but please understand mine. I'm in the middle of a murder investigation here, and my goal is to catch the person responsible. That takes priority over all else, and your daughter's continued cooperation may be important."

"Cooperation? In what way could she help?" Vicky Salerno paused. "Oh my God, you think he did it, don't you?"

"Who?"

"My husband, of course. You think Ray killed Scooter. I can't *believe* this!"

"It's not a matter of what I think. It's a matter of what I can prove. Right now I have no reason to suspect your husband."

"But you think he had a motive, I can see that, because of ... what happened to Angela. But he couldn't have killed Scooter. It just isn't possible."

"Is there any light you can shed on that?"

"What do you mean?"

"Well, for instance, if you and your husband were

someplace other than southern Arizona in the summer of 1995, then that would rule him out. Rule out both of you, actually."

There was a silence. It continued long enough that I thought perhaps we had been disconnected.

"Mrs. Salerno?"

"Yes, I'm still here. Just thinking, that's all. And no, we were around that summer. Ray was still deeply involved in the Bobcat Creek Estates development. He was working with the builder, Jay Hancock, on final plans. I wish I could say otherwise, but I know you'd check and find out."

"And I appreciate your candor, Mrs. Salerno. I know this is difficult."

"Mr. Creede, I think you're a good man, and I know you're just doing your job. But you must believe me when I say that Ray could never do anything like take another person's life. He comes across as hard and gruff sometimes – I know that, and I apologize for his recent behavior towards you. But he's just doing that to hide his grief and worry over Angela. He's a good man. Please believe that."

I had an idea. "There may be a way that I can help you get in touch with Angela. Why don't you write her a letter and send it to me? Then I'll add a note explaining the circumstances and forward it on to her."

"Oh, that's a wonderful idea! I'll do it right away. And God bless you."

I decided I liked Vicki Salerno, and that I might have underestimated her. I hoped that no one in the family, including Angela, had anything to do with the murder of Scooter McLeod all those years ago. But my job was not to root for one suspect over another. My job was to find out who killed the man.

~ ~ ~

Our party returned this day from its expedition up the Babocomari River, and rejoined the main force still camped near its joining of the Nexpa. We were pleased to learn from Don Pedro Tovar that all was well in the camp, and that the horses were substantially replenished from eating the fine grass. Surely God in his wisdom will now permit us our return to New Spain without further distress. As to our trip up the Babocomari, once again we met with the sort of misfortune that seemingly has plagued our expedition from the start. We had ridden up the valley for two days, and our Indian guide was becoming increasingly vague about how far and in what direction might lie the curative spring in which our suffering Captain-General Coronado had hoped to bathe and restore himself. The valley was fine and green, in striking contrast to the dry and relatively barren uplands adjacent. A broad marshland followed the stream that meandered through its center. We rode beside the marsh through heavy stands of a tall grass that reached well past the bellies of our horses.

At the end of the second day we reached a point where the stream course was joined by a substantial tributary flowing in from the south. It was lined with tall Alamo trees. We determined to make camp some distance up this creek, because of the shade and because, while the horses could easily reach water to drink, there were far fewer of the mosquitoes that had plagued us along the broader Babocomari marshland.

That night we were awakened by a strange sound. It was like the roar of a distant cataract. It became louder and louder, and suddenly a wall of water was upon us. There being no clouds and no rain overhead, we did not expect and could not comprehend this event, though in *retrospect it must have come from an unseasonably early downpour in the distant mountains.*

*Fortunately we lost none of our party and only three of our animals. However, we had to abandon our saddles, most of our weapons, and all of our supplies as we fled to higher ground. Most tragically, the Captain-General's breastplate and helmet were swept away by the flood, these having been put aside while he slept. His magnificent trappings were not found despite a lengthy search at first light and after the water had subsided. Dispirited by his loss, the Captain-General determined to abandon our search for the curative spring, and he ordered a retreat back downstream. Now, not only would his return to New Spain be without news of gold or other riches, but he would be forced to suffer the further humiliation of riding without his fine armor.*

- from the diary of Pedro de Castañeda,
May 14, 1542

~ ~ ~

*Hit the jackpot today in the San Carlos Wash. This could re-write the history of Arizona. One of the best days of my life. But there's something spooky going on around here. I have a bad feeling about things.*

- from the diary of Jeremiah McLeod, Jr.,
July 10, 1995

# Chapter 41

### Sheriff Luis Mendoza

**T**he note from Lucinda Trujillo, now called Sister Magdalena, had said to find a man in Mexico named Hector Morales. The note had not said why Luis might want to do that, but since he had been asking Lucinda and her mother about the death of Paco Trujillo in the Nogales County Jail in 1993, he decided that was the place to start.

The records had been hard to find, but the warden finally dug out the old logbooks. They showed that a man named Hector Morales had in fact been locked up at the same time as Paco. He'd been arrested on a drunk and disorderly charge, which subsequently was dropped. The logbook didn't say why. So it looked promising, except for the fact that there were several people named Hector Morales in the Nogales phone book. It had taken several of the Sheriff's many contacts, but eventually he'd located a likely individual. The man owned a small liquor store and pharmacy just across the border. It was one of many such places that specialized in selling alcohol and drugs like Viagra and penicillin at bargain prices to the *gringos*.

Once again Luis Mendoza crossed into Mexico with his passport and badge, but without a gun. He suspected the guards on both sides of the border knew who he was, but they did nothing to stop him either coming or going. In fact, they seemed to avoid making eye contact.

It had just quit raining in Nogales, Sonora, and the sun was back out. The heavy air smelled of warm wet concrete. The storm sewers had backed up as usual, and there were deep puddles at nearly every street corner. A man with whom he was familiar was selling homemade tamales and green chili burros from a pushcart. The Sheriff bought a tamale and asked directions to the Morales Pharmacia. He ate the tamale while he walked. It was delicious.

Hector Morales was an old man in a wheelchair, bent and disabled by age and perhaps by a life of violence. He made no effort to come out from behind the counter when Luis walked in. No one else was in the store. The Sheriff made a pretext of examining the shelves lined with dusty bottles of tequila and vanilla, along with the glass-fronted cabinets full of medicine bottles. Then he locked the door and pulled down the shades. The man appeared startled, but he did not speak.

Luis shifted to vernacular Spanish. "Are you Hector Morales?"

"That is my name."

"And would you be the same Hector Morales who spent time in the Santa Cruz County Jail in the fall of 1993?"

The man probably thought he was going to be robbed. Obviously he was not expecting to be asked about this. He seemed at a loss for words.

The Sheriff persisted. "Please, sir. I believe that in fact you were a guest in my jail back then. I need to ask you about something that might have happened. If the information you give me is satisfactory, and if it is consistent with what I already know, then I will leave you alone."

Now Hector Morales was puzzled. "I was in *your* jail? How was it *your* jail?"

"It was not my jail then, but it is now. I am the Sheriff of Santa Cruz County. So once again sir, please answer my question."

"And if I do not? This is Sonora, not Arizona. You have no authority here."

"Technically you are correct. But I have many friends on both sides of the border, some of whom would be very disappointed to learn that you sell drugs to the *Americanos* even when they do not have prescriptions. Even more important, I know that some of the drugs you sell are counterfeit. If word of that got out, I expect that your business might suffer. They might even close you down. On the other hand, I have no particular interest in these matters, so I am hoping that we might come to an agreement."

The old man thought about that. Everybody he knew sold drugs to people without prescriptions, and it rarely if ever caused trouble. And as far as he knew, most shops also sold some counterfeits. Still, he didn't need the hassle, and the Sheriff was not asking for much. It was a long time ago. He decided to take a chance.

"All right. Yes, I was once jailed in your county. I do not exactly remember the year. But 1993 you say? It was about then."

Having established that he had found the right Hector Morales, it was now time for the Sheriff to run his bluff.

"We know you worked for the Trujillo family back then, and we know they arranged for you to be arrested at the same time that Paco Trujillo was being held in jail awaiting charges on drug smuggling. So this is not my question."

Now Hector Morales realized he was being drawn into truly dangerous, perhaps even lethal, territory. He weighed that against the possibility that his business would be shut down, and eventually he spoke: "Then just what is your question?"

"I want to know what you were expected to do while you were in the jail."

"I was supposed to start a fight in the eating hall, to create a disturbance. That is all."

"Did they tell you why?"

"No. But they promised me that afterwards I would be released. That the charges against me would be dropped."

"Did anything unusual happen during that disturbance?"

"Yes. Somebody killed Paco with a knife."

"Who?"

Hector Morales did not answer, and Luis could appreciate the dilemma the man faced. He decided to give him a way out. "I do not need his name, but I would like to know if he also worked for the Trujillos."

"He did, *señor*. We both did. And afterwards, they arranged for us to disappear into Mexico."

"And you no longer worked for the Trujillos?"

"That is correct."

"Do you know Pedro Trujillo?"

"I know of him, of course, but I have not met him. I was at a very low level in their organization."

"Do you know what happened to the man who used the knife?"

"I heard that he ... died."

"Have you ever wondered why you didn't die as well?"

"Many times, señor. But that was more than twenty years ago, and I have not worried much about it recently."

"Are you worried now?"

"More than yesterday. But I am an old man without a family, and you can see that I am not well. So perhaps I am not as worried as you might expect."

Luis despised the drug traffic for what it did to his county and to his people, and he wished the Trujillo family nothing but misfortune. But Hector Morales had been a mere underling, one of dozens like him trapped in something beyond his control, probably out of economic

256

necessity. The man had been surprisingly forthright and helpful.

"I have only one more question, Señor Morales. Then you have my word - and I do not give it lightly – that what you have told me today will remain between us."

"And what is that question?"

"In the years you worked for the Trujillos, did you ever encounter a man named Barney Stroud?"

"I am not sure. That name has a familiarity. Who was he?"

"He was a deputy in my department."

Once again the old man hesitated. "Ah yes, I may remember such a person, but I was never sure of his name. Was he a tall thin man, without much hair but with a big belly?"

That was a pretty good description. "What else do you remember about him?"

"There was only one time, but I remember that he accepted some cash money. I believe that if he truly was your deputy, then you would not be wrong to consider him a traitor."

~ ~ ~

Luis thought about things as he walked back across the border into Arizona. He was relieved, because he knew that now they could go after the Trujillos for their real crimes and not for a possible revenge killing of Scooter McLeod in 1995. The death of Paco Trujillo in the Santa Cruz County Jail had been a hit, most likely arranged by his brother Pedro in an attempt to take control of the family business. He probably couldn't prove it, even with the testimony of Hector Morales. And he wasn't about to ask for that, for two reasons. First, he had just given his word. Second, he didn't much care if one Trujillo killed another one.

Somebody who obviously did care was Sister

Magdalena. She must have loved her brother Paco as much as she hated her brother Pedro for his fratricide. Their father was now gone, and mercifully so from what Luis understood. But he wondered about their mother Camarilla, and how she made it from one day to the next knowing what she did about her own family.

Barney Stroud, a former deputy in his department, clearly had been on the take. But what for, if it had nothing to do with the death of Scooter McLeod? And why would the Trujillos want him dead now, after all these years? The Sheriff was pretty sure of one thing. Barney's death had come just a few days after he, Luis, had visited both Pedro and Camarilla Trujillo. It could not have been a coincidence.

# Chapter 42

**I**t was Monday evening, but I decided to break tradition and go to Maria's for a quick bite before heading back for two-fers night. For one thing, I missed her. For another, I was curious to see if the video camera had picked up anything out in the San Carlos Wash. It hadn't, except for a deer, a javelina, and something scuttling away that could have been a jackrabbit.

I drove away from the Obregon homestead to the sound of bleating. Maria was out milking, and evidently somebody was complaining about it. The sun had just dropped below the skyline of the Santa Ritas as I pulled into my usual spot in front of the namesake saloon. Based on the number of cars, it already was busy inside.

When I came in, Frenchy Vullmers was behind the bar talking to Al Treutline and Sally Benton. Most of The Regulars were there. I exchanged nods with the portly proprietor, then sat down alone at a booth near the door.

He nodded in my direction. "The usual?"

"Just the *Bohemia*, thanks. I already ate something."

Frenchy feigned offense. "What? Does my cooking no longer meet with your approval? I could not help but notice that you sent your young colleague last Monday instead of coming yourself."

"I'm sure your steaks are as good as ever. In fact, Larry Hernandez said so. It's just that I had something to do at home."

"Home these days being Ms. Maria's goat farm, no?"

I decided not to take the bait. "Just get over here with my beer, okay?"

"But of course, my friend. In my business it does not

pay to keep *les gendarmes* waiting."

I cast an eye over the crowd once again, while I waited for my beer. I was surprised to see Sandy McLeod and Ray Salerno sitting together at a small table near the back wall, behind the pool tables. I hadn't seen either one of them in here before. The two men were deep in conversation, and they didn't seem to be eating the food that had been placed before them. I could not hear what they were saying, but Ray was doing most of the talking and he didn't look happy.

Al Treutline came over and eased himself into the other side of my booth. "So how's it going, Deputy?"

"It's going, Al. More or less as usual."

"That's not what I hear."

"What have you heard?"

"I've heard you figured out that it was Scooter McLeod for sure who was dead in that pickup. And I've heard you're up to your neck in suspects, but pretty much stuck for evidence."

"Sounds like the jungle drums have been beating. Where did you get all this?"

"Oh, from different places, but mostly from Barney Stroud. I heard about Barney. We're gonna miss him around here. You got any idea what happened?"

"Nope. The Sheriff is handling that case. I don't think they've come up with anything so far."

"The last time I saw Barney, he said he needed to talk to you again about the McLeod case."

I was not pleased that the Regulars had been gossiping, and I wondered how much Barney Stroud had revealed.

"What did Barney say?"

"I don't remember exactly, but it was something about Ollie Swade."

That was interesting. "What about him, Al? This could

be important."

"I think we've all heard stories about Ollie going around digging up things, especially in the old days. I knew lots of folks back then who went treasure hunting. Never saw much harm in it myself."

"Maybe yes and maybe no. But I'm more interested in why Barney thought this had anything to do with the McLeods."

Al Treutline thought about that for a minute. "Here's what I remember, but don't hold me to it because we'd both had a bunch of beers that night, and it's all a little vague." He paused and scratched his head. "Barney said the McLeod boy had come to see him just a little while before he went missing. That he wanted to report on somebody he thought was digging up stuff illegally in the valley."

"And that somebody was Ollie Swade?"

"Yep." At that point somebody over at the bar called Al's name, and he got up and left.

Suddenly loud voices erupted from the back of the restaurant that I recognized as belonging to Sandy McLeod and Ray Salerno. Chairs scraped as the two men stood and faced each other over the largely uneaten remains of their steak dinners. Ray's face was red and he was shaking an accusatory finger. Sandy looked around like he hoped nobody would notice. I couldn't hear all of what they were saying, but at one point Ray shouted something like "no more extensions!" Then he turned his back on Sandy and headed for the bar. As he did so he called back over his shoulder "Now go pay the bill and get the hell out of here!"

The Regulars got real quiet and made a point of inspecting their beers.

I was surprised when Sandy McLeod stopped by my table on his way out. "Sorry about that. Ray and I had a little disagreement. But everything'll be okay. He just gets excited sometimes."

I must have seemed skeptical, because instead of leaving the man took a seat in my booth and kept talking. "We're involved together in a couple of my housing projects, and things are just a little slow right now, with the downturn and all. But it's gonna work out."

"I didn't know Ray was a partner of yours. How long has that been going on?"

"I don't know why it's any of your concern, but we've been working together on things right from the start. I mean, from back when I first began to develop the Rocking M. He had so much good luck with his Bobcat Creek Estates, and he was looking for a place to invest, so I let him. But I wouldn't call him a partner exactly. He's more like an investor."

I'd been waiting for just such an opportunity to ask a key question. "What about your brother?"

"Scooter? What about him?"

"Was he in on any of your projects?"

"No. And by the way, when do you think you might come over to my mall and pick out a suite for your new office? I can't hold 'em forever you know. Things definitely are picking up."

"Pretty soon, Sandy. I've been real busy lately."

"You mean trying to figure out what happened to my brother?"

"Mostly, that's right."

"Have you gotten anywhere? I mean, do you have any idea who might have killed him?"

"We have lots of ideas, but nothing concrete."

"Who is we?"

"Sheriff Mendoza and me."

"Oh, sure. Well, goodnight then." Sandy McLeod rose, walked to the door, and stepped out into the dark.

For his part, Ray Salerno didn't seem in any hurry to

leave the Santa Rita Saloon. Instead he stayed at the bar drinking straight shots of bourbon. At one point Frenchy Vullmers gave me the look that said 'we may have a problem here.' But Ray stayed quiet, and for about another twenty minutes nothing happened.

Then Ray Salerno fell backwards off his barstool. Fortunately Al Treutline was walking past on his way to the men's room and cushioned the fall. "Jesus!" said Al, as the two men lay sprawled across each other on the floor.

I got up in a hurry and elbowed my way through the other Regulars, who had quickly gathered around to survey the damage. I bent over the two men, who were in the process of struggling to their feet. There didn't seem to be any blood, but Al was rubbing the side of his head. Ray Salerno lurched back against the bar and mumbled something that might have been an apology. After two failed attempts he got out his wallet, threw some bills on the bar, and staggered toward the door.

I blocked his way. "Excuse me, Mr. Salerno, but you're in no condition to drive."

Ray stopped and blinked. He swayed unsteadily on his feet and attempted to focus. "Well then Deputy, just what do you expect me to do? Spend the night here in a booth?"

"Is there somebody local who could come and get you? Maybe put you up for the night?"

Ray seemed puzzled, like he was trying to think of a name. Then he shook his head. "About the only person I know around here anymore is Sandy McLeod, and I'm not about to let that sonofabitch do me a favor."

I made a decision. "Tell you what. There's a place you can bunk for the night over at the Pitchfork Ranch – my folks place. I'll drive you over there and bring you back to your car in the morning. Now give my your keys."

"Why should I do that?"

"Please. Just give me your keys. And you should call

your wife."

Ray Salerno must have decided that was a bad idea, because he passed out again, falling right into my arms.

Al Truetline and Sally Benton helped me load Ray into the Blazer, and then offered to help get him back to my place. I declined. Once back on the Pitchfork ranch, it took me another half hour to get Salerno settled down. Then I got back in my vehicle and headed for Maria's. During the short drive a strange thought occurred: "Wouldn't it be funny if I just tucked a killer into my old bed?"

# Chapter 43

**E**arly the next morning I filled a thermos with coffee and put some energy bars and a handful of aspirin in my shirt pocket. Then I headed for the Pitchfork Ranch to deal with Ray Salerno and what was likely to be the man's world-class hangover. He was still unconscious when I arrived. As far as I could tell, he hadn't moved all night.

I shook him awake, and he blinked up at me. "What?" Then he turned back to the wall, closed his eyes, and drifted off again.

I shook him again. "Excuse me, Mr. Salerno, but we really need to get you moving. I called your wife last night and told her what happened. She's worried. She said she would come over this morning with a man named Alfredo – that he would drive you back. I think he works for you. Anyway, we're supposed to meet at the Santa Rita, and I expect they're already on their way. So, you need to get up. I've brought you some coffee."

It took three cups and two aspirin, but Ray Salerno eventually managed to get out of bed and stagger to the bathroom. He came out looking gray but a little less bleary-eyed. He sat down hard in a kitchen chair, refusing the offer of an energy bar. "Sorry about last night. That doesn't usually happen to me."

"You just had too much to drink. It can happen to anybody. I'm glad you're okay."

Ray rubbed his bloodshot eyes and pawed at his tangled black hair. "No, I hardly ever drink that much. I've got some sort of allergy to alcohol. It was Sandy McLeod. I think he did it on purpose."

"Did what?"

"Tried to get me drunk. He was the one that said we should go to the Santa Rita last night. He said he would buy, said he had some good news about the financial situation."

"You mean about his housing developments?"

"Yeah, that and his damned mall. Talk about a stupid idea. I never should have let him talk me into it."

"So you're a partner of his?"

"You could say that. It's mostly my money. It's his land, but my money. Last night he said he was going to pay off a big chunk, a quarter million dollars. He said we should celebrate. But even if he does make the wire transfer today like he promised, it still wouldn't be half of what he owes me. That's why we got into that fight over dinner. I gave him an ultimatum. I said I wanted out, period."

"What did he say to that?"

"It's not what he said, it's what he did. He got me to drink, and he knew I couldn't handle it. Not and drive, that is."

"How could he make you drink?"

"I think he knew if he got me started that I wouldn't be able to stop. And he was right."

"So let me be sure I understand. You're suggesting that Sandy McLeod did this deliberately? That he hoped you might try to drive home and ..."

"Sure, isn't that obvious? I know I can't prove it. But the man's in a hole, and I think he'd do just about anything right now to try and dig his way out."

Ray Salerno coughed and shook his head. Then he went on. "I need to apologize, Deputy. I've been short with you, tried to blow you off in fact. I know you're just trying to do your job. And really, it isn't the money so much. I've got lots of it, probably more than Vicki and I will ever need."

"Then what is it?"

"For heaven's sake, can't you figure that out?"

"I suppose I can. It's about Angela, isn't it?"

He sighed and nodded. "You got it. She's my daughter, my only child for God's sake. She won't forgive me for what she says I did to her. She won't even see me or her mother. It's pretty much ruined our lives. And I know what you're thinking."

"What's that?"

"You're thinking I killed Scooter McLeod. That I blamed him for all of this."

"*Did* you kill him?"

"As God is my witness, no." Ray Salerno buried his face in his hands.

I wasn't sure why, but I believed the man. A cloud may have been lifting over Ray Salerno, but at the same time another much larger one was building over the head of Sandy McLeod.

# Chapter 44

**A**ngel Corona was in the office talking with Larry when I got back from delivering Ray Salerno to the parking lot at the Santa Rita Saloon. A pang of guilt shot through me as I remembered that I had not spoken to Angel since the death of his grandson Oscar four days earlier.

I looked the man in the eye and shook his hand. He held my gaze and his grip was firm.

"Hello Angel. I want you to know how sorry I am about the loss of your grandson."

"He was a good boy, Cal. But he made some bad decisions, and he paid for it. We're all paying for it now, especially his grandmother."

"I'm sure. Please give her my deepest sympathies."

The Rocking M foreman seemed anxious to change the subject. "There's something we need to talk about." He glanced in the direction of Larry Hernandez. "In private, if that's okay."

Larry got the hint. "I'm just on my way out on patrol."

"Thanks. Check in with me later today." I invited Angel to sit. "Is there something I can do to help?"

"This isn't about Oscar. It's about Sally Benton's bull."

I'd almost forgotten about that, what with all the other stuff that was going on. "Good news, I hope?"

"Yes and no. This gets a bit complicated, and it is not a short story."

"I'm listening."

"Last week I got a call from a nephew of mine. He's foreman of a big *rancho* down in the northeastern part of Sonora. He wanted me to know that my brother – his father – is not well. He lives in a village nearby."

"I'm sorry to hear that. Is your brother going to be all right?"

"Probably not. But that's not what I wanted to tell you about."

I could see that the man was very uncomfortable. "Then what is it?"

"My nephew told me about a new bull they got on the *rancho*, and that the bull carried two brands. One was the Rocking M, and that is why he thought I would be interested. The other brand was the V-9. So of course I wondered if it might be Sally's Benton's lost Hereford."

My mind was racing. "Seems likely. But how do you suppose it got your brand? Did your nephew say how his ranch happened to buy this bull?"

"He said it was through a dealer, and that the man was vague about where it had come from."

"This is complicated. I need to get a photograph of the animal and show it to Sally. Then, if she can identify it, we need to get it back. The problem is, I have no idea how to go about retrieving stolen property from Mexico. Maybe the sheriff will know."

Angel Corona shook his head. "Actually, that isn't going to be a problem."

"Why not?"

"Because the animal is in my barn."

I was startled. "How did that happen? I mean, how did it get back from your cousin's place in Sonora?"

Angel Corona hesitated. "The owner of the *rancho* is very wealthy, and even more influential. There are ways of getting things across the border unofficially, even something as large as a bull. I met my nephew in Naco, on the Arizona side. He had the bull."

"Was there any paperwork? I mean like a bill of sale or a certification from a brand inspector?"

"No. There was no paperwork. My nephew said the owner of the *rancho* was highly embarrassed when he learned that the animal had been stolen – that he just wanted the problem to go away without any official investigation. I expect he'll deal in his own way with the man that sold him the animal. And, if you will take my advice, it also would be best if you just let the matter drop."

The last thing I wanted was some big messy international investigation, so I was inclined to take the foreman's advice. On the other hand, it seemed as if somebody at the Rocking M had gone to the trouble to re-brand the animal – probably to make the sale appear legitimate.

Angel Corona apparently read my mind. "You know, if that bull carried only the V-9 brand, I probably would have returned it to Sally and made up a story about finding it wandering around on our ranch. But that Rocking M brand means I couldn't really do that."

"It means more than that, though, doesn't it?"

"I know. But you've gotta believe me. I didn't steal that animal. Otherwise, why would I be here?"

"And that leaves only one likely person, doesn't it? So you're really in a jam here, aren't you, because now you're in the position of having to betray your boss."

"I suppose it could have been anybody who knows our brand. But you're right, Sandy is the most obvious person." Angel looked down at his hands. "My god, Cal, I could lose my job over this! The only reason I'm here right now is I happen to know that both Janet and Sandy are up in Phoenix today. If he even saw my truck outside your office ..."

I made a decision. "Here's what I want you to do. I want you to go home and stay there. I'll call Sally and have her send somebody over to get the bull. Don't get involved in that. I'll do everything possible to keep you out of this. But before you go, I have one question. Which of the Rocking M vehicles most likely would have been used in the theft of the Benton Hereford? Assuming, of course, that somebody on your ranch was involved."

Angel thought about that. "We have only one trailer big enough to haul that bull, and that's the same one I used to pick him up in Naco. It's red and white, and it's parked outside the barn where I put the bull. As for a truck, there's only one besides mine with a hitch, a big silver Dodge. Sandy uses it when he's not driving his Mercedes. It's usually parked by their house. But why does this matter?"

"Just a hunch, Angel. Now get the hell out of here."

As soon as I was alone, I phoned Sally Benton and told her the news.

"Oh thank you, Cal. That's wonderful! Where is he? I'll send my foreman right away. Was it on a neighbor's place? I'll bet one of those water gap fences went down again."

"It's a bit complicated. It's in the barn at Rocking M headquarters. So go ahead and send your foreman. But I need some favors."

"Sure, anything. What do you need?"

"First, don't tell anybody where you got it. Second, don't ask me about the brands on the animal, and don't try to change them."

"Why not?"

"They may be evidence."

"I see."

I guessed she probably did see, because Sally Benton was no fool and she asked no more questions.

"Oh, and one more thing. I'll need to be riding out on your place again, if that's okay. Probably this afternoon. I'll bring my own horses, and I think Larry Hernandez will be with me."

~ ~ ~

I called the sheriff and brought him up to speed on the

case of Sally Benton's prize bull. At first, he seemed incredulous. "You think Sandy McLeod did this? That's one hell of an accusation."

"The evidence points in that direction. And he may have had a motive."

"What would that be?"

"Money." I explained my suspicions about Sandy's financial situation, and the fact that I wanted to look around the Rocking M for evidence of rustling.

The sheriff sighed. "Well, if you want to go in that direction, you're going to need a search warrant."

"That's why I called. And while you're at it, see if you can get me one for Ollie Swade's place too."

"While I'm *at it*? These things don't just grow on trees you know. We'll need a judge to sign both warrants, as you damn well know. And anyway, what does Ollie Swade have to do with Ms. Benton's bull?"

I felt sorry for the sheriff, who understandably was having trouble getting his head around the full variety of things happening in my end of the county. I caught him up on the possibility that Ollie might have been involved – might still be involved - with looting, and his possible motive for killing Scooter McLeod. "I think we really need those warrants, Luis, and I'm confident you can make it happen."

All I got in response was a growl, but within an hour the old fax machine in my office came to life, and copies of the two search warrants were on my desk.

# Chapter 45

I got Larry on his cell. "Hey, it's Cal. Are you busy?"
"I just pulled over a bass fisherman who was in too much of a hurry to get on the water at Lake Patagonia. Otherwise it's dead quiet. What's up?"

"How would you like to help me with some forensic botany?"

There was a pause. "What's that?"

"Using botanical materials in criminal investigations. I saw a program about it on TV the other day. I may need you to sign off on some evidence, so get back up here as soon as you can. We have a time issue on our hands."

"Botanical you say? That's something about plants, right? I don't know much about plants."

"That makes two of us. But if this goes like I expect, that shouldn't be a problem."

~ ~ ~

I explained to Larry what I was up to as we drove out to Rocking M headquarters. Angel Corona's pickup was in front of his house, but I was more pleased to see that Sandy McLeod's silver Dodge was in the yard up the hill beside their big adobe. There didn't seem to be anybody around, but I went to the door and rang the bell just to be sure. I waited a minute and rang it a second time before I was satisfied that we were alone. Then I turned my attention to the Dodge. From the back seat of the Blazer I extracted a camera, a box of sturdy paper bags, a large pair of tweezers, a flashlight, and a permanent marker pen. I handed the pen to Larry, and then I got down on the ground and scooted back under the front end of the pickup.

"You're gonna get your shirt dirty doing that."

"It's an occupational hazard for a forensic botanist."

Just like it had showed on the TV program, the underside of Sandy McLeod's truck was a tangled mess of vegetation, especially up in the wheel wells, around the springs and axles, and under the radiator. It was the inevitable consequence of driving off-road in a grassland. I took some flash photos. Then I poked and tweezed at the plant materials, collected several items into one of the paper bags, and finally repeated the process under the rear wheels and axle.

I crawled out from under the truck, stood up and dusted myself off, and examined the cab, especially the floorboard on the driver's side. But it was clean. Just as I had expected, the truck had been washed and vacuumed, but whoever did it forgot about the undercarriage.

I turned to Larry. "Now, we'll both sign and date these bags, with you as a witness. And then let's go take a look at that big red-and-white livestock trailer we saw by the barn on the way in."

If anything, the underside of the trailer was an even bigger mess, and I made another substantial collection. "This may help, too. But anybody could have used this trailer. It's the stuff from the Dodge that links it to Sandy. Now let's get the out of here before somebody spots us."

Larry looked puzzled. "But hasn't Angel Corona seen us?"

"Probably, but that doesn't matter. He's under orders to lay low."

"Whose orders?"

"Mine." I explained why I wanted to keep Angel out of things.

Larry seemed to accept that. "What do we do next?"

"Next we go for a horseback ride on the V-9."

We went back to the Pitchfork Ranch, borrowed horses

from the people who currently leased the property from my parents, and trailed them to V-9 headquarters. From there it was only a short ride north across the mesa to the same spot where Sally Benton had taken me a week earlier to show me where she thought someone had rustled her bull.

I dug up several specimens of New Mexico feather grass, put them in paper bags, and once again asked Larry to date and witness the collection.

"I think I'm getting what you're up to. But how's it going to tie Sandy's truck to this particular place?"

"Two things, one of which is going to be lots simpler than the other. This plant here, that we just collected, is called New Mexico feather grass. I think we got some off the Dodge too. Sally says it is very rare in this part of Arizona, so rare that there may be no stands like this one anywhere else in the valley. But even if there are, we might be able to get a DNA analysis showing that the samples we got off the Dodge are genetically similar to the plants we see here."

"But I've heard those DNA tests are really expensive. Do you think the sheriff will spring for it?"

"That's what I intend to find out."

~ ~ ~

Back in the office, I phoned Nogales and brought the sheriff up to speed. "So the plant material we found under Sandy McLeod's pickup looks just like a grass growing at the place where somebody loaded up Sally's bull. I'm sure we can prove that even if you don't want to pay for DNA work, but you're probably gonna have to find a forensic botanist to make it official."

It took some time to explain all of this to the sheriff. I guess he'd missed the TV show, and he still didn't seem all that satisfied.

"As I told you, I think Sandy is about to go under water. If you can get a peek into his financial dealings, I'll bet you find a wire transfer of $250,000 from somewhere in Mexico, and maybe by now another transaction moving that money to an account belonging to Ray Salerno."

"I'll be damned. Looks like you've really done your homework on this one. Still, it makes me edgy going after somebody as prominent as McLeod unless we have solid evidence. But I'll talk to the DA, and if he's good with it then we'll ask a judge for a court order to check into the financial aspect. Hopefully we'll be able to keep it confidential. I don't want Sandy to find out about this unless your hunches turn out to be right."

"Thanks. I appreciate your handling it from Nogales. I'm not trying to duck anything here, but the more distance we can put between this investigation and Angel Corona, the more likely he won't lose his job because of it."

"I'm with you on that one. The Coronas have had enough bad news lately. But back to the McLeods, I wanted to let you know that you can eliminate the Trujillos as suspects in Scooter's murder."

This was a surprising development. "Really? How can you be sure?"

"Because they had no motive."

"But Scooter got Paco Trujillo sent to jail, where he died. Isn't that a motive for another family member to kill Scooter?"

"I told you from the beginning that I'd handle this aspect of the case. I guess maybe you weren't listening."

I'd been listening all right. "But it's just that ..."

The sheriff interrupted. "I'll tell you this much, and then we're finished here. The Trujillos had no motive because Paco's death was an inside job."

"You mean the family *wanted* him dead?"

There was no reply, and I realized, once again, that the sheriff had hung up on me.

# Chapter 46

"hat camera over in the San Carlos Wash got something interesting this morning."

"Maria?" I had been sitting in office eating a ham sandwich when the phone rang.

"Oh sorry. Yes, it's me. I came home for lunch and the red light on the computer was flashing. You need to see this."

"I'll be right there."

~ ~ ~

It took less than my usual 20 minutes to drive from Sonoita to the Nanny Boss goat dairy. Now I was sitting in front of the computer screen, with Maria standing behind me. I double-clicked on the desktop icon the way Dr. Rincon had showed us, and a list of choices appeared that were arranged by date and time. We had seen all the earlier clips before, where a deer or a jackrabbit or something unknown had triggered the camera. Those taken during the day were in color. The others, taken a night, had the eerie greenish glow of night vision technology.

I clicked on the most recent recording. It had been made at seven-fifteen that morning, just after we had both left for work. At first all that was apparent on the screen was a slightly out-of–focus figure in the background, perhaps fifty yards from the camera. But it definitely was a human. Over the next five minutes he or she gradually moved closer to the camera, though not in a straight line. Soon it became obvious what was happening. The figure was that of a man, and he was carrying both a metal detector and a shovel. He was sweeping the ground with the detector, but he never stopped and he never used the shovel. No hits, apparently. I thought the man looked familiar, but I couldn't be sure.

Suddenly the man stopped and stared. He dropped the detector, raised the shovel over his left shoulder, and ran straight at the camera. The last image transmitted to the computer was unmistakable. It was Ollie Swade swinging the shovel. Then the screen went blank.

Maria put a hand on my shoulder. "Should we go out there?"

"I expect he's long gone."

"Then what do you want to do?"

"I think you should go back to work. On a hunch yesterday I got the sheriff to fax me a search warrant for Ollie's place. Now I'm gonna go use it."

"What if he's there?"

"So much the better. He was on state land. If he knew it, he was deliberately breaking the law. That old man is a looter, and he just destroyed a very expensive piece of equipment. Maybe he's done worse things. It's about time he got busted. If we're lucky, he doesn't know the camera sent us an image before he smashed it, and so he might still be at home packing up his goodies, if he has any."

~ ~ ~

I tried to raise Larry on both the radio and my cell, but there was no response. He'd gone out that morning heading for Gardner Canyon to check on a reported burglary. It was rough country, and apparently he was out of range. I thought about calling somebody else for backup and decided against it. Ollie Swade might be a thief and a little crazy, but it didn't seem likely he was all that dangerous. I left Larry a message on his phone, and got in the Blazer.

As I approached the Swade homestead I spotted an old gray Ford Econoline heading north on the county road at a high speed. It was Ollie. I gunned my SUV in pursuit and called Arizona State Patrol with a vehicle description and a request for any units on route 82 to apprehend.

Ollie never made it that far. I had tried an easy approach, using neither the siren nor the lights, and staying back at least a hundred yards. But the old man only drove faster, until he missed a curve. The van somehow cleared the roadside ditch, broke through a barbed wire fence, and ploughed out into the grassland. Then it spun sideways and smashed broadside into the trunk of a large mesquite. The impact was directly into the driver's side door, and I feared the worst.

Before walking out to the wreck, I got on the radio to Nogales, gave dispatch my location, and told them to contact emergency services for an ambulance. Then I got back in touch with State Patrol and told them to call off the APB for Ollie's van. At my request, they patched me through to the trooper nearest the accident scene. That turned out to be Bob Melvin, who was over at Mustang Corners in Cochise County, about twenty minutes away. I told Bob what was happening, and asked that he join me to help secure the site.

# Chapter 47

Ollie Swade was unconscious but evidently still breathing. The EMTs got him out onto the ground and began taking vital signs. I thought they looked worried, and my suspicions were confirmed when I heard one of them get on the radio and request a helicopter.

"Any chance you could fly him to the hospital in Nogales?"

One of the emergency crew nodded. "Sure, I suppose so. But why?"

"Because he's a suspect in a crime, and I would like to have a deputy from our department assigned to his room so we can get a statement when he wakes up. And then we'll want to book him, and possibly put him in the county jail."

"That may be optimistic. I think this guy's pretty badly hurt."

"Hurt how?"

"Can't be sure. There's not much sign of external trauma. It's probably brain damage. He's definitely not responding like he should."

Just then Larry arrived. "Sorry I didn't get here sooner. I was in a dead space over in the Santa Ritas. Is that Ollie Swade? What happened?"

I filled him in on the essentials.

"Anything I can do?"

"Yeah. Go over to the Swade place and secure it as a crime scene. Don't let anybody in. I'm gonna get a look in his van and I'll meet you over there as soon as they fly Ollie out. Oh, and call the sheriff for me. Tell him what's happened and to have an officer ready to be stationed in the hospital room once Ollie gets out of emergency. Assuming he does, that is."

"It's that bad?"

"Could be."

~ ~ ~

As soon as the helicopter had departed with a still-comatose Ollie Swade, I turned my attention to the crumpled van and its contents. Based on the speed with which Ollie had been driving, it seemed obvious he had been carrying something he didn't want the law to see. Was it some sort of a find from his morning treasure hunt in the San Carlos Wash? Had he been on the way somewhere to make a sale? I went back to the Blazer for latex gloves, my camera, and some evidence bags, just in case. Trooper Melvin was still on the scene, and I asked him to string up crime scene tape.

"So this is more than just an accident?"

"Yeah, we think it is. I'm gonna check out the contents of the van, then head over to the place where the victim lived. Can you stay here until we get somebody up from Nogales to impound the vehicle?"

"Sure, I guess so. You got any coffee?"

"No, sorry. But thanks for your help."

The vehicle contained a daunting jumble of junk: old magazines and newspapers, soda cans, plastic water bottles, a rusted toolbox, an axe, two empty paint buckets, and a length of frayed garden hose. Ollie Swade might have been headed for the county landfill, except that he had been driving in the wrong direction. There was no sign of a metal detector or a shovel, but there was a cardboard box on the back seat that was taped shut.

I photographed the inside of the van. Then I put on my gloves and pulled the box out onto the ground. I slit the tape with my pocketknife and carefully pulled back the flaps. The box was filled nearly to the top with a real hodgepodge. There were some bits of pottery, a plastic bag filled with arrowheads or spear points, and various metal things that were rusted almost beyond recognition. I photographed the box and then put it inside my vehicle for safekeeping. Someone far more competent than me needed to examine the contents. I already had decided that person would be Dr. Julio Rincon from the State Museum.

~ ~ ~

Larry was waiting on Ollie Swade's front porch when I pulled into the yard. I got out, carrying the cardboard box.

"What's that?"

"It was inside Ollie's van. Apparently he filled it with some special treasures acquired during his looting career. But there could be more. Have you checked inside?"

"I looked in through the front door, which was unlocked by the way, but I didn't go in. Didn't see anything unusual."

"You got gloves?"

"Nope. But I didn't touch anything except the doorknob, and I used my bandana for that."

"Then follow me."

The inside of Ollie Swade's house was pretty much as it had been the other times I had been in there. In other words, it was still a mess. There was the same or at least a similar stack of dirty dishes in the sink, and piles of dirty laundry on the floor. But it was the basement that I really wanted to see. I laid the cardboard box on a chair in the living room and invited Larry to follow me downstairs.

One look inside the unfinished basement, and we both realized we needed help. It looked just like the inside of Ollie's box, only bigger. A lifetime of accumulated stuff stared us in the face. To my untrained eye it mostly resembled junk, and I guessed it had long-since been culled of anything valuable. But there was no way to be sure.

"Let's get out of here and call in the right kind of help to go through all this."

"What kind of help?"

"Archaeologist help."

Larry looked skeptical. "It just looks like a bunch of crap to me."

"Me too, but that's because neither of us knows what the hell we're doing. For all we know, there's something stashed around here that could change history."

It turned out there was, and it did.

# Chapter 48

**I** phoned the State Museum in Tucson and asked to speak with Dr. Rincon. The secretary said he was up in Phoenix at a meeting hosted by the State Land Department. The subject was looting artifacts on public land, and finding better ways to stop it. Interesting coincidence.

"May I try his cell?"

"Sure. But he probably has it turned off. One of his 'things' is having phones ringing in the middle of meetings. Can I take a message in case you don't get through?"

"Please have him call me at his earliest convenience. Tell him it's about that thing we installed in the San Carlos Wash."

I punched in the number Rincon's secretary had given me. Not only was the man's phone turned off, but the message box was full. I hoped that he checked in with his office at some point during the day.

Larry and I went outside into Ollie Swade's yard, and I asked him if he'd gotten hold of the sheriff.

"Oh yeah, and I almost forgot. He wants you to call him. There's some sort of a problem about that stolen bull."

"What sort of a problem?"

"He didn't say. But it sounds like you may need to go down to Nogales."

"Okay, but I was hoping to stay here and guard Ollie's house. Now it looks like you're going to have to do that job."

"You think we need to stay here round the clock?

We've got it marked as a crime scene."

"I have a funny feeling about this one. So yes, please sit tight and I'll be back to relieve you as soon possible."

~ ~ ~

Fifty minutes later I was in the sheriff's office down in Nogales. There were four of us in the room, including Sergeant Joe Ortega, the head of criminal investigations, and the county District Attorney, a big heavy-set man named Bancroft. Following introductions, we all took seats lined up across the front of the sheriff's desk.

The purpose of the meeting was twofold. First, Luis wanted to bring everybody up to speed on the matter of Muffy Davenport and Oscar Corona. The Davenport lawyers were trying to find somebody to sue, but they weren't getting anywhere. Oscar Corona had been driving, and he was dead. The Border Patrol might have been chasing them, but there wasn't any proof, and in any event it didn't have anything to do with the Sheriff's Department. Luis suggested we all just sit tight, that there wasn't anything we needed to do at this point. We all agreed.

The group then turned its attention to the case of Sally Benton's Hereford. Ortega spoke first. "So all you've got is an altered brand and a handful of grass plants, and that's it?"

Obviously the ball was in my court. "That and some testimony that Sandy McLeod may be in financial trouble. So if we could ..."

D. A. Bancroft interrupted. "Which at this point is only hearsay."

"But that's why we need to get a look at his financial dealings. I understand your reluctance, but I wouldn't be asking for this if I wasn't convinced McLeod is a rustler. The plant evidence alone can make the case that his vehicle was at the crime scene. It just can't absolutely prove he was driving, but if we ..."

Now it was Ortega's turn to interrupt, which led me to suspect that he and the DA had rehearsed things in advance. "This plant evidence – how reliable is that? I mean, can you really tell one grass blade from another? Are there any expert witnesses who can do that sort of thing and make a jury believe them?"

I had read up on the subject, and I was ready for his question. "There are people who do exactly that. They're called forensic botanists, and they have been cleared to testify all across the country, including Arizona. The particular plant growing on the Benton ranch, and the pieces of it that got caught under the McLeod vehicle, they are very distinctive and very rare. It should be an easy case."

Up to this point the sheriff had just been sitting there like an observer at a tennis match, watching the ball bouncing back and forth between the players but not getting involved. He got our attention by standing up. Then he walked to the window as if to look outside, but instead turned back to face the District Attorney. "Bill, it's your call, but I agree with Cal. We have at least enough evidence to ask a judge for a court order. Let's do it."

"All right, Luis. But let's just put a toe in the water here. If you don't come up with something solid right from the start, then we drop it, okay?" The DA turned in his chair and looked directly at me. "And in the mean time, we talk to nobody else about any of this. I mean *nobody*."

I got the message, but the sheriff cut me off before I had a chance to respond. "By solid, you mean evidence of a wire transfer from Mexico?"

"Exactly. And we'll probably need to get the feds in on this, since it involves another country's banks."

The sheriff turned to Ortega. "Joe, I want you and your team to handle this, once we get a court order. Find out what you can, and get back to me ASAP."

Ortega nodded back at the sheriff. "Will do." Then he shot me a look. He didn't say anything, but the message seemed obvious. It was about time his department took charge of things.

After the other two men left I moved over to the chair centered directly opposite the sheriff's, the one previously occupied by DA Bancroft.

"Thanks, Luis."

"For what?"

"First, for supporting my plan regarding Sandy McLeod. And, more generally, for your confidence. I realize you have a choice here, in terms of who does what in this investigation."

The sheriff nodded. "You're the right person for this job, among other reasons because you know the people involved and what's going on in your corner of the county. I'll handle Ortega. Just don't screw it up."

No pressure there. Or had I seen the trace of a grin on the man's face? I asked him about Ollie Swade.

"He's in intensive care. I've got a deputy at the hospital keeping an eye on things. Last I checked, the man was still out of it. It may be one of those cases where he never wakes up."

"I'd like to go over to the hospital in any event."

"Sure. But tell me something first. Why do you think Ollie took off like he did?"

"I think he figured out we had him identified on the camera that Dr. Rincon set up in the San Carlos Wash. Plus, he had that box of artifacts with him. My guess is he grabbed the things he thought were most valuable out of his basement, and he was making a run for his dealer, whoever that might be."

The sheriff scratched behind one ear. "Sure, I suppose that's what happened. But the penalties for looting aren't all that stiff, just a misdemeanor on the first offense I believe. Hell, he could be in bigger trouble just for attempting to evade the law when you were chasing him."

"That and for destroying the video camera. But you've got a point. That's why I'm hoping he wakes up so we can talk to him about what's really going on. Did I tell you that he had a run-in with Scooter McLeod way back when?"

The sheriff's bushy black eyebrows rose. "Really? What about? And how did you find this out?"

"Barton Hampstead was the first person who told me about it, and one of Barney Stroud's friends confirmed the story. Apparently Ollie approached Hampstead and Scooter about selling them some artifacts the summer they were living together on the Rocking M. Scooter had a fit and threatened to turn Ollie in for looting. And I guess he did that, but Stroud didn't think it was important and he never followed up."

The sheriff rolled his eyes. "Sounds like Barney. So Ollie Swade had a motive to kill the McLeod boy. Not a very strong motive, but you can never be sure with odd ducks like him. I can see why you'd like to talk to him."

"Speaking of Barney Stroud, are you getting anywhere with his murder?"

"So far, it's a total blank."

"But you suspect the Trujillos, don't you?"

"Suspicions are one thing. Solid proof is another. I'll keep you posted. But like I've said before, Cal, you stay out of it."

"You're serious about this? The Trujillos don't scare me. I'd like to help. After all, Barney used to have my job."

The sheriff frowned, then pivoted in his leather swivel chair and looked out the window. I followed his eyes. A gust of wind was blowing debris across an undeveloped acre or two of former desert next to the county building. The shredded remains of plastic bags flapped in the breeze, tangled in the thorns of some half-dead mesquites. We weren't all that far from a big box store that handed out plastic bags like it didn't matter.

Luis swung his chair back in my direction. "You agree I'm the sheriff don't you? And that you work for me and not the other way around?"

"Sure."

"Then here's a direct order. Stay the hell away from the Trujillos."

~ ~ ~

It was a short drive across town to the Catholic hospital. Short, but not fast given the late-day traffic. I parked under a spreading mesquite, and walked in the main entrance. It was cool and clean inside, but the place still gave me the creeps, just like all hospitals. I showed my badge to a security guard and was directed down a hallway to the intensive care unit.

The door to Ollie's room was easy to find, because it was the only one with a deputy sheriff standing in front of it. I nodded to the man, knocked, and walked in. Swade was lying in his hospital bed, hooked up to all sorts of tubes and monitors. He was pale and gaunt. The doctor on duty told me that his condition was stable, that there was minimal swelling of the brain, but there was no way to be sure when he might come out of it. They had diagnosed his condition as a severe concussion. It could have been a lot worse, but they were contemplating putting him into an induced coma. It sometimes helped with the recovery in cases like this.

"Has he said anything at all?"

"A couple of times when I've been in here he's made a sort of groaning sound. And one of the nurses said he might have spoken a couple of words. But that was when they first brought him in. He's been dead quiet ever since, as far as I know." The doctor, who was young and probably

*292*

just out of medical school, clearly was embarrassed. "Sorry. Bad choice of words."

"Any chance I could talk to the nurse who heard him speak?"

"Sure, if she's still on duty. Let me go check."

The doctor returned shortly with a middle-aged Hispanic woman. I introduced myself and asked whether she had heard Ollie Swade say anything since he'd been admitted to the hospital.

"I wouldn't know about when he first came in, down in emergency. But up here, when we were transferring him from the gurney into this bed, he groaned and maybe said a couple of words. It was hard to tell. We were pretty busy getting him settled and then attaching him to the monitors and drips."

"Could you understand the words he said? Even a guess would help."

"We were real busy around here, and I wasn't paying all that much attention. But it was strange. I think he said something like 'durn loud.' Kept saying it over and over."

I grinned, and thanked the nurse. Durn loud? Maybe Ollie was going to make it after all. "If he starts talking again, please notify the officer out in the hall. I'm really anxious to speak with this man."

It was only later, on the way back to Sonoita, that it occurred to me what Ollie Swade might actually have said.

# Chapter 49

**M**aria wasn't happy when I announced at dinner that I was planning to spend the night at Ollie Swade's house.

"You said yourself that all you found in his place was a bunch of junk."

"I said that's what it looked like to Larry and me. But Dr. Rincon is coming tomorrow, and then we'll know for sure. In the mean time I don't want to take any chances that somebody might break into the place. I have a funny feeling about this."

"Funny how?" She didn't look amused.

"There are too many people involved with this thing. Given where Ollie had been digging, and maybe for a long time, and the history out there ..."

Maria raised her eyebrows. "You think this might have something to do with Scooter McLeod?"

"It's possible."

"What about Larry? Couldn't he pull the night duty?"

"He could, but he's been there all day and he deserves a break. I'll have him come back at dawn so I can catch a couple hours sleep before Rincon gets here. I expect by tomorrow night we'll know a lot more about all of this."

I got to the Swade place about seven-thirty. Larry was on the front porch taking in a sunset highlighted by thunderheads that had first risen in the late afternoon over the Santa Ritas. I parked next to his jeep, got out, and joined him on the porch. "Anything happening?"

"Nope. But I'm glad you got here because I'm starved. What about you? Did you get a chance to talk to Ollie?"

"I saw him, but he wasn't talking. When I was there he

didn't even move. Listen, you go on and get out of here. I'll see you in the morning."

I settled into one of the old wicker chairs on Ollie's porch to watch the last of the sunset. There were two or three lightning strikes followed by the distant rumble of thunder, but the storm quieted down before it got dark. The whole thing was too far away to bring any rain to the valley anyway, even if it had kept going. I went inside.

Nothing happened until about 11 o'clock, when Maria arrived with snacks, a thermos of coffee, and Boomer, who wagged his tail and gave me a lick in one ear. Maria hinted around that she might stay the night, but I put her off.

"What's wrong?"

"You'd be a distraction."

"That's what I had in mind."

"I know. Now get out of here. But if it's all right with you, I'll keep the dog."

~ ~ ~

I had no clear idea how long I'd been asleep when Boomer barked and woke me up. There was light coming in through the screen door from somewhere outside, and I heard the sound of a vehicle.

Somebody had started down the road toward the house.

I shook myself fully awake, then ducked down behind an overstuffed chair and rubbed my eyes, hoping to make out what sort of a vehicle it was. But the glare of the headlights was too bright. Suddenly the vehicle stopped, backed out onto the county road, and sped off. The driver must have seen something, most probably the county seal and star on the front door of my SUV. I regretted not having parked somewhere out of sight, but now it was too late. Big mistake.

I jumped in the Blazer. By the time I got out on the county blacktop the other vehicle was nothing but a pair of taillights fading into the distance. Then even they blinked out, and I realized the driver had decided to run in darkness. There was no moon to help. I radioed State Patrol, but there was nobody in the area. I gave chase along the same route where I had pursued a fleeing Ollie Swade earlier that day. It was ironic that my first two car chases of the year would be in exactly the same place.

Despite my best efforts, I never caught up. I drove on the county road to the junction with State 82, then took a guess and turned left. I drove clear back to Sonoita, where everything was dark and quiet except for the usual lights around the businesses, all of which were long-since closed down for the night. I never spotted the mysterious vehicle again, and I had no idea who might have been behind the wheel. One thing was for sure, though. It couldn't have been Ollie Swade.

# Chapter 50

**J**ulio Rincon and two assistants arrived at the Obregon homestead about nine o'clock the next morning. I was just finishing my third cup of coffee. Despite my best intentions, I hadn't managed to get any sleep at all. Larry had relieved me at the Swade place about 5 AM, so that Boomer and I got home in time to have breakfast with Maria. I tried to take a nap after she left for the post office, but it didn't happen. I just lay there, staring at the ceiling, thinking about last night and about the sheriff's admonition earlier in the day not to screw things up. Obviously, something big had slipped through my fingers.

Whoever had driven onto Ollie Swade's yard at three o'clock in the morning hadn't been there by accident. Somebody must have known, or at least suspected, that there was something valuable or perhaps incriminating in the old man's house. It was likely they also knew that Ollie wasn't there. But who was it? At least I'd protected the evidence, whatever it was.

Rincon rode with me to Ollie's place, while his assistants followed in the museum van. I asked the curator about his plans for the day.

"The first thing we'll do is a preliminary sort through everything in the house. Then we'll go back and catalogue objects of particular interest. It could take most of the day, depending on how much we find."

"That sounds good, and I hope you'll be liberal about deciding what things are interesting."

Rincon laughed. "You don't have to worry about that. Catching looters of state property happens all too rarely. If

Mr. Swade has been digging around on that Rocking M lease for as long as it appears, there's nothing I'd like better than to throw the book at him." Rincon paused. "I take that back. There is one thing I'd like better, and that is to catch the sonofabitch who's fencing the stuff. Pardon my language."

Once again I relieved Larry Hernandez on Ollie's front porch. I settled down to wait while the archaeologists went to work inside.

There was a mild breeze from the south, and the old windmill creaked and groaned, dribbling a little water into the rusted stock tank. The sky was an interrupted pale blue with no hint of a cloud, not even over the Huachucas or Santa Ritas. But then it wasn't ten o'clock yet, so it was too early to predict what the afternoon or evening might bring. On a local scale, even a good inch of rain wouldn't produce much of anything except mud and wet rocks on Ollie's land.

Two hours passed without a word from anybody inside, when I noticed a handful of cows and their calves hanging around a shed out behind the house. It occurred to me that they might be expecting to be fed. With so little natural grass left, Ollie might have resorted to buying feed just to keep his meager herd alive. That cost money, and it was no way to be in the cattle business. But maybe money wasn't as much of a problem for the old man as most people assumed.

I walked over to the shed and pulled open the door. I peered inside, waiting for my eyes to adjust to the darkness. I was unaware that two of the older cows had followed right behind me, and they promptly knocked me off my feet in an effort to get at the alfalfa hay stored inside. These animals were hungry, and with Ollie gone they would soon be starving. I made a mental note to set up a feeding schedule with Larry. One of us would have to come by regularly and put out a bale or two. Maybe I could talk Maria into helping out.

I carried part of a bale outside for the cows and their calves to eat. On a hunch, I went back inside, and it was only then that I noticed an old wooden trunk against one wall. I'd seen trunks like it in antique stores, the kind that the pioneers used. I bent down, pulled open the latch, and lifted the lid. At first glance it looked empty, but then I saw something old and rusty in the bottom, barely visible in the windowless gloom of the shed. I picked it up and carried it outside for a closer inspection.

It was a horseshoe, rusted almost to oblivion. But even in its present condition, I could see there was something odd about it. The metal plate was too wide and too thick. There was something wrong about the overall shape, too, but I couldn't put my finger on just what it was.

I went back inside the house. Julio Rincon was in the basement writing notes on a clipboard, standing amidst a pile of debris.

"Any luck?"

"Not much, I'm afraid. There are some chards of broken pottery that probably date to pre-Columbian times, but nothing intact. There's lots of newer stuff: purple glass, shell casings, a folding knife, things like that. I have no doubt Swade has been digging someplace around here, and probably for a long time. But there isn't much left here of any value or interest."

"What about that cardboard box I found in his van?"

"That's a different story. There were a couple of good spear points and some stone fetishes that could have been game pieces. They were mixed in with the usual assortment of junk, but at least we should be able to charge him with trafficking in historically significant artifacts. There will be enough to prosecute, but I'm disappointed we didn't find anything obviously dating to the Spanish period. You know, something to go along with the Clarksdale Bell that Maria discovered."

I held out the horseshoe I'd just retrieved from Ollie's shed. "What about this? I haven't ever seen one like this before."

The curator took the horseshoe and held it up to the light. "Where did you get this?" I noticed his hands were shaking.

"It was in Ollie's shed, out behind the house. I found it in a wooden trunk. Why? Could it be old?"

"Old, you say? That's an understatement. Deputy, you may just have hit the jackpot. This shoe came off a Spanish horse, or possibly a mule. The animal could easily have walked in this valley right around 475 years ago."

"No kidding. But why 475 years? I mean, why not 400 or 500?"

"Because it was 475 years ago that Francisco Vásquez de Coronado came north out of old Mexico."

"You mean the Spanish explorer? I didn't know he was around here."

"Nobody knows for sure just where he went, but it's a definite possibility. The whole thing is an unsolved mystery. The record of his expedition doesn't make it clear what particular route he followed when he crossed into what now is Arizona."

I was anxious to learn more. "Did Coronado write about his travels?"

"No, or at least nobody's ever found such a document. One of his soldiers, a man named Castañeda, wrote an account of the expedition, but it's pretty vague about just where they were when they got to this part of the world. For one thing, most of the place names Castañeda used don't mean anything in terms of modern geography. So there's a big debate. And it's an important one, because Castañeda described a lot about the native peoples they encountered, and anthropologists would love to be able to link those people with specific places."

"Weren't there other Spanish riders who came later than Coronado, who would have used that same kind of horseshoes?"

"You're right, of course. I'm not saying this *was* a horseshoe lost during the Coronado expedition, just that it *could* be. But it certainly speaks to an early Spanish presence around here, along with Maria's bell. And for sure we've caught Mr. Swade with something valuable. Funny it was in that old trunk out there, all by itself. He probably had no idea what he'd found."

I was curious about one other thing regarding the horseshoe, and I asked the curator about it. "That old shoe is made of iron, right?"

Rincon nodded.

"So why didn't it just rust completely away, after all this time?"

"Good question. I can think of two possibilities. First, it might have been buried someplace that was anaerobic – that is, a place without oxygen. That can happen in deep soil in certain sorts of bogs or marshes. The second possibility is that it actually hasn't been out in this country all that long."

"You mean like it might have been in a collection somewhere, maybe for centuries, and then somebody brought it out here and buried it?"

"Something like that."

"But why would anybody do that?"

Rincon shrugged. "I have no idea."

# Chapter 51

**B**y late morning the clouds had begun to build over the hills and mountains that surrounded the Sonoita Valley. Thunder started about eleven, and by noon the sky lit up and it began to rain. I was waiting under cover of Ollie's Swade's front porch when Julio Rincon came out to tell me they had finished sorting and cataloging what they had found in the old man's basement.

Rincon gave me a handwritten list. "I'd like to keep custody of these items for safekeeping up at the museum. You will see that it includes the horseshoe, along with the contents of that box you found in Swade's van."

"Sure, no problem. I have a custody form that you should sign. Did you find anything else in the shed?"

"Nope."

"Do you think I need to keep somebody posted out here?"

"I guess that's your department's business, but we did a pretty thorough search. It's unlikely there's any more evidence around. The only other possibility is that he buried stuff somewhere else on the property. I'm thinking of coming back out here with a metal detector some time in the next couple of days, just to take a look."

"That would be fine. I'll have Deputy Hernandez keep an eye out when he's patrolling the area, and we'll leave the crime scene tape around the house. Let me know when you might be coming out with the detector."

~ ~ ~

Maria was soaking wet when she came in to my office for a late lunch.

"What happened?"

305

"The rain came while I was putting the mail out in the boxes at Elgin."

"Why didn't you just get back in your car until the storm let up?"

"Because at least six people were circling around waiting for me to finish, that's why. One of them was Janet McLeod, and she acted kind of funny."

"What do you mean, funny?"

"Well, she's usually real chatty. But today she didn't say anything. She wouldn't even look me in the eye. She just grabbed her mail and drove off. Is something going on out there? At the Rocking M, I mean?"

I thought about that. There was something going on of course – like maybe the fact that her husband was a cattle rustler. But would Janet know about that? It didn't seem likely. On the other hand she might well have some idea about Sandy's money troubles, because it could be affecting their finances. I had not yet discussed the case of Sally Benton's Hereford bull with Maria, because rustling is such a serious local matter and I didn't want to put her on the spot.

"I'm not sure why Janet was upset. Maybe it was just the weather."

Maria raised her eyebrows. "Since when does rain make a rancher's wife grumpy? There's something you're not telling me, isn't there?"

"There may be a financial problem Janet knows about, but I can't be sure."

"And so you're not going to share it with me?"

"The case is in the hands of the District Attorney down in Nogales, so I probably shouldn't at this point."

"Then I probably shouldn't be wasting your time." She picked up what was left of her sandwich and stomped toward the door.

"Oh hell, Maria, come on back. I'm sorry about this.

It's just that the DA swore all of us to secrecy. And besides, I've got something interesting to tell you about what we found this morning out at Ollie's place."

She had one hand on the doorknob, but that stopped her. "What?"

I told her about the horseshoe.

"And Rincon thinks it might be really old?"

"Yep."

"As old as the Clarksdale Bell I found?"

"He didn't say, but I guess so."

Maria came back, sat down, and finished her sandwich. It was quiet for a while as we both listened to the rain on the roof. Thunder still rolled in the distance, but it sounded like the storm was receding.

"You know, there's something spooky about the San Carlos Wash. I felt it the first time I ever went down there."

"Spooky how?"

"I can't say exactly. But when I walk along that creek I always get the feeling that somebody or something is watching me. And now with the bell and the horseshoe, well, I wonder if maybe something happened out there a long time ago. Something important. It's almost like the place is haunted."

I had always thought of Maria as a rational person. It was one of many things I admired about her. And now she was talking about ghosts or something out along the San Carlos Wash? I had the good sense not to share these thoughts aloud, instead offering a logical explanation for her feelings.

"Ollie Swade has been spending a lot of time out there, and perhaps other people too. Maybe somebody actually has been watching you."

"No, that's not what I'm talking about. This is something different, something out of the past. I've never had a feeling like it anyplace else."

I decided to drop the matter. For one thing, I was pretty sure Maria was right. It seemed likely that something important *had* happened out there in the San Carlos Wash, a long time before the murder of Scooter McLeod. But was there a connection?

# Chapter 52

**T**he slopes of the Mustangs were loosing the last of their evening color, under a darkening gray-blue sky. The rains had long-since ended and a full moon, enormous and yellow, had broken the horizon behind the Dragoon Mountains off to the east. As had become our habit, Maria and I were sharing a beer and enjoying the view from her front porch before we went inside for dinner.

I wanted to probe her knowledge of southwestern history. "What do you know about Coronado?" It seemed like a nice neutral subject, and one I hoped would divert her attention from our unpleasant interaction earlier in the day about Janet McLeod.

"I took a class at the university about Spanish explorations in the New World. The professor gave several lectures about him. And I've been to that Coronado Monument place over on the south side of the Huachucas. They have a pretty good little museum there. Why?"

"When I found that horseshoe in Ollie Swade's barn today, Dr. Rincon said it could be from the Coronado era. He was pretty excited, so I just wondered."

"What I remember is that Coronado led this big expedition up out of Mexico into what is now the American Southwest. It was in 1540 or maybe 1541, I'm not sure which. They were looking for a place called Cibola that was supposed to have all this gold, but didn't. The next year they got as far as a place called Tiguex on the Rio Grande. I think it was someplace near present-day Albuquerque. Then they rode even farther east, out onto the Great Plains. But they didn't find any gold there either, and so they went back to Mexico, not in disgrace exactly but really disappointed."

"Where was Cibola?"

"I'm not sure, but I think it was supposed to be in eastern Arizona, north of the Gila River."

"So is it possible that Coronado could have been here? I mean right here in the Sonoita Valley?"

"I suppose it's possible, but nobody knows for sure just exactly where they went. Somebody on the expedition named Castañeda wrote a book about it. It was for sale in the visitor center over at the monument, and I bought a copy. It's around here someplace. There are notes in the back by different scholars."

"Did you read the book?"

"Some parts. I remember Castañeda talked about how they followed a river on the way north, but it isn't clear just what river. It might have been the San Pedro, in which case they were pretty close to here. But maybe it was the Santa Cruz, or even some other river. Apparently there is no physical evidence that can be directly tied to the expedition that might prove exactly what route they followed. So it's sort of a mystery, I guess."

"That's just what Dr. Rincon said this morning. And now we have a mystery inside a mystery."

"How do you mean?"

"Well, let's suppose that horseshoe in Ollie's shed did come from one of Coronado's animals. And let's suppose that Ollie found something else around here that was even more convincing, and he tried to sell it to Scooter McLeod back in 1995."

"And somehow that got Scooter killed?"

"That would be the other mystery I'm talking about."

After dinner, I was browsing through the book about Coronado, when the telephone rang. Maria was out in the barn tending her goats. I picked up the phone and identified myself. It was Sally Benton.

"Hi Sally. What's up? It's not your bull again, is it?"

"No, he's doing fine, thanks. But I just saw something out here I thought you should know about. You remember that old shack we rode past the other day? The one just across the fence on the Rocking M, down near the place where my bull was taken?"

"Sure I remember it. Why?"

"Well, you may recall I said I could see it from my window, and a funny thing happened this evening. It's a long ways off, but I swear I saw a light coming from down there. It was only there for a few minutes, and then it moved off. But you seemed interested in the place the other day, so I thought I'd let you know."

"Thanks. Maybe I'll go down there tomorrow. Just in case."

"In case what?"

"I won't know that until I get there."

"It was probably just some illegals trying to get out of the rain and dry off. We got soaked good today. Lyle Canyon is running hard."

I wasn't so sure about Sally's explanation for the light, knowing what I did about the history of that old line shack down in Lyle Canyon. But I decided for the time being not to share my suspicions. "Thanks, Sally, I'll let you know if I find anything."

# Chapter 53

**T**he next morning I called the Border Patrol station in Sonoita and told them about a possible break-in at the McLeod shack over in Lyle Canyon. My goal was to get a look in the old place, with a search warrant in hand, but to do it under the pretext of looking for border crossers. This way I hoped Sandy McLeod would not get suspicious about my real reasons for poking around down there.

I met Border Patrol Agent Virginia Dale at the turnoff to the Rocking M Ranch, and we drove to headquarters together, with her following behind in a late-model Dodge Durango. We pulled up in front of the McLeod home and got out. Dale was short and blond, somewhere in her early twenties. She had a round face and ruddy complexion, and looked like someone who would be facing weight problems later in life.

We went up to the door and I rang the bell. I hoped Janet might be home alone, so I could follow up on Maria's observation about her odd behavior the day before. But it was Sandy who appeared first, with Janet standing behind him. I introduced them both to Agent Dale and explained the reason for our visit. Sandy didn't seem interested in whatever might have been going on the night before over in Lyle Canyon. "You're right, it's probably just some illegals. We haven't paid any attention to that old place in years."

I thought about the light that Sally Benton had seen. "Is the power still on down there?"

Sandy shook his head. "No. We lost the poles in a fire years ago, and never put them back up. Go ahead on down there if you want, but all you're going to find is an old empty shack." Then he muttered something about needing to get in to the office, and more or less shut the door in my face. I thought it was odd he didn't make his usual pitch about leasing me a suite in his shopping mall. Maybe it was the presence of the Border Patrol that put him off.

The road east down the Babocomari River was well-maintained and showed no damage from the recent rain. The same could not be said for the fork leading south up into Lyle Canyon. It was little more than two muddy ruts squeezed in between a sacaton floodplain and the adjacent slope. There were fresh tire tracks that had been made since yesterday's rain. I regretted having to drive over them, but there didn't seem to be a choice. At one point I got out for a closer inspection.

Agent Dale stopped immediately behind me, and we checked the area together. The tracks suggested that a vehicle had passed in both directions, so it seemed unlikely anyone would still be at the cabin. We got back in our respective vehicles, and continued driving. After about a mile the road climbed out of the bottomland and up onto the adjacent mesa. I could see the cabin as soon as I crested the rise. The grass there was fresh and green, and it showed little sign of any recent grazing. The tire tracks were still there, and now we could avoid them by driving off to one side. It was not something I did ordinarily, because good manners said you never drove over somebody else's grass in cattle country. But this was not an ordinary occasion, and I had noticed before that Border Patrol personnel pretty much drove wherever they wanted to go in any event. So we avoided the old tracks as we carved our own.

The one-room structure was about two hundred yards away, and just inside the boundary fence separating McLeod from Benton land. I drove carefully and slowly, watching for any signs of movement. There were none, and in about three minutes I parked and got out of my vehicle. Agent Dale did the same, and we approached the shack together.

She called out "hello in the house," but there was no response.

I suggested we walk around the old shack before going inside, and she agreed. She headed left toward the back of the place, and I went right, toward the front door. The only tire tracks I found were the single set we had followed in, suggesting that the place was visited only rarely. There was one set of footprints leading to and from the door, which was ajar. I was pretty sure it had been closed the day Sally Benton and I had been riding on the other side of the fence. The footprints were good sized, without any obvious tread, and rounded at both the toe and heel. They definitely were not made by cowboy boots, and the soles were not made for any sort of traction. It was unlikely a border crosser had left the prints because those people, even the drug runners, rarely traveled alone. The tire tracks didn't make any sense either, unless there had been some sort of a pick up.

Agent Dale came around from behind the shack and joined me at the doorway. I asked her if she had seen anything out in back.

"Not a thing. Let's check inside."

I had hoped to avoid this, but before I could say anything she pulled a flashlight out of her belt, stepped to the door, and peered inside.

"Anything?" I asked from over her right shoulder.

"Nope. Place looks empty, and there's only the one room."

Sometimes luck plays a role in how things work out, and this turned out to be one of those times. Just when it seemed I was going to have to tell Agent Dale the actual reason for our visit – and I *really* didn't want to do that – the radio in her Durango came to life. It was an urgent call about a possible group of border crossers spotted behind the winery in Elgin, not all that far from our present location.

"I'd better get over there," she said. "And besides, there doesn't seem to be anything going on here any more, if there ever was."

"Sure, sounds good. But I think I'll stay here for a while and just poke around. I'll let you know if I find anything. Thanks for your help."

~ ~ ~

I congratulated myself on remembering to bring water and plaster for making casts of the tire tracks and footprints. I mixed a batch of solution and poured it over the best examples of each. The material would set while I explored the shack. It was unlikely the casts would be all that useful, but you never knew.

I walked to the doorway of the little cabin and looked inside. The place was a mess, but Agent Dale was right, it was not a human mess. A pile of vegetation better than four feet tall occupied one corner. It was a woodrat nest. These plump rodents obviously had long-since taken over the cabin, and the size of the nest was testimony to the years that must have passed since the last person had lived there. The inside of the shack was shrouded in cobwebs.

A rough countertop with a small sink and an old derelict hotplate occupied the back corner of the cabin opposite the woodrat nest. An old-fashioned hand pump was attached to the counter next to the sink, mostly rusted but with bits of olive-green paint still showing through. Other furnishings included a pot-bellied stove stuck back in one darkened corner, a pair of small cots, and the remains of two wooden chairs. There was no bathroom. The shack obviously had provided sparse living conditions even in the best of times, and those times were long gone.

The mattresses were shredded, and bits of stuffing were scattered everywhere, as if the place had been recently ransacked. Other than that, I could see no sign of recent human occupancy.

I walked inside. The first clue that something was wrong was a strange rubbery feeling under my right boot. Then came a great blurred frenzy of hissing and flailing. The next thing I actually remember was being outside the cabin, sitting down in the mud. It had been a full-out adrenalin rush, and my heart raced. Just inside the cabin, with its head and neck pulled back into a taut arc, was the biggest diamondback rattlesnake I had ever seen, still rattling furiously. The thickest part of its body was bigger around than my calf.

I struggled to my feet and looked down. There were two wet spots about six inches above the right cuff of my jeans. I carefully pulled up my pants leg and saw fang marks in the leather. It was pure luck that I had stepped on the snake close enough to its head that it couldn't reach up very high when it struck. Never again would I have a bad thought about cowboy boots.

It was a standoff that ended peacefully enough. I kept a snake stick in the back of the Blazer for just such occasions. It had an adjustable noose at one end that I managed to slip over its head without incident. Then it was just a matter of picking the animal up and hauling it outside. The rattler thrashed violently back and forth, but it could not escape the noose. I carried the animal about a hundred yards away from the shack, and released it under a small mesquite. I wouldn't say we parted friends, but at least neither of us was hurt.

People say rattlesnakes are useful around ranches and ranch buildings because they eat rats and mice. They're right about that. I also could respect these animals as a part of the natural scene, whether or not they justified their existence by killing things we didn't want around. But still, I've always found it hard to actually *like* something that turns your insides to jelly, and I have deep suspicions about people who claim to have a fondness for snakes of any sort. That includes Maria. Maybe it's the only thing about her I just don't understand.

This particular diamondback probably had grown large and fat by eating woodrats, and I didn't expect to find any left in the cabin. However, these plump rodents are notorious for accumulating odd bits of things in their nests. Some people call them packrats for this reason. Scooter McLeod and his friend Barton Hampstead may well have been the last human occupants of the shack. If they had left behind any unusual objects, there was a good chance the first woodrat on the scene would have added them to its nest.

I set to work, systematically taking apart the nest and setting aside anything that looked out of the ordinary. It was painstaking work, not least because I couldn't rule out the possibility that there could be another snake or two living inside.

It took over an hour, and by the time I was finished the cabin floor was littered with an assortment of items that could be traced to people. In addition to multiple bits of broken glass and scraps of aluminum foil, there were two pop bottles, three tin cans, a spoon, a corroded D-cell flashlight battery, a small folding knife, and the remains of an old pocket-sized transistor radio. All of these things clearly were contemporary. But there was one object I could not identify, and it looked old. It was metal, about two inches long, pointed at one end and hollow at the other. Based on the blue-green color, it must have been made of copper. I put it in my shirt pocket.

Careful inspection of the rest of the one-room shack

turned up nothing more of interest. I was ready to leave when I remembered the potbellied stove. It probably held only ashes, but maybe there was something inside that had not completely burned. Then I remembered that Scooter and his friend had used this old place in the summer, and maybe they'd never built any fires. I tried to open the door on the front side of the stove, but it was corroded shut. I got a screwdriver out of the tool box I kept in the Blazer, and by working all around the edges I finally succeeded in getting the old door to swing open on what remained of its hinges.

I bent over and looked inside, half expecting to discover that a scorpion or a spider had taken up residence. Nothing moved, but there was something stuck way in the back. I reached in and pulled it out. It was a metal box, about twelve inches square and four inches deep. I pried it open and looked inside. What it contained was a small book, wrapped in heavy plastic. Surprisingly, it seemed to be intact. Evidently the old stove had been sufficiently sealed off that nothing – and obviously no one – had gotten inside.

I carried the book out into the sun, pulled it carefully out of the plastic bag, and opened the front cover, which appeared to be made of leather or vinyl. The first page included just three lines:

Jeremiah McLeod, Jr.
Rocking M Ranch
Summer, 1995

The pages of the notebook were old and brittle. I handled each one only by its edges in order not to disturb either fingerprints or possible DNA. Under strict protocol I probably should have delivered the whole thing untouched to the forensics lab down in Nogales. But I just couldn't help myself.

The notebook was filled with handwriting, and there were dates at the top of every second or third page. I had found a diary. Some of the entries included maps and drawings. I skipped to the back page, which was blank, and thumbed my way forward until I found the last one that included any writing. The final entry in the diary of the late Scooter McLeod was dated July 17. I read that last page, and then carefully put the whole thing back into the metal box.

Now I was pretty sure who had been around that old shack the night before, and why. If I was right, there was no time to waste.

# Chapter 54

**M**y cell drew a blank, so I got on the radio and asked Nogales dispatch to get me through to the sheriff. He was surprised to learn what had just turned up in Lyle Canyon.

"I'll be damned."

"Believe me, I wasn't expecting it either. Listen, I need your help with a search warrant, and probably an arrest warrant too, just in case. And my gut tells me we need to move right away on this, in case our suspect decides to skip town."

"I'll get right on it. Who besides me do you want from down here?"

"You're coming?"

"Damn straight, and I'd better bring Joe Ortega along too."

"Well, then, I suppose nobody else. But I'll take Larry if that's all right. He deserves to be in on this. I know the police are going to have to be there too, since its their jurisdiction, and I hope you can persuade them to meet us a little ways from the house. We don't want to spook the guy ahead of time. Do you think you can get this set up in the next couple of hours?"

"I'll do my best. I know their chief of detectives from way back, so he and I will be in on this. And I expect he'll mobilize substantial backup. From what you've described there shouldn't be much of a problem getting the warrants. Good grief, Cal, this really is hard to believe."

We agreed to meet at the Sonoita office and drive up together.

I loaded up the Blazer with the things I had found in

the shack. I left everything else inside the cabin, and wrapped yellow tape around the whole structure. Then I radioed Larry, who was someplace down near Patagonia, and told him what was up.

Nobody was home back at the McLeod's place, but I found Angel Corona out in their horse barn, working on a saddle. I told him the old shack in Lyle Canyon was off limits until further notice, and I made up a story about the real reason.

One thing was puzzling me as I drove back to Sonoita. Why hadn't that visitor from the night before already looked in the stove? Then it occurred to me. This may have been the first time that a rattlesnake had helped to secure a crime scene. It must have scared the pants off the guy, assuming he'd been wearing any.

~ ~ ~

Three hours later I was driving up a familiar winding road in east Tucson, with Larry as a passenger. Luis and Joe Ortega were following behind us, and everybody was armed. As promised, the sheriff had acted quickly and effectively in securing the warrants and mobilizing the police. Chief of Detectives Art Blumenthal and three uniforms were set to meet us about a quarter mile below the house. It seemed to me like overkill, but clearly that wasn't my call. The Tucson part of the team would not approach until our arrival, but they would pursue and apprehend the suspect should he try to exit the scene. There was no reason he should guess we were on to him, but neither was there any guarantee he'd be at home. We'd know soon enough.

I pulled in behind an unmarked cruiser and a police van parked about where I had expected to find them. We all got out of our vehicles. Luis and Detective Blumenthal greeted each other like old buddies. Larry and I were introduced to Tucson Police Officers Becky Ramirez, Tim

O'Rourke, and Mike Preston. Ramirez acted like a veteran. O'Rourke looked like a rookie. I couldn't get a bead on Preston.

I described what we would be searching for in the house – something big enough that it would be difficult to hide. Then, with a nod from Luis, I suggested a plan of action. We would drive into the compound together, with the Sonoita contingent parking in front of the garage door, and the Tucson cops using their cruiser and van to block the driveway. Larry and Preston would go directly up onto a small knoll at the back of the house to wait and watch, in case the occupant tried to flee. That proved to be a fateful decision. Ramirez, O'Rourke, and I would go to the front door and ring the bell, while the sheriff, Ortega, and Blumenthal would wait out of sight. Because the city department had jurisdiction, Ramirez and O'Rourke would show the search warrant if anybody answered, and they would enter first and secure the house whether or not it was occupied. Only then would I conduct the actual search.

Detective Blumenthal approved the plan, and Joe Ortega grunted something that I took as positive if not enthusiastic. Blumenthal also insisted that we all put on Kevlar vests, and the sheriff agreed. I was not altogether happy about this, because I thought we might get something useful out of suspect before we raised his suspicions.

~ ~ ~

Things started out like they were supposed to.

Bartie Hampstead was home, and he came to the door after the second ring. He had on blue jeans, a red t-shirt, and black running shoes – nothing like what he'd been wearing on my previous visits. He looked startled. "Yes?" Then he recognized me standing behind the two uniforms. "You again? Haven't we been all through this? I've already told you everything I can remember about Scooter McLeod. And why in God's name did you need to bring the local police this time?"

"Mr. Barton Hampstead?" asked Officer Ramirez.

"Of course. You obviously know that. Really, I just don't see ..."

"Mr. Barton Hampstead, we have a warrant to search your house and grounds." Officer O'Rourke held out the document. "Please step aside and let us in. And you're not to disturb anything until we have completed our work."

Hampstead accepted the papers, glanced briefly at the signature on the last page, and stepped backwards into his living room. "Well, you might as well come on in. Let's get this over with, and the sooner the better. I have nothing to hide." He gestured toward his extensive collection of Native American and Spanish-era objects. "All of this was obtained legally, as I have explained on numerous occasions."

Officer O'Rourke stayed with Hampstead while Ramirez and I started through the house. The shelves in the main living area were cluttered with artifacts as they had been on my previous visits, but I didn't see anything new. Certainly there was no sign of the extraordinary object that Scooter McLeod's diary suggested ought to be someplace in the house – assuming it hadn't already been sold.

I moved next to the master suite, which included a bathroom and a large walk-in closet. I looked under the bed and inside the bathroom cabinets, but nothing unusual turned up. There were three large storage trunks in the closet, but they were empty. I found an opening in the closet ceiling that led up into an attic crawl space. It took a good half hour to explore all of that area. It was dusty and hot - and a good place to hide something – but there was nothing up there.

I met Becky Ramirez back in the main living area. She had gone through the kitchen, including all the cabinets and a large pantry, with an equal lack of success. There were no other rooms on the main floor.

I had thought next of going to the garage, but then I noticed the stairs leading down to what presumably was a basement. I invited Officer O'Rourke to accompany me while Ramirez stayed with Hampstead, who was sitting in one of the large leather chairs in the living room. He looked bored, and not the least bit worried. I wondered if we were on a cold trail. There were any number of other places the man could have hidden his treasures.

The basement was unfinished, and it was cluttered with the usual sorts of things such places tend to accumulate. It took a long time to go through the whole mess, including a dozen or so boxes full of clothing that were more appropriate for a place like Connecticut than they were for Arizona. There also were cartons full of books and magazines. I decided the man was a compulsive packrat, which was ironic in light of my experiences with the real thing just that morning.

There was a door on one wall of the basement, and it was locked.

I went to the base of the stairwell and called up. "Mr. Hampstead? Could you come down here please? I need to have you unlock a door."

"Just a minute. I'll get my keys from the bedroom."

Barton Hampstead came downstairs slowly and with apparent nonchalance, followed by Officer Ramirez. He inserted his key into the lock, swung the door open, and stepped back. I reached inside, fumbling unsuccessfully for a light switch.

Hampstead explained. "You won't find a switch. There's a string hanging from the light socket. Just go on in and you'll find it."

O'Rourke and I walked into the darkened chamber. The next thing I knew, Becky Ramirez came tumbling in behind us and landed heavily at my feet. The door slammed shut, and I heard the sound of a key in the lock. We were trapped, and it was totally dark.

Becky Ramirez struggled to her feet. "Shit! That was all my fault."

"What the hell happened?"

"As soon as you went inside he just grabbed me and threw me inside."

I found the light string and pulled it, illuminating a finished room lined with shelves on brackets attached to the walls. The shelves were cluttered with more artifacts, but again there was no sign of the object of our search — not that I spent that much time looking. I tried the door, first the knob and then the whole thing with my shoulder, but it would not open. We shouted for help, but there was no response.

Things were very quiet for a time, and then I heard the distant but unmistakable sound of gunshots. Both O'Rourke and I put our shoulders to the closet door, but it still would not budge. Then I heard a voice, not all that close.

"Cal, are you down here?" It was Larry, probably at the head of the stairs.

I needed to warn him, and did so as loudly as I could. "Hampstead locked us in a closet down here, and took off! I think he has a key. I heard gunshots. Are you all right?"

There was a pause. "I'll be right back."

Another minute or two passed, and then I heard a key being inserted into the lock, and the door swung open. Larry was standing there, and he didn't look right.

"What happened?"

"He had a gun and I had to ... and I shot him. I didn't mean to do it, but he came at me with a pistol and fired it."

*326*

"Are you okay? What about Hampstead?"

"I think he must have hit my vest. I'm fine, but he's not. My god, Cal, I've never even used my gun except at the range, and ..."

This was not the time for a discussion with Larry about his experiences with firearms. "Where is he?"

"In the kitchen. He's in the kitchen. That's where ..."

I ran upstairs, with everybody else following me.

Barton Hampstead lay on his back in front of the refrigerator. He was alive, but just barely. A large dark stain was spreading across the front of his shirt. His breathing was raspy and irregular, and he was blowing bloody bubbles. Luis, Detective Blumenthal, and Mike Preston were standing over him. Preston was in the process of holstering his sidearm. It was obvious that the man no longer posed a threat.

The sheriff turned to me. "We've called for an ambulance. Did you find anything in the house?"

I ignored the question. Instead I knelt at Hamsptead's side, bent close to his left ear, and asked: "Where is it?"

Hampstead actually grinned, but he didn't say anything.

"Come on man, we both know your dying here. Tell me where it is. You want to be famous don't you?"

That seemed to work, because he stopped grinning and his eyes took on an eerie far-away look. "It's in my car, out in the garage. I was leaving." He took several more ragged breaths. "You promise to tell them I found it?"

"Yes. But why did you have to kill him?"

Barton coughed. Blood flowed from one corner of his mouth, running down the side of his face and onto the floor. "It was mine, that's why."

Another bloody cough. "It was mine, and he just wanted to give it away, ... to some museum or something. I didn't want to do it, but I had to. You can see that, can't you? I had no choice. It was mine."

"How did Scooter end up buried in his truck?"

Barton Hampstead did not answer. He only repeated himself. "It was mine."

"It was you at the cabin the other night, wasn't it? Why did you wait so long to search that place?"

Again, there was no answer. Hampstead didn't say anything, ever again. He just gurgled and then exhaled one last time.

~ ~ ~

Barton Hampstead drove a late-model Range Rover. I could see nothing on the front or back seats. The rear cargo area was stacked high with cardboard boxes, and on top of one of the boxes there was something wrapped in a towel. I opened the back hatch, reached in, and carefully unfolded the towel.

The object that lay before me was metal, and it looked very old. It was rusted and covered with dents, but any schoolchild would have recognized the domed crown and narrow upturned brim. It was a helmet all right, and this particular one was inlaid with fine patterns of silver, gold, and brass. These were relatively untarnished, and doubtless they had helped retain the original shape.

My hands were shaking as I wrapped the helmet back up in its towel, and carried it out to the Blazer.

Luis had been outside talking with Art Blumenthal. He saw me and walked over. "Is that it?"

"Could be."

"Can I see it?"

I laid the towel and its contents on the hood of my vehicle, and carefully unwrapped it. The sheriff leaned in for a closer look. "Wow. Do you suppose that really belonged to Coronado?"

"Maybe. We'll have to wait on the experts for an answer to that one."

# Chapter 55

**T**he ambulance came and went, with the body of Barton Hampstead on board. The crime scene was unusual to say the least, as well as unusually busy. For one thing, Larry Hernandez had been way out of his jurisdiction when he shot Barton Hampstead, and so lots of extra brass from the Tucson police had showed up, including a pair of detectives from Tucson Internal Affairs. They interviewed Larry about the shooting, following department protocol. Larry told the detectives that at first he had stayed outside as instructed. But eventually he'd begun to wonder what was going on, and he'd left his post on the little knoll behind the house and come inside. There he encountered Hampstead in the kitchen, and they had exchanged pistol shots. It seemed like a clear case of self-defense, and one of the detectives said as much, even though they weren't supposed to until the case was closed. Sheriff Mendoza agreed strongly and vociferously, but it didn't seem to help Larry all that much. He clearly was still shook up.

With permission from the sheriff, I made another phone call. About an hour later, Dr. Rincon and a half dozen archaeologists from the State Museum showed up. They huddled with the Tucson cops, and agreed on a plan.

It was an open question as to who eventually would own the artifacts, pending a search for Hampstead's will and for his heirs, if there were any. Artifacts originally taken from public land belonged to the state, of course, but that would be almost impossible to prove after the fact. Rincon's people photographed everything and left it in place for the time being, under assurance that the police would keep the house under guard. Everything, that is, except the helmet. Rincon argued, successfully, that it was very fragile and of incalculable value to historians and archaeologists. He would take it to the museum vault for safekeeping.

About eight o'clock somebody came with sandwiches and coffee. Two hours later the archeologists, the crime scene investigators, and the internal affairs team had completed their work. Luis met briefly with Larry and me in Barton Hampstead's driveway, while the Tucson police locked up the house.

Larry clearly was still upset, so Luis did his best to assure the man. "Don't worry about this. You shot in self-defense. There will be a hearing and some paperwork, but you have my word the department will back you one hundred percent. In a couple of weeks this will all be over."

"I'll be on paid leave?"

"Yes, but that's just routine. And congratulations, Cal. You have solved a very cold case, and they're the hardest kind. I'll admit I had my doubts about this one from the start. But stumbling onto Scooter McLeod's old diary was the key, wasn't it? Oh, and speaking of the McLeods, I have some interesting news about Sandy. Give me a call sometime tomorrow when you get a chance."

It had been a very long day for the two of us from the Sonoita Valley, one of whom had suffered a life-changing trauma. I told the sheriff I'd talk to him tomorrow, then turned and put my arm around Larry. "I'm bushed. Let's go home."

# Chapter 56

**M**aria and I were on her patio sharing a single beer. It was well past midnight. There was no wind, and it was dead quiet except for a chorus of spadefoot toads that had found a rain pool in which to breed somewhere down the San Carlos Wash. Scattered clouds filtered the light from the moon, casting mottled shadows across the Sonoita plain, like black sheep in a gray pasture.

I brought her up to speed on the bizarre case of Barton W. Hampstead III, and I was surprised at her first question.

"Did you ever have to kill anybody?"

"Not around here, maybe in Afghanistan. But that was sort of long distance, so you couldn't be sure who actually did it. I haven't experienced what's going on with Larry tonight, which is what you're asking about, right?"

"Of course it is."

"Luis and the Tucson cops were good about it, but I think he's pretty shook. Maybe the worst part is he has to be on leave until the case is settled, so he'll just be sitting around thinking about what happened."

I sipped from the bottle and handed it to Maria. No doubt she had a hundred more questions, but maybe she sensed I wasn't feeling all that talkative.

"You're a hero."

"How's that?"

"Don't be obtuse. You solved two mysteries today, one dating back twenty years. The other one has been around for better than four centuries. Tell me the name of the last deputy sheriff in Santa Cruz County that did something even a little bit like that."

I grinned in spite of myself and put an arm around her.

She leaned closer. "So now that I've successfully buttered you up, can I ask you about a couple of things?"

"Okay, I guess so. Sure."

"Well first, how did Scooter McLeod end up in that truck?"

"Good question. I asked Hampstead about that, but he died without telling me anything. They must have been in the truck together, and Hampstead hits him in the head with the rock hammer. That part is easy. The hard part is what happened afterwards."

"I've got a theory. Mind if I try it out on you? After all, I'm the one that found him."

"Say, that's right. If it hadn't been for you and Boomer ..."

"So here's my idea. They're in the truck and Hampstead kills Scooter with his rock hammer, because they've found the helmet and had a big fight about what to do with it. They're in the San Carlos Wash looking for more artifacts, when a flash flood comes around the bend. It happens so fast and so unexpectedly that Hampstead has no time to do anything but escape from the pickup before he drowns."

"Sounds reasonable. But then why didn't he come back the next day and get rid of the body?"

Maria paused. "All right, how about this? He does come back, but there's no sign of the truck because side of the wash has collapsed in the flood and buried it. So he figure's he's safe. He gathers up his stuff from the cabin, including the Coronado helmet, gets in his car and leaves the ranch without anybody spotting him. The next thing anybody knows he's back at Yale in time for summer school."

"Well however it happened, Hampstead made one big mistake."

"What was that?"

"He couldn't make himself get rid of the helmet, probably because of his giant ego."

"Ego is part of it I suppose, and maybe greed. But there's something else going on with people like him that hoard stuff."

This puzzled me. "What do you mean?"

"It's a type of personality I've run into among biologists and archaeologists. They just have to collect things and then live surrounded by their possessions. I had a prof once who collected butterflies, and he was a real expert. Turns out he also collected stamps and coins and matchbook covers. He even collected license plates."

"License plates?"

"Sure, he'd keep a running list of license plates from different states that he spotted as he drove around. And when he'd tallied up all fifty states, then he'd start over again. You've heard of crazy people that die and somebody finally gets into their house and discovers it's jammed to the ceiling with newspapers, old magazines, empty boxes, rubber bands, you name it? They just can't throw anything away. Well, it's the same thing with people like Hampstead, except their collections are valuable. And if you're rich like him, then all the value is in the possession."

"So to somebody like him just *having* Coronado's helmet was more important than any fame or glory that might come from sharing it?"

"Exactly."

I was skeptical. "Maybe you're right, but from the way he was acting just before he died, he seemed pretty interested in the fame and glory part of it too."

I yawned, but Maria didn't take the hint. "I guess the thing that is really bothering me, if I have your story right, is this: Why didn't Hampstead find the diary in that old shack? Surely he must have seen Scooter writing in it. Why didn't he think to go back in there and look? Didn't you say he's been poking around down in this country for years after that last summer with Scooter?"

"That's what Sandy said. And I've been wondering the same thing. I guess he thought he was safe. He had the helmet and whatever else they had dug up in the San Carlos Wash. Nobody had discovered Scooter's body, and the case was closed. Or so it seemed until you and Boomer made your discovery. It must have been a helluva shock when I showed up at his door with the news."

Maria nodded. "And that got him mobilized. I mean then he knew something might turn up, so he went back to the cabin for one last look. And, do you think it was Hampstead that came into Ollie Swade's yard that night you were guarding the place?"

"I expect so, but we'll probably never know."

"How much do you suppose Ollie was involved in all of this?"

"Good question, Maria. Maybe we'll find out, if he ever wakes up. I don't think there's any doubt Ollie knew that Scooter and Hampstead were on the trail of something. That's why he tried to sell them some of the junk he'd dug up on his own, and I'm sure that's why he has kept digging around in the San Carlos Wash himself. But if I had to guess I'd say Ollie was only a bit player in this whole thing. He's only interested in money, not in hoarding. And while he's a grumpy old guy, and sort of weird, I don't think he's a killer."

~ ~ ~

We were still outside, maybe an hour later, when a coyote howled from someplace far off in the Huachucas. Boomer, who had been asleep on the patio, raised his head and said 'woof.' He'd heard coyotes many times before. He knew from the way their tracks smelled that they were relatives, and a little part of him was jealous. Those were the real dogs out there, doing real dog business. All he ever did was lie around the house waiting for Maria to come home. That other kind of dog had to work hard for a living, and it had to stay outside in the heat and the rain and the cold. The coyote howled again. Boomer gave one more little woof, then put his head down on the bricks and went back to sleep.

I tried to wrap things up. "So, what are your other questions?"

"They'll keep. You're tired and a bit troubled, even though you've got no reason, and I think I know a way to distract you."

"I was hoping you might."

# Chapter 57

**I** was surprised to get a wake-up call from Luis early the next morning, and doubly so when I learned he was at the office in Sonoita.

The sheriff was apologetic. "I know it's the weekend, and I know you had a long night to say the least, but there's somebody here that needs to talk to you. It's kind of important."

I rolled out of bed and began the process of rubbing the sleep out of my eyes. Maria barely moved. "I'll be right there. Just give me a minute to get dressed and grab a cup of coffee."

"Skip the coffee. I'll get some going down here."

Clearly, something was up.

~ ~ ~

The sheriff met me at the office door, and there was another man behind him. He wore a dark suit that was wrong for summer and pretty much wrong for Sonoita no matter what the season.

"Sorry I'm late."

Luis nodded to the man in the suit, but spoke to me. "No problem. This is Special Agent Barkley from the FBI. He's from their Tucson office."

That explained the suit, but why was he here?

Barkley came forward and shook my hand. His grip was firm, but slightly damp. "Pleased to meet you, Deputy. And I understand congratulations are in order. That was good work you did solving that old murder case. I'm here about something else, but I think it involves the same family."

"How's that?"

337

"I'm here to talk about a case of livestock theft."

At first I wondered why the FBI would be involved in a rustling case. Then the light came on. Something funny must have turned up in Sandy McLeod's finances.

"You mean about Sally Benton's bull?"

"That's right," interjected Luis. "We've been able to trace the transfer of $250,000 from a bank in Mexico City to one of McLeod's accounts in Arizona. It was complicated as hell because the money apparently was moved several times on both sides of the border. And then most recently there was a transfer of $200,000 from one of McLeod's corporations into an account belonging to Ray and Vicki Salerno."

Barkley didn't seem all that pleased that the sheriff had inserted himself into the conversation. "I'm not sure your deputy needs to know all those details, Sheriff." Then he turned to me. "But in any case, what can you tell me about that?"

There was something about the FBI guy that rubbed me the wrong way, which I suppose was the reason I got a little smart-ass. "There's probably not much you don't already know."

"Why don't you just tell me about it anyway?"

I looked at Luis, who gave me a barely perceptible nod.

"Well, I think it all fits. McLeod is a local real estate developer. He seems to be in a financial bind, and Ray Salerno is one of his biggest backers, so that would explain the payment. A while back a prize bull belonging to a lady named Sally Benton went missing, and the next thing I learned about it was when the foreman at the McLeod ranch came to see me. He had Sally Benton's bull in his barn, and he told me a story about how it had turned up in Mexico. Do you need me to tell you that story too?"

Luis probably could see I was heading for trouble, and did his best to calm the waters. "Please tell the man everything you know, Cal."

I proceeded to relate what Angel had told me about the bull ending up in the hands of an influential and wealthy Mexican landowner, and how it had gotten back on this side of the border.

Barkley nodded. "The sheriff tells me you have some plant evidence that might have a bearing on this case?"

I thought he looked skeptical.

"That's right. Sally showed me a place on her ranch where the bull likely was rustled, and it had some very unusual grass. I collected some of that same grass from underneath Sandy McLeod's pickup. I've got it here in the office."

"We're going to need that evidence, Deputy. Could you get it for me please?"

Again, Luis gave a positive nod. I went to a locked cabinet, removed several plastic evidence bags, and placed them on my desk. Agent Barkley gave them only a cursory glance, and then turned back to me.

"Everything you've told me is consistent with what we have learned. But I am wondering about something."

"What's that?"

"I'm wondering why you didn't suspect this Angel Corona of taking the bull himself."

Here it comes, I thought. It would be easier to go after a Hispanic ranch foreman than to take on a member of one of Arizona's most prominent families.

The sheriff was squirming in his chair. Barkley stood silent and motionless. Clearly the ball was in my court.

"I thought about that, of course. But there's at least two things wrong with that theory. First, if Angel had taken the bull, why did he get it back and then come to tell me about it?"

"And the other thing?"

"Angel Corona is an honest man. I've known him all

my life, and so has my family."

Luis Mendoza grinned, but it was Agent Barkley who replied.

"That's hardly evidence, Deputy. But I take your first point. And to tell the truth we'd pretty much come to the same conclusion because of what our investigation uncovered about Mr. McLeod's financial dealings."

"So what happens next?"

"We've shared what we know with the appropriate Mexican authorities, and it's up to them whether and how to pursue the middle man who got the bull to its new owner. As for McLeod, we're planning to raid his home and offices day after tomorrow, to search for more records of his financial dealings. And we'll probably arrest him for international theft and fraud. That's one of the reasons I'm here, since it will be happening in your territory."

"What's the other reason?"

"To take this plant evidence."

Without saying another word, Special Agent Barkley picked up the plastic bags, put them in his briefcase, and pulled out a piece of paper. "We both need to sign this chain-of-evidence slip. Do you want to be there when we go out to the McLeod place?"

"You bet I do. And I have a favor to ask."

"What's that?"

"Well, I understand that you'll probably need Angel Corona to testify when this case comes to trial. But in the mean time, could you leave him out of it?"

"No guarantees on that, but we'll try. Why does it matter?"

"Because," interjected Luis, "even if you arrest Sandy McLeod he's going to be out on bail right away, and he could make life really difficult for his foreman. Angel's an old man who's already had plenty of trouble in his life." The sheriff turned to me. "You've got my word on this one.

We'll keep him out of it for as long as possible."

Barkley clearly was ready to leave. "Well I guess that's it for now. See you in a couple of days."

The man was already at the door when the sheriff spoke up. "Can you give me a minute alone with my deputy? I want to talk to him about a couple of other cases."

Barkley shrugged. "Sure. I'll be outside."

# Chapter 58

As soon as we were alone, the sheriff took the opportunity to try to calm me down. He actually poured me a cup of coffee, and then he ordered me to sit down. "He's just doing his job. And frankly in this case I'm just as glad, because now the whole thing will be handled by the feds. Sort of lets us off the hook for the bad feeling this is bound to generate in the county, no matter how it turns out."

I wasn't buying it, because I wouldn't have minded at all being the one who threw the book at Sandy McLeod. But I decided to change the subject.

"What else? You said you wanted to talk to me about other cases?"

"Mainly just to tell you again what a great job you did tracking down Barton Hampstead. Thanks. Oh, and I had a call from the hospital last night. Ollie Swade is in an induced coma, so it's going to be a while before we find out what connection he might have had with Hampstead, or with Scooter McLeod for that matter."

"I hope he comes out of it all right. And not just for what he might be able to tell us. In spite of it all, I kind of like that old geezer."

"Why? I thought you really had it in for looters like him."

"You're right, I do. And from what Dr. Rincon said about the stuff he had, he was really tearing things up over in the San Carlos Wash. So I don't know, Luis, it's just that he seems like a really sad case. We talked once about what it used to be like around here, before it got all cluttered up. I kinda' feel sorry for him. "

If the sheriff had any clue what I was talking about, he must have decided not to let on. "Do you think he had anything to do with the murder of Scooter McLeod?"

"No, I don't. All the evidence points to Hampstead. He killed Scooter for that helmet, and maybe for some other stuff."

At that point Luis Mendoza got contemplative in a way I had not seen before. "You know, it was a funny case."

"Funny how?"

"Not *funny* funny. But we had all these suspects who had a motive – Ray Salerno for what Scooter did to his daughter, Ollie Swade because Scooter threatened to expose him as a looter, Pedro Trujillo because Scooter might have contributed to the death of his brother, and Sandy McLeod himself, because Scooter's environmental leanings threatened to disrupt his plans for developing the Rocking M. And then it turns out to be Barton Hampstead, who didn't seem like much of a suspect at all until you found that diary."

"Just shows it's better to be lucky than good."

The sheriff shook his head. "You got that wrong."

"I got what wrong?"

"The part about being lucky. Well, you might be lucky, but that has more to do with your choice of girlfriends than it does with being a detective. You're pretty damned good, Cal. You've more than proved that on this case. I'm glad to have you around. Maybe one of these days you'll take my advice and move down to headquarters in Nogales. I'd make a slot for you in criminal investigations."

"Not gonna happen."

"Why not?"

"Well, among other things, I like being out in the country. And then there's the aforementioned girlfriend and her goats."

# Chapter 59

As I said before, Maria Obregon lived in the original adobe home built by her late husband Tony's great-great-grandfather. Jorge Obregon had chosen the site because of the shade cast by some enormous old mesquites, and also for its proximity to water. The San Carlos Wash ran pretty much year-round back then. What he had failed to notice was that the spot also was in the bottom of an old oxbow, completely inside the floodplain. It had taken better than a century for that mistake to cause any trouble, but today was the day.

~ ~ ~

I had heard the first rumble of thunder during my conversation with the sheriff and the FBI agent, but I hadn't paid all that much attention. It wasn't until they had both left that something caught my eye out the window. A single cloud had built over the Canelo Hills. It towered to a great height, which of itself was not all that unusual. The odd part was that everywhere else the sky was clear. I went outside for a better look.

It was an unusually humid day, even for mid-summer. The single cloud built higher and higher into the Arizona sky. Then it began to dump rain, and lots of it from what I could see. Still, it was the monsoon, and rain was normal enough for this time of year, so I didn't pay all that much attention.

I went back inside to get started on my report about the Hampstead case. About forty-five minutes later I looked back out the window. In all the years I'd lived in the Sonoita Valley, I'd never seen anything just like this. It was still raining hard, but only in that one spot. Then I heard a siren, and about the same time the radio came to life.

"Hello Cal? This is Irma from dispatch. Listen, we've

*345*

had a 911 call reporting the state highway washed out in your area. Somebody ran off the road. They're okay, and they called it in. I've notified rescue and they're on their way. Is there a storm going on?"

I looked out the window again. "Sort of. There's a huge thunderhead, but it's just in one place over the Canelo Hills. Is that where the washout happened?"

"I think so. You'd better get down there."

I packed up and got ready to leave the office. Then I remembered something. The San Carlos Wash originated in those hills. In fact, it was right about where the cloud was dumping all that rain. Where was Maria? I tried both her cell and the home phone, but nobody answered. I called Larry, explained the situation, and told him to go look out the window.

"Yeah, I can see that cloud. Looks really weird. Do you want me to help out? I'm supposed to be on paid leave."

"This is an emergency, so you're officially back on duty. Get down there right away. Set up roadblocks around the washout. Give fire and rescue whatever help they need, then start a search of the whole area. Call Nogales for backup if you need it. Hard to say what other damage this thing might be doing. I think we could have a major flood on our hands, and people won't be expecting it because the sky is clear most places. And keep in touch."

"Where will you be?"

"I'm headed over to Maria's."

"Why there? I mean her place is nowhere near ... oh, Jesus, Cal, you think this thing might be running down the San Carlos Wash?"

"Seems likely. I gotta go, Larry."

~ ~ ~

I knew something was wrong as soon as I got to Maria's turnoff, because her car was parked clear out by the road. I drove down the drive as far as I could, and got out.

*346*

The whole place was flooded.

"Maria?"

Nobody answered. I started to run, but it was hard going. I was only halfway to the house, and the water already was above my knees. I kept calling and running.

Finally there was a response. "Is that you Cal? Oh, thank God! I'm in the barn! My goats are trapped in here, and they're going crazy. Please hurry!"

"I'm coming!"

I couldn't believe the mess that until an hour ago had been the old Obregon homestead and attendant Nanny Boss Dairy. The flood was thigh-deep everywhere. I could hear a roar coming from over in the San Carlos Wash. Here the water barely flowed, but it was everywhere – all around the house, in the milking shed, in the barn, and in the corrals.

Maria was out in one of the goat pens when I finally reached her. "What can I do?"

"Find some rope in the shed. We need to tie these animals up someplace, or they're going to run off. And hurry, please! I think they're going to hurt themselves trying to get out of here!"

It took us about a half hour to get all the goats out of the barn and tied to some mesquite trees on higher ground between the compound and the San Carlos Wash. Only then did we enter the house.

It was a complete, heart-wrenching mess. The furniture, the tile, the walls up better than two feet, everything was soaked. Only after the water receded would we know whether the old adobe bricks had survived.

Maria was ashen-faced. "I've got to get out to the shed. All my records are in there."

I think we both knew what she would find. It was only then that Maria began to cry. "My god, Cal, everything is ruined. What am I going to do?"

*347*

"How did you happen to come out here?"

"What? Oh, I just came out to have lunch, and when I turned off the road I saw ... What difference does *that* make? What am I going to *do*, Cal?"

"I'm going back to my place and I'll get a big horse trailer. We'll take your goats to the Pitchfork Ranch. The barns and corrals are still good there. And you'll move in with me. Then, if you want, we'll set to work fixing up this place. We'll get out of this mess, I promise."

"Really? You promise? I'm not sure my insurance is going to cover all this."

We were back outside now, standing in the water. At least it didn't seem to be getting any higher. I looked back toward the Canelo Hills and noticed that the cloud was gone. "I promise. And one more thing, Maria."

"What?"

"Will you marry me?"

"Now?"

"Well I suppose not today, no."

Maria looked up into my face, laughing through her tears. "No, you stupe. I mean of all the times you could pick to ask me to marry you, *this* is the one?"

"I'm an idiot."

"But you meant it?"

"About getting married? Of course I meant it."

Maria surveyed the remains of her house and property, then turned and looked me straight in the eye. There was only a moment's hesitation.

"You've got a deal. Otherwise, where the hell am I gonna to live?"

~ ~ ~

Fortunately, nobody died in what came to be known as the San Carlos Flood. Larry and I, along with fire and rescue crews - even Border Patrol agents on their days off – we all pitched in to help people who lived along the wash to dig out and start getting their lives back together. For some it would be a tough decision about whether to restore and rebuild or to move someplace on higher ground.

Things in the Sonoita office of the Santa Cruz County Sheriff's Department gradually returned to normal. Sandy McLeod was arrested for stealing Sally Benton's bull and for some financial skullduggery that I did not fully understand. He got a fancy lawyer, but at the very least it was clear that his whole Sonoita Valley enterprise was going down.

Dr. Rincon reported that the helmet was looking more and more like it had come from the Coronado expedition. Very possibly it could have belonged to Coronado himself, or at least to one of his officers, given its ornate design.

As far as anyone could determine, Barton Hampstead had no will and no heirs. Rincon and his staff were going to make replicas of the helmet and other artifacts, and then give the originals to a museum in Mexico City, which seemed appropriate.

~ ~ ~

Maria and I were busy for several weeks getting settled on the Pitchfork Ranch and salvaging what we could from her place. More than a month passed before either of us thought about taking a walk down the San Carlos Wash, to see if the flood had brought anything interesting up out of the sand.

Thank you for reading.
Please review this book. Reviews help others find Absolutely Amazing eBooks and inspire us to keep providing these marvelous tales.

If you would like to be put on our email list to receive updates on new releases, contests, and promotions, please go to AbsolutelyAmazingEbooks.com and sign up.

# Authors' Note

The Sonoita Valley, the setting for our novel, is a real place in Santa Cruz County, Arizona, with a landscape much as we describe it. However, *Coronado's Trail* is entirely a work of fiction, including all of its characters and events. Most particularly, we are aware of no evidence suggesting that the Spanish explorer actually visited the valley during his 1540-42 expedition into what is now the southwestern United States. However, it is plausible that he did so, given what is known about the history and likely route of his travels. Someone named Pedro de Castañeda was part of the expedition, or at least there exists a book about it largely attributed to his authorship. Our quotes from his supposed diary are entirely products of our imagination, but they are informed by what we have learned about the journey. A substantive literature about Francisco Vásquez de Coronado is available. For interested readers, here is a start:

Castañeda, Pedro de, et al. 1933. The Journey of Coronado, translated and edited by George Parker Winship, with an introduction and additional notes by Frederick Webb Hodge. Grabhorn Press, San Francisco, California. [Reprinted in 1990 by Dover Publications Inc., Mineola, Minnesota.]

Bolton, H. E. 1990. Coronado, Knight of Pueblos and Plains (foreword by J. L. Kessell). University of New Mexico Press, Albuquerque (originally published in 1949 as Coronado on the Turquoise Trail, Knight of Pueblos and Plains, by H. E. Bolton, University of New Mexico Press).

Flint, R., and S. C. Flint (editors). 1997. The Coronado Expedition to Tierra Nueva: the 1540-1542 Route across the Southwest. The University Press of Colorado, Niwot, Colorado.

Flint, R., and S. C. Flint (editors). 2003. The Coronado Expedition, from the Distance of 460 Years. University of New Mexico Press, Albuquerque.

# Acknowledgments

Our thanks to the following individuals for their advice, encouragement, and assistance:

- To our many friends in the Southwest, especially those who helped most to broaden our understanding of both the natural and cultural history of the region: Ariel Appleton, George and Sis Bradt, Bill Brophy, Winn Bundy, A. T. and Lucinda Cole, Sara Dinham, John Donaldson, Mary Peace Douglas, Anne Gibson, Patricia Hoffman, Linda Kennedy and Dan Robinette, Cynie and Joel Murray, Ron and Janice Pulliam, Joe Quiroga, Steve and Karen Strom, Joe and Helen Taylor, and our many students over the years, too numerous to mention;
- To fellow members of the Red Herrings writers' group, Beth Eikenbary, Milt Mays, and Jean McBride, for doing their best to make us better at the craft, and for encouraging us through lean times;
- To our family, Laura, Larry, Anthony, and Dominic Hernandez;
- To Stephen Strom, who saw *Coronado's Trail* in his mind's eye and provided just the right cover photograph;
- To Toni and Vince at The Steak Out, for perfecting the art of mesquite-grilled ribeyes and margaritas "rocks and salt;"
- To Shirrel Rhoades and Chuck Newman of Absolutely Amazing eBooks. Without them *Coronado's Trail* would have remained hidden to all but a few.

# About the Authors

**Carl and Jane Bock** are retired Professors of Biology from the University of Colorado at Boulder. Carl received his PhD in Zoology from the University of California at Berkeley, while Jane holds three degrees in Botany, a B.A. from Duke, and M.A. from the University of Indiana, and a PhD from Berkeley. Carl is an ornithologist and conservation biologist. Jane is a plant ecologist and an internationally recognized expert in the use of plant evidence in criminal investigations. She is co-author with David Norris of "Forensic Plant Science" (Elsevier-Academic Press, 2016).

"Coronado's Trail" is the Bocks' first published fiction. However, they spent nearly forty years studying the natural history of the region in southeastern Arizona that is the setting for this novel. They have co-authored numerous articles and two books based on their fieldwork in the Southwest: "The View from Bald Hill" (University of California Press, 2000), and "Sonoita Plain: Views from a Southwestern Grassland" (with photographs by Stephen Strom; University of Arizona Press, 2005).

Now largely retired from academic life, the Bocks presently divide their time between Colorado, Arizona, and the Florida Keys, mostly fly fishing (Carl), fighting crime (Jane), and writing.

**ABSOLUTELY AMAZING eBOOKS**

AbsolutelyAmazingEbooks.com

or AA-eBooks.com

Made in the USA
San Bernardino, CA
16 September 2016